BLACK NOON

BLACK NOON

ANDREW J. FENADY

PINNACLE BOOKS
Kensington Publishing Corp.
www.kensingtonbooks.com

PINNACLE BOOKS are published by

Kensington Publishing Corp.
119 West 40th Street
New York, NY 10018

All Kensington titles, imprints, and distributed lines are available at special quantity discounts for bulk purchases for sales promotions, premiums, fund-raising, educational, or institutional use. Special book excerpts or customized printings can also be created to fit specific needs. For details, write or phone the office of the Kensington sales manager: Kensington Publishing Corp., 119 West 40th Street, New York, NY 10018, attn: Sales Department; phone 1-800-221-2647.

ISBN-13: 978-0-7860-3473-4
ISBN-10: 0-7860-3473-4

First printing: December 2015

10 9 8 7 6 5 4 3 2 1

Printed in the United States of America

First electronic edition: December 2015

ISBN-13: 978-0-7860-3474-1
ISBN-10: 0-7860-3474-2

for

The Three Mesquiteers

GARY GOLDSTEIN
"ol' Faithful"

BOB ANDERSON
"ol' Trail Duster"

DUKE FENADY
"young Trail Compadre"

and of course

MARY FRANCES

PREAMBLE

As when a misty dream unfolds—out of the darkness of the mind; black, impenetrable, until—the face of a cat appears, lambent, saffron eyes glinting, mouth distended, then twisted.

The cat screeches.

An unearthly sound.

The cat creeps noiselessly on its pads, then stops in front of something burning; the flames fling leaping towers, yellow and blue, behind the hunched feline as it looks at something, or someone, and emits an audible purr of contentment while its gaze travels ever slowly upward—the length of a human figure.

The figure of a young woman—she wears a gossamer white gown that slithers across her long and sinuous body, and her face is the fulfillment of the promise of the upward journey. Silver-blue eyes illuminated by the flames, flowing flaxen hair, a claret mouth, and sensuous alabaster skin all molded into a living mask of mythic perfection. She watches, fascinated by the trident flames.

The cat leaps effortlessly, and just as easily, the beautiful young woman catches the purring animal, presses and softly *strokes its flanks. The cat purrs even louder as it is stroked by tapering white fingers, while ascending flames, glowing against the chocolate night, reach up to a burning cross atop the tower of a church that is on fire.*

The curling flames turn to sable.

AND THE BLACK FLAMES RISE INTO THE STARLESS DESERT NIGHT.

Reverend Jonathon Keyes woke abruptly, stared at the ribbed top of the Conestoga, then at the stirring figure of his wife, Lorna, lying next to him.

"What is it, Jon?"

"Nothing, dear."

"Nothing?! You're trembling . . . was it that dream again? The war? The battle of Yellow Tavern? The wound?"

This was not the first time since he had come home from the war with a head wound that his sleep had been breached by a bad dream. She reached out and gently touched the back of his head as she had done before.

"No, Lorna. It was a dream, but not about the war. Something different this time," he tried to smile.

"Then tell me about it. They say that dreams often have some meaning . . . sometimes about something that's happened, or even about what's going to happen . . ."

"Or," he said smiling, "as Dickens's friend, Scrooge, said, 'the result of an undigested bit of beef, a fragment of underdone potato.' Let's just forget about it."

"But, Jon . . ."

"Actually, I thought I heard something, something out there. Probably the cry of a lonesome coyote."

"Well, I'll never be lonesome, Jon . . . so long as we're together."

"That makes two of us." He moved and kissed her forehead. "Now, go back to sleep. It's only midnight, and we've still got a long way to Saguaro."

CHAPTER 1

It was a long way from Monroe to Saguaro, much longer than they had anticipated as they journeyed by creaking wagon—pulled by a two-up team, through Missouri, southwest into Kansas, across the one hundredth meridian, to the panhandle of Texas, then the desolate New Mexico Territory and its arid, unforgiving terrain.

There had been a few respites such as Amarillo and Santa Fe, too few and too far between, and they had so far averted sudden, deadly threats from hostile red natives, who resented trespassers coming into their ancient domain.

This was Dry Tortuga—although they didn't know it—and no one really knew where it began and ended—a worthless span of earth where God had stomped the dirt and dust off his boots, with little or no water to provide nourishment, no game to provide food, or no fertile fields to provide crops.

And so they faced the vast emptiness between the winds—grassless, barren, rock hard, boiling windless days under a blistering sun, and relentless freezing nights under the worn canvas of the Conestoga.

Still, there were forced smiles, mostly from the young bride, unaccustomed to such trials.

"Jon, tell me more about Saguaro."

"There's not much I can tell except what was in the letter from the retiring reverend that we served together in the war . . ."

"Served gallantly."

"Most of those who served gallantly are dead."

"But not all, those medals you . . ."

"The war's over, Lorna. That's all in the past."

"But not our honeymoon. That's just beginning." She smiled.

"Some honeymoon." Keyes barely smiled. "Hundreds of miles in nowhere, to a place we know little about . . ."

"Except they need a minister named Jon Keyes."

She rested a soft white hand on his muscled arm that held the reins.

After a strained silence, he spoke without looking at her.

"But, Lorna . . ."

"What, Jon?"

"I've been thinking . . ."

"About what?"

"You and me. You mostly . . . did you make the right choice? You could have had your pick of rich young men in Monroe, of the elite society you were born into, with all the comfort you're used to, with everything . . ."

". . . Everything except the man I love . . ."

". . . Maybe your family was right . . ."

"As you said, Jon, about the war . . . all that's in the past. Our future's in Saguaro."

"Saguaro . . . you know what's been said. 'There's no God in Saguaro.'"

"Reverend Jonathan Keyes can do something about that."

"We'll see." Then he added, "If we ever get there."

"We'll get there. I have no doubt about that . . . or you."

But after what seemed like infinite days and nights, the prospect of Saguaro became less likely and more doubtful—much more doubtful.

The parched earth of the desert had claimed countless pilgrims wasted into dried-out meatless bones, picked clean by ravenous, far-seeing blackbirds who preyed on those who had prayed in vain—until they could pray and breathe no longer.

After scores of unnumbered days and nights lost in the no path terrain, with far away mountain peaks that never came closer—but vultures that circled ever nearer, it seemed inevitable that two more bodies and souls would soon surrender to the fate of those who had gone before.

CHAPTER 2

It was a burning day with a bald desert sky, cloudless, as if painted, but pierced by the hot circle of sun that sent shimmering waves across jagged, burnished peaks bleached for a million years by the same immemorial sun.

Nothing moved, until . . .

For the first time there was motion.

Circling in the distance, death's patient sentinels, several black buzzards . . . drifting . . . waiting . . .

And below, the team of horses, unhitched but with barely enough strength to stand on the desert crust. The Conestoga wagon. A wheel broken off. All its contents emptied. Trunks. Tables. Chairs. The remnants of civilization—and the bent figure of a man.

Jon Keyes managed to waver toward the side of the wagon where a barrel was tied. He had a red scarf in one hand, and with the other hand he twisted the spigot of the barrel.

Nothing. It was empty.

Desperately he placed the scarf under the spigot,

hoping for even a single drop. He shook the barrel with fading strength—to no avail.

With face parched, lips cracked, he breathed heavily and looked off in another direction.

Lorna lay motionless in the shade he had managed to fashion from some of the wagon's unloaded contents.

Keyes staggered back toward the inert figure of his bride. As he did, his stumbling feet inadvertently kicked an empty canteen on the ground—and nearby was the Bible he had carried for years. He picked up the Bible and moved on, then fell to his knees beside Lorna, unconscious and probably much worse. He placed the scarf on her brow, he held the Bible in both hands.

"Lorna."

But there was no answer.

There had been none for a long while.

With the Bible still in his grasp, his face tilted upward.

"Lord in heaven . . . we beg of you . . . deliver us," he whispered.

That was all the prayer he could manage.

He placed the Bible near her, then struggled to his feet. Keyes weaved toward the heavy wheel that was off the wagon. With all the might of his remaining strength, he tried to lift and roll the wheel closer to the Conestoga but lost control and collapsed as the wheel crashed hard on top of him.

He did not move.

But something else did and landed on a nearby jagged rock.

A buzzard, one of the desert sextons, without so much as a blink over its vast graveyard, gazed at the buckled body of Jon Keyes. The gold watch he wore on his vest had fallen out, but was still attached to the button hole by a heavy gold chain.

Before the vulture moved, as the other blackbirds circled, there appeared, as if out of a mirage, through the undulating heat waves, a large buckboard wagon.

Cheated, the buzzard flew off.

CHAPTER 3

As the squadron of buzzards winged away, the large buckboard drew closer to the crippled Conestoga.

Three people were aboard the approaching wagon.

At the reins, Caleb Hobbs, middle-aged, tall, clean featured, with a smooth, almost saintly face.

On the far side, Joseph, rope-thin, with a long elfin visage, creased by a thin-lipped smile.

And in between the two men, Deliverance, the young woman out of the dream, and even though her garments now were much less revealing, and her hair was pulled taut from her forehead, there was still a soulful, suasive look about her.

Caleb Hobbs tugged gently at the reins and the twin white horses obeyed his silent command to stop between the unconscious woman and the man under the fallen wheel.

All three stepped off of the buckboard, not fast, not slow, with just the right effort for people who knew the desert. Deliverance and Joseph each carried a canteen.

"From the looks of 'em," Joseph said, "none too soon."

"We'll do what we can," Caleb replied.

As they approached, Joseph noticed something on the ground next to the inert woman.

He picked up the Bible.

"See here, Caleb."

The tall man nodded and bent over Keyes. He looked for just a moment, then reached down and lifted the gold watch on which there was an inscription. He read it with a voice just above a whisper.

"'To Reverend Jon Keyes. Mother and Dad.'"

His voice was still soft, but deeper as he looked at Deliverance and Joseph.

"Literally sent from heaven. This man is a minister." Caleb glanced in the direction of Keyes's wife. "Joseph."

Joseph nodded and walked toward Lorna as Caleb put the watch into Keyes's vest, rose, and moved toward the buckboard.

Deliverance knelt beside Keyes with the open canteen in one hand and placed her other hand gently on the left side of Keyes's bruised face.

Suddenly there was the sound of a nearby rattle, then the warning hiss.

Deliverance looked up, but not abruptly, at the uncoiled snake about to strike. Her expression remained unchanged, her eyes unafraid. She did not move, except for her eyes ever so slightly, and not really a movement, more a penetration.

The snake ceased its rattle, recoiled . . . then slithered away.

Caleb at the buckboard had unhinged a chain and

started to lower the tailgate. Joseph was still at Lorna's side. If they were aware of what had just happened they displayed no reaction.

And neither did Deliverance.

She poured water from the canteen into her palm and fingers, then softly pressed her long, milk-white fingers across Keyes's sun-scorched lips . . . until his face moved tenuously.

His eyes fluttered and opened out of some bottomless graveyard pit, into the blinding glare of the sun, and finally into focus came the face of Deliverance . . . cool and beatific . . . the haunting face in his dream.

But this was not a dream.

Or was it?

Then he heard a dim voice.

Not hers.

"It's all right, Reverend," Caleb said, "we'll take care of you."

CHAPTER 4

There are journeys . . . and journeys.

Journeys of gladness and joy, even in the long voyage home, with the anticipation of welcoming relatives and friends.

The downhill journeys of sadness and gloom, to the resting place of those same relatives and friends.

Journeys of wine and roses—to journeys' end with lovers meeting.

Journeys where autumn winds succumb to winter's wrath.

For Jon Keyes there had been journeys to and from battlefields with only stone markers left behind for those whose journey in life was closed within death's dream.

But he had survived those battlefields and had vowed that his days of killing other men were over . . . and he had taken other vows: to become a minister, and to marry the one he wanted to spend the rest of his life with.

But now he was not certain they had both survived.

What was real?

And what was death's illusion?

Keyes thought to himself—*It's strange, the things you think of when you're not really sure if you're dead or alive.*

And Lorna . . . had she survived?

With effort he turned his face and saw Lorna lying next to him in the moving buckboard. He managed to lift his arm, place his hand on her shoulder, and squeeze with what strength he could.

At first, nothing . . . and then an ever so slight stirring, and a muffled sound came as her lips moved.

Alive.

More reassurance that they were still in the realm of the living.

But as he lay, sometimes barely conscious, on the bed of the buckboard, he remembered that face out of a dream, or nightmare, that now brought salvation.

He had heard that they had called her "Deliverance," and they had delivered the two of them from certain death.

Deliverance had spoken not a word; but those silent lips and beautiful face were what he most remembered.

Jon Keyes was aware that he and Lorna were on another journey. But to where?

And to what fate that awaited them?

CHAPTER 5

Reverend Jon Keyes had only a hazy, billowing recollection of the journey from death's doorway on the desert—as a cat sitting on its haunches with its forelegs straight like a statue, neck extended—watched in the large comfortable bedroom appointed in New England décor.

The feline had placed itself near the foot of the canopied bed and gazed toward the unconscious form of Lorna lying on the bed.

Keyes sat on a chair, still showing the effects of their ordeal, still weak, but running his fingers through his thick thatch of auburn hair, his present thought only of Lorna's condition.

He spoke to the others in the room without looking at them.

"Have you sent for a doctor, Mr. . . . ?"

"Hobbs. Caleb Hobbs." The tall man smiled.

"Yes, of course, Mr. Hobbs . . . have you . . ."

"Dr. Moody had a much better offer in North Fork. He and his family moved there just a few weeks ago. We're still looking for a replacement . . ."

"Do you think Lorna will be all right?"

"I'm sure she will, m'boy. Our housekeeper, Bethia, will look after her. Won't you, Bethia?"

"Of course, Mr. Hobbs." Bethia, a middle-aged, dignified woman dressed in New England tradition, was placing a damp cloth on Lorna's brow.

"Bethia did quite a bit of nursing," Caleb said, "in a veteran's hospital when the war ended."

"I'll take good care of her, Mr. Keyes."

"Thank you, Bethia." Keyes turned his attention to Caleb Hobbs standing nearby. "I haven't any idea of how long we were out there. Lost all track of time."

"The important thing is that you're both here now . . . and safe."

"Thanks to you. Kept moving as long as we could . . . but never seemed to get anywhere."

"The desert all looks the same."

"The mountains appeared never to get closer."

"You must've taken a wrong turn. It's happened before, but with worse results . . . much worse."

"If you hadn't . . ."

"Don't even think about that, Reverend."

"How did you know," there was a quizzical look on Keyes's face, "that I am a minister?"

"Your watch, it had fallen from your pocket. The inscription . . ."

"Oh, yes. Mr. Hobbs . . . something else . . . I seem to remember . . ."

"Now, m'boy, you mustn't strain yourself. We'll have time to talk about all of it as Mrs. Keyes recovers."

"You're very kind, Mr. Hobbs, and you're right . . . as of now I'm not really sure . . ."

"You can be certain of one thing, but first of all I'm

not *Mister* Hobbs. Please call me Caleb, and we only did what . . ."

"You said 'we' . . . I do seem to remember . . ."

But before Keyes went on, his attention was drawn to the sound of the doorknob turning as the cat bolted from the foot of the bed and stood in front of the opening door. Deliverance entered without speaking.

She stood not as in the dream, but dressed as she had been in the desert, except her flaxen hair now flowed onto her shoulders, still as chimeric, with those silver-blue eyes directed at Keyes, who rose from the chair, looked at her, and brought his fingers to his lips in remembrance of her touch as he lay in the wasteland.

Caleb Hobbs took a step closer to the minister.

"You'll have to excuse my daughter, Reverend. You see Deliverance has . . . an affliction."

Keyes's eyes remained on Deliverance. Whatever the "affliction," it certainly was not evident.

"She can't speak," Caleb continued. "But she can hear and understands everything we say. However, she is unable to speak."

Deliverance's long expressive fingers moved in a rhythmic pattern as she looked at her father, who nodded in response.

"Very good, my dear." Caleb smiled at Keyes to interpret her message. "I sent Joseph and some of the other men. They've brought back your wagon."

"Oh, I'd . . . I'd like to thank them."

"You're still weak. It might be better if you wait."

"I'm all right. I'd like to."

"Very well."

As the two men spoke, Deliverance had moved toward the bed near Bethia, but looked down at Lorna, then at her father, as once again her hands and fingers sent a silent communication.

"Well, Deliverance," Caleb smiled, "it appears that Mrs. Keyes is going to be all right, but she'll need some time to recover."

Deliverance nodded.

"Thank you for your concern," Keyes said to Deliverance. "My wife and I are grateful to all of you for saving our lives and for all you've done."

Deliverance acknowledged with a slight nod and smile.

"Well, Mr. Hobbs . . . Caleb, shall we go to see Joseph?"

"Certainly." Caleb touched Keyes's shoulder and led the way toward the open bedroom doorway.

Deliverance watched them leave and looked toward Bethia—then to Lorna—and then to the cat, who was already looking at her.

CHAPTER 6

The street with its buildings looked nothing like what Keyes had seen since he and Lorna had started on their journey through the West, nor did its citizens.

The buildings were scrubbed and freshly painted, constructed in a New England style, and the people, young and old, were dressed more like pilgrims debarked from the *Mayflower* or some other vessel newly arrived from abroad. The citizens carried no weapons, and Keyes noted the absence of any sign of a saloon that inevitably adorned other western streets.

But before he could take it all in, he saw a faintly familiar figure standing beside the battered Conestoga with several other men nearby.

"Reverend," Caleb said, "do you remember Joseph? He was with Deliverance and me when we found you."

"Yes, yes, I do . . . now."

Keyes extended his hand.

"Joseph, we are beholden to you and to these other gentlemen."

"You'll get to know the others later," Caleb said as

Keyes and Joseph shook hands while the other men nodded and walked away. "They'll take the wagon over to Sam Hawkins's stable. He's a blacksmith who can fix anything."

"Happy to help you, Reverend." Joseph smiled. "Like the Book says, 'Gather up the fragments that remain, that nothing be lost.'"

"Yes," Keyes said. "And if you hadn't gathered up my wife and me and brought us to . . ." He realized he didn't know where he was.

"San Melas." Caleb smiled as Keyes took further note of the surroundings.

"San Melas," Keyes repeated. "We've passed through many a western town, but . . ."

"I know what you're thinking." Caleb motioned. "Things here are a little . . . different and so are we. We're from New England. Connecticut. Some of the buildings we've constructed, our dress, even our speech . . . it's hard to break old ties."

"It's charming," Keyes said. And as his glance swept the street a young boy of seven or eight years, on crutches, hobbled toward them accompanied by his mother and father. In spite of his handicap, the youth's face had a happy aspect.

"Hello, Mr. Hobbs," the young boy greeted. "How are you today, sir?"

"Just fine, Ethan. And you?"

"Never better, sir." Ethan smiled as his parents drew closer.

"Oh, Reverend Keyes, this is the Bryant family. Pricilla and William. William is in charge of our grocery-hardware store."

The Bryants were a handsome couple, both in their thirties.

"Good day, Reverend." Mr. Bryant nodded. "We heard what happened. Welcome to our little community." Bryant pointed to the Conestoga. "If you need anything please come and see me. Just across the street."

"Thank you, Mr. Bryant. You've all been very kind. A pleasure meeting you . . . and you, too, Ethan."

"Thank you, sir," Ethan replied as he made his way just ahead of his parents.

"Poor lad." Caleb shrugged at Keyes. "Injured by a runaway wagon. He'll never be able to walk without those crutches . . . only one of a series of misfortunes that's lately struck our village."

"Misfortunes?" Keyes repeated.

"There's no need to trouble you, Reverend."

"I'd like you to tell me."

"Well, as I told you, our doctor moved away . . . and then there's the mine . . ."

"What sort of mine?"

"Gold. We worked a shaft near here. Oh, not the richest by far, but it helped sustain the town. Now it's played out. Doesn't pay to work it anymore."

"Tell the Reverend about the church, Caleb," Joseph added. "Tell him."

"Yes, please do."

Caleb hesitated, but it was evident that Keyes wanted to hear.

"Some time ago, our church burned down and unfortunately our minister, Reverend Courtney Joyner, perished while trying to save it."

"Like the Book says, Reverend," Joseph's voice quavered, "'We have suffered many things in vain.'"

"The Good Book, also, says, 'this too shall pass.'" Keyes's voice was calm and confident.

"That's true, Joseph," Caleb affirmed, "we must look on the brighter side. And Reverend, when we found you in the desert . . . a minister . . . we did hope you might stay with us and . . ."

But before Caleb could go on, one of the townspeople ran toward them. There was fear in his eyes and shrill alarm in his voice.

"Caleb! He's coming!"

"What is it, Jacob? Who . . ."

"It's Moon! Moon's coming . . ."

"All right, Jacob." Caleb Hobbs took a deep breath and squared his shoulders. "I'll go to him."

Jacob Brahmwell wiped at his mouth as Caleb took a step.

"What do you think he'll do? What . . ."

"I don't know. Now, please, try to stay calm. Tell the others to do the same."

Jacob Brahmwell was anything but calm as he pointed.

"There he is!"

"Yes, I see. Excuse me, Mr. Keyes. This may well be the worst of our misfortunes."

As he started to walk ahead, Joseph followed.

"I'm going with you, Caleb."

The two men moved, and Jon Keyes stood with a perplexed expression on his face, looking at the approaching rider.

Reverend Jon Keyes had never seen anyone or anything like the man to whom the terrified citizens of San Melas had reacted . . . from the sound of his name to the sight of his approach.

Keyes had read the exaggerated tales of fabled gunfighters in penny-dreadful periodicals, men who killed without conscience or compunction, of gunmen for hire, immune to emotion—men whose only law was the gun, men with no place in the corner or crevice of their mind or body for any feeling of friendship, tenderness, sorrow, or sympathy.

But these were, for the most part, fictional, manufactured in the mind of some wildly imaginative writer while in the comfort of his eastern home or office—with blood dripping from his pen, to stimulate some reader in the safety of his overstuffed chair or lantern-lit bedroom.

However, this was real. Not a fiction of the mind—but a living danger.

A man called Moon, riding slowly into town, dressed in foreboding black garb, astride an imposing black stallion.

His saddle glinted with gold ornaments. His hatband decorated with gold moons. His belt buckle a golden half-moon. The handles of both his revolvers plated in gold with carved moons.

Moon's mask-like face was dark, with a full mustache curved downward past deep creases—a face that was handsome, yet repellent. His eyes, cold-steel blue.

The townspeople, cowed in terror, watched from what they hoped was a safe distance. It was evident that they had earlier known the effect of Moon's presence.

Caleb Hobbs walked to the center of the street

followed by Joseph. They stood in stiff anticipation as Moon approached. His horse stopped without either verbal or physical command from its rider.

Moon looked down at Caleb but said nothing.

After a strained silence, Hobbs had mustered all his art and did his best to appear calm. He removed a leather pouch from his pocket that he had readied in anticipation of the confrontation and extended it toward Moon, who looked at it a moment . . . then reached down slowly and took it.

Moon let the pouch weigh in his palm as he looked down at the two men. His stark eyes conveyed a negative message. *Not enough.*

"There's no more gold," Caleb said. "We're shutting down the mine."

Moon said nothing.

"That's the last of your share." There was a tremor in Caleb's voice.

Still Moon was silent.

Caleb lifted both his empty palms toward Moon.

"I'm sorry . . . there isn't any more."

Moon spoke for the first time with a voice sibilant, but harsh, almost a hiss.

"There better be."

Keyes's eyes were fixed on Moon's face. He had seen ominous, forewarning, sullen faces in the war, laden with hate, but never had he seen, or felt the presence of evil incarnate, as etched on the face of the man called Moon. And seldom had he had such a feeling of helplessness as Caleb implored the dark rider.

"Moon . . . it's no use . . ."

Moon spoke just above a whisper; still everyone on the street could hear.

"I'll be back."

"But," Caleb pleaded, "we haven't anything to give you!"

Moon looked to his left across the street, looked at Deliverance standing in front of a doorway. By far she was the most desirable figure in sight. Slim, but radiant in the sunlight. Her face impassive, calm, her eyes, catlike, enigmatic.

There was a slight trace of a smile across Moon's tight lips, but sinister, as he repeated.

"I'll be back."

Again without overt command, Moon's stallion backed a couple of steps and Caleb pressed forward in desperation.

"Moon, please! Let us be . . . we've done everything you've asked. Leave us alone!"

In response, Moon's right hand, with a single, swift, dazzling motion, lifted the gold plated revolver and fired into a post, close, too close, to where Deliverance stood.

The post was ornamented by decorative knobs. Three shots smashed into three knobs shattering them and sending some of the debris flying across Deliverance's face.

She did not move or react.

Keyes did, involuntarily taking a step forward.

But Moon holstered the revolver.

Joseph paced out from Caleb's side.

"Moon," Joseph said, "'Wickedness proceedeth from the wicked. But our hand shall not be upon thee, for in heaven . . .'"

He never finished. Moon's foot slammed against Joseph, catching him in the shoulder and sending him sprawling onto the street.

Keyes ran toward the fallen man as Moon looked down, and Caleb lifted both arms in a plea.

"Moon. He's an old man. He meant no harm . . . he's just an old man."

By then Keyes was at Joseph's side helping to lift the dazed man to his feet.

"Thank you, Reverend," Joseph uttered. "Thank you, kindly."

"*Reverend?!*" Moon noted. "So . . . we got a preacher among us. Well, what do you know about that?!"

Moon's lariat was off the saddle horn. He swirled it and threw a loop around Joseph, pulling him off his feet.

Moon's horse backed away, slowly at first, dragging Joseph along the ground.

Moon smiled. The horse backed faster.

Keyes grabbed hold of the rope, and he, too, was pulled along, stumbling but still standing.

"No!" Keyes shouted. "Let him go!"

"Sure, Preacher Man." Moon laughed. "When I'm ready."

"Turn him loose!" Keyes hollered out. "You'll kill him!"

Moon stopped laughing, but his eyes were yet fierce. He gave the rope a wicked jerk. The stallion accelerated.

Keyes lost his balance and fell to the ground, still managing a grip on the rope as the two men were being dragged along through the dirt at a pace that mounted faster and faster.

In vain Keyes exerted all his strength against the taut rope stretching through his grip while their two bodies twisted and whirled against the dusty street. He could hear the tormented voice of Joseph.

"Deliver us, oh Lord, from our enemy in our time of need, we beseech thee . . ."

And suddenly the rope slackened its tug, and both he and Joseph came to rest on the ground.

Keyes looked up at Moon and was about to voice thanks that their ordeal was over, but it wasn't. Moon was still smiling that malevolent smile as once again the stallion bolted ahead, propelling its human cargo even farther through the coarse ground.

Keyes's strength was spent. He was about to let loose, when once again the rope slackened and both he and Joseph lay twisted, panting for breath.

The rope was slack, but Moon was not quite through.

He snapped the rope in a whiplike motion and it larruped across Keyes's face.

Moon's eyes swept around the crowd on the street and anchored on Keyes.

"I'll be back . . . Preacher Man."

Moon dropped the rope and rode off.

Even before he was out of sight, Caleb, Deliverance, and a dozen others rushed to the fallen men as most of the townsfolk stood nearby, still stunned by what they had witnessed.

Caleb and Deliverance helped Keyes to his feet while Jacob and William Bryant tended Joseph.

"Reverend," Caleb's voice was little more than a harsh whisper. "I'm sorry."

Keyes placed a palm on Joseph's shoulder.

"Are you all right?"

For a man of his age and condition, Joseph seemed more than all right, but he staggered a bit to maintain his balance.

"I'll make it, Reverend. Thanks be to you."

"I'm sorry, Jon." Caleb shook his head in concern. "We didn't mean for you to get involved in this . . . you . . ."

". . . did what I had to do."

"More than that, my friend, much more. We're grateful."

Caleb turned his attention to his fellow citizens.

"We all knew something like this might happen, but . . . there's nothing more we can do here and now. Please, go back to your homes and tasks. We'll call a meeting later and see what we can come up with to cope with . . . with our situation. May the Lord be with us all."

As Keyes turned to leave he found Deliverance standing close to him. She paused a moment, reached up, and gently touched his face, then looked at the blood smeared on her tapered fingers.

Her lips were silent.

But her eyes said it all.

CHAPTER 7

Jon Keyes, for most of his adult life, had not been a man of the cloth.

The decision and transformation took place in the course of the war between North and South—and was completed on his return to Monroe, Michigan—and Lorna.

Monroe, for over a century, had been a quiet, little more than a village-like settlement, ever since the Red Man moved out of the area because the White Man had moved in—by force of arms. Divided by the banks of the Raisin River, and situated between Detroit, Michigan, and Toledo, Ohio—Monroe had a reputation for nothing in particular until what was called the "Civil War" by the North and the "War for the Confederacy" by the South.

During that unpleasantness, headlines and stories abounded in northern newspapers with mention of Monroe. Not because any remembered battles were fought in, or around the town, but because of the exploits of one of its young citizens—who was no longer just a citizen.

Born in New Rumley, Ohio, and born to be a soldier, he had moved to Monroe as a young boy to be with his sister, Lydia, and to go to school. Some considered him "wild," others settled for "spirited," as he set a new record for outlandish pranks. Still in his teens, he petitioned Senator John A. Bingham for an appointment to West Point where he graduated last in his class of 1861—last in academic study and first in demerits, mostly due to a series of roguish shenanigans, which he made up for by being first in marksmanship, fencing, and horsemanship.

By then the war was in full fury and the army was less in need of scholars and more in demand of soldiers, leaders who could shoot straight and inspire their troops.

The young lieutenant filled the bill—and then some—at Bull Run, the Peninsula Campaign, the Battle of Antietam, and at Chickahominy, where he led a valiant charge against superior forces and emerged a captain—then at Chancellorsville—after distinguishing himself, boldly and aggressively at Brandy Station, he was promoted to brigadier general—then came the defeat of General J.E.B. Stuart's "Invincibles" at Gettysburg, where he prevented Stuart's attempt to join Pickett—and at Culpeper, where he had two horses shot from under him, then continued the victorious charge while wounded in the leg.

After that he was sent back to Monroe to recover—the youngest general officer in the U.S. Army.

That's when Jon Keyes met Brigadier General George Armstrong Custer.

And that made all the difference until the war was over.

But there were different kinds of wars, and here in San Melas, Keyes found himself in the middle of one of those wars.

CHAPTER 8

Deliverance, holding a moist handkerchief, touched Keyes's face where it bled, a gentle, soothing touch, as he looked at her graceful eyes and wistful smile while he sat at the table.

The two others in Hobbs's parlor, Caleb and Joseph, sat in silence, as Caleb relit his pipe.

The silence was interrupted when Keyes's fist slammed against the table.

"It's hard to believe," Keyes muttered.

Caleb and Joseph reacted.

Deliverance did not.

"It's hard to believe," Keyes repeated louder, "that one man . . . one lone man can exact tribute from an entire town."

"He's not just a 'man.'" Caleb said. "He's a monster . . . you saw how he used those guns and that rope. Moon is a killer. A sadistic, soulless killer."

"Wasn't for you, Reverend, I most likely would not be among the living. Came close, too close." Joseph rubbed his shoulder and neck.

"Where's the law?" Keyes asked.

"In Moon's guns." Caleb puffed.

"Don't you have a sheriff?"

"Only a mayor. Me."

Keyes rose past Deliverance and began to pace the room.

"All right, then it's up to you . . . and the rest of the citizens."

"To do what, m'boy?"

"To stop him."

"How?"

Keyes ceased pacing and turned directly to Caleb Hobbs.

"Moon has two guns. Don't the people of San Melas have weapons? Don't they have guns?"

"Reverend." Caleb shook his head. "It's against our religion. We don't believe in violence."

"He who lives by the sword . . ."

"Yes, I know, Joseph. But do you believe in surviving? Or to just paying tribute to evil . . . and for how long?"

"You're right about that, Reverend." Caleb nodded. "Moon is evil. But so long as we had the gold to give . . . it seemed the easier path."

"But that is no longer the path. You haven't any gold. Now what are you going to do . . . besides call a meeting?"

"I . . . don't know . . ."

"Moon said he'd be back. Suppose he comes back in the middle of your meeting? Then what?"

"For the time, all we can do is hope he doesn't . . . and pray."

"Can't you send for a marshal?"

"We're such a small community and so far off the

beaten path . . . this is a vast territory. What few marshals there are . . . are not just on call."

"It's your *home*."

"We've moved on before."

"*If* Moon gives you the opportunity . . ."

Keyes glanced at Deliverance. "Or if he doesn't take something or someone instead of the gold."

"We realize that." Caleb shrugged, "But our hands are tied."

"*Un*-tie them."

"How? Our fate is in the hands of the Almighty . . ."

"As Joseph would quote, 'The Lord helps those who help themselves.' You can't wait around hoping that Moon gets hit by a bolt of heavenly lightning!"

"Reverend, Joseph said that there is a rifle in your wagon . . ."

"Yes, for hunting . . . in case we run out of food on our journey . . ."

"I understand, but . . ."

"What is it, Caleb? Say what's on your mind. Do you want me to give the rifle to you? To . . . the town?"

"Not exactly . . ."

"Would *you* . . . use it . . . if Moon came back while you are here?"

There was a deep silence as Keyes looked around the room, and the others looked at him.

"Suppose he confronted you . . . and your wife, Lorna?"

Finally, Keyes spoke.

"Some time ago I made a covenant . . . a vow."

"What kind of a . . . vow?"

"You'll have to excuse me, Caleb, if I don't answer your question."

"Yes, of course, my friend. It was unfair of me to ask that question. You've already done more than we could expect. But, Reverend, may I ask, what are your plans? Where were you and your wife . . . what was your destination?"

"A place you might never even have heard of, Saguaro."

"Yes, we know of Saguaro."

"The minister there is retiring at the end of the year. I'll assist him until then."

"Very good." Caleb looked from Joseph to Deliverance. "In the meanwhile, since you'll be here for a time . . . until Mrs. Keyes is fit to travel . . . I was wondering . . ."

"Yes?"

"There is a different way you can help . . . if you're willing."

"How?"

"As you've seen, the people here are so depressed, and since our minister died they even seem to be losing faith. I'm sure it would be a great comfort to San Melas if you would conduct services this Sunday."

"A great comfort," Joseph added.

Deliverance moved forward slightly and nodded, her eyes importuning.

"We have no church to offer you," Caleb said, "but there is a shady knoll. Would you consider . . ."

"I would consider it an honor, Caleb, after all you've done," he smiled. "I haven't had the opportunity to conduct a service since we began our journey. Only silent prayers . . . and you good people have answered one of my prayers."

"And, in a way, you've answered one of ours, just by being here."

"I may be a little . . . rusty."

"Reverend, you will be received with great favor."

"With great favor." Joseph beamed, as Bethia entered the room.

"Excuse me, sir," she addressed Keyes. "It's your wife . . ."

"Is something wrong?"

"To the contrary," Bethia brightened, "she's awake. She's been asking for you."

"That's wonderful news." To the others. "Please excuse me."

Keyes moved quickly out of the room.

The parlor remained silent for a time.

"He certainly is a fine young man." Caleb's pipe had gone out.

Deliverance took a match from the table, struck it, and brought the flame close to her father's pipe.

As Keyes climbed the stairs, thoughts rushed through his mind, thoughts of their desperate journey, a journey that for a time became hopeless. His wife, debilitated, unconscious, near death; he, himself, devoid of strength, felled in the desolate wilderness with buzzards circling in anticipation as he lay with no chance of survival . . . and then three strangers, out of that desolation, carrying them to a haven of survival. And now Lorna was awake and calling for him.

In time they would resume their journey. When Lorna was well.

But in how much time . . . and what might happen until then?

CHAPTER 9

The bedroom was mostly illuminated by a large ornate candle on a bed stand. Lorna was leaning back on two oversized feather pillows. Her face still bore the effects of her ordeal, eyes circled darkly, cheeks sallow and sunken, and it was evident from the shape of her shoulders that she had lost too much weight.

Keyes sat at her bedside holding her hand.

"Jon . . . don't let go of my hand. Keep holding it, please . . ."

"I'll never let go, Lorna. We're together . . . and we're going to stay together."

"It's . . . it's a miracle . . ."

"You might call it that." He smiled.

"What . . ."

"What happened?"

She nodded.

"The last thing I remember was the broken wagon . . . and the sun. Oh, Jonathon, that sun is still burning in my brain . . . I thought that we . . ."

"Now, Lorna don't think about it. We're in a nice,

cool room; you're safe and you're going to get well soon . . . very soon. It's all worked out."

"Are we in . . . Saguaro?"

"No, not yet. But we're with friends . . . in a place called San Melas."

"San Melas." She noticed the rope bruise on his face. "Jonathon, your face . . . what happened?"

"It's nothing . . . nothing at all. I'm all right. But most important, so are you."

"But how did you get us here?"

"I didn't . . . some people found us."

"In the middle of the desert?"

"Yes. We were very lucky. They've asked me to deliver a sermon this Sunday. They have no minister since their church burned down. But now, you've got to rest." He started to rise but still held her hand.

"I will . . . but please stay here for just a little while. I want to tell you something."

He sat back on the side of the bed.

"What is it, dear?"

"Jonathon . . . I never lost faith in you. Never. Do you remember in Monroe when you were going away . . . ?"

They both remembered.

During the fiery heat of hostilities, Keyes had been away to get his law degree and came home to visit his fiancée, Lorna Benton. It was at the same time Brigadier General George Armstrong Custer came home to recover from his wounds at Culpeper—and to see his fiancée, Libbie Bacon.

And at that time Monroe, Michigan, was no longer

the semi-somnambulate little town it had been since its inception. After Gettysburg and Culpeper the tide was sweeping overwhelmingly in favor of the North. In fact, it was declared by most strategists that the war would have ended at Gettysburg if it were not for General George Meade's reluctance to pursue Lee and decimate the torn, defeated, and retreating Confederate troops. Meade had been tabbed the "Reluctant General" and would soon be relieved of command.

But it was just the opposite with Monroe's war hero, the "Boy General," George Armstrong Custer. The town had turned out to bask in the reflected glory of its returning celebrity. Champagne. Liquor. Parades. Rallies and hurrahs. For Custer and his beloved Libbie, all through the days and into the nights, they were surrounded by celebrants, well-wishers, and sycophants. It seemed that for them, there was no solitude . . . no escape—but the "Custer-Boy" had another strategy in mind . . . that didn't quite work out.

Keyes and Lorna were picnicking at an isolated location on the banks of the Raisin River and in the midst of an embrace, when they were interrupted by a voice from behind one of the trees.

"Say there, Sport. Suppose you retreat to some other spot? This area is restricted."

"Suppose we don't," Keyes replied to the voice. "This is public property."

"Not anymore." The voice shot back.

"Says who?"

"The U.S. Army."

A young man dressed in civilian clothes stepped out from behind the tree.

"I don't see any uniform," Keyes said.

"It's resting and recovering . . . and so am I."

"Rest and recover someplace else. We were here first." Keyes motioned as he took a closer look at the intruder.

Just then a beautiful young lady carrying a picnic basket stepped into sight.

"Lorna." She smiled.

"Libbie!" Lorna stood up. So did Keyes.

Lorna Benton and Elizabeth Bacon had been friends since childhood.

"Lorna, this is my fiancé, George Custer." Libbie's smile broadened.

"And this is *my* fiancé, Jon Keyes." Lorna matched Libbie's smile.

"I'm sorry, General," Keyes stammered. "I didn't recognize you out of uniform . . ."

"That's the whole idea," Custer said. "We wanted to get away from all the hoopla. Haven't been alone since I got back. And looks like we're not alone now."

"General," Keyes repeated. "I'm sorry."

"You already said that. And it seems like our fiancées already are acquainted." Custer reached out his hand.

The two men shook.

"We might as well get acquainted too," Custer said. "Mind if we join you?"

"Not if you don't, sir."

"Don't 'sir me' . . . unless you're in the army, too."

"No, si . . . No, General, getting my law degree. . . ."

"That so? My commanding officer used to be a lawyer, named Abe Lincoln. Ever hear of him?" Custer repressed a laugh.

"Voted for him," Keyes said.

"I didn't," Custer reposted. "Let's go on with the picnic . . . together."

They did.

Keyes had, from time to time, caught a glimpse of Custer in Monroe during the past years, but most of the time either he or Custer had been out of town a good deal of those years and in different schools, Keyes studying law and Custer at West Point, but Lorna and Libbie traveled in the same social circles and had become good friends. However, Keyes was surprised and pleased at how affable the Boy General was on such short acquaintance.

"This is my favorite spot along the Raisin," Custer pointed out toward the middle of the river. "When we were kids on a school picnic, I damn near drowned there, right Libbie?"

"Well, yes. Autie was an excellent swimmer, but he'd eaten more than his share of apple pie and got a severe cramp showing off swimming across . . ."

"Libbie saved my life . . . jumped in and pulled me out, didn't you, sweetheart?"

"Not exactly."

"But you did pump the apple pie out of me once I landed—while everybody else was making bets on whether I'd survive."

"Autie's prone to exaggeration, but it was a close call." Libbie smiled.

"May I ask you something, General?" Keyes inquired.

"About Libbie?" Custer grinned.

"No, about your . . . nickname. I've heard some, matter of fact, most of the people around Monroe call you Autie . . ."

". . . among other things best not repeated when ladies are present."

"But why Autie?" Keyes said.

"Let me tell them," Libbie volunteered.

"Go ahead."

"Well, when he was a cute little fella, barely able to talk, he tried to pronounce his name; George Armstrong Custer, but Armstrong came out 'Autie,' and it stuck. He's been Autie ever since."

"So both of you might just as well call me Autie, too," Custer added.

They shared the contents of their picnic baskets, which included chicken, fruit, and cake. Custer had given up liquor after an unfortunate incident during one of his earlier visits to Monroe, but he consumed much lemonade amidst humorous tales of his shenanigans in Monroe and West Point, but inevitably the topic of war was broached.

"How long do you think it will last, General?"

"It could've been over if it weren't for Meade and McClellan before him. Neither of them would attack unless he outnumbered the enemy fifteen to one. But Grant's in charge now—general of the armies of the United States. He split the South when he took Vicksburg, and he's sending Sheridan to the Shenandoah and Sherman to the South through Georgia to take Atlanta. But those Rebels are determined and will go on fighting till Lee has nothing to fight with. It'll take every fighting man we can muster, and the sooner we do, the sooner the war will be over and the more of our men—and theirs—will survive."

Custer looked directly at Keyes but said nothing more about it.

"General, I have another year to go at law school, do you think . . ."

"I think we'll need more lawyers someday. But right now we need soldiers . . . fighting men to get the job done sooner. And, Jon, if and when you're ready, I'd be glad to have you wear a red scarf and join an outfit called the Wolverines."

Days later, after Custer left Monroe to rejoin his Wolverine Brigade, Jon Keyes had made a fateful decision that deeply involved his fiancée, Lorna Benton.

"Lorna, I've made up my mind, and I hope you'll understand."

"I think I know what you're going to say."

"I can't go back, not now. Law school can wait, but you don't have to. I don't know when, or if, I'll be back. Under those circumstances . . ."

"Under those circumstances—what, Jonathon?"

"The engagement ring," he took her hand, "if you want to take it off . . . until we see what happens . . . I'll understand . . ."

"Understand this, Jonathon. Libbie is wearing her engagement ring until her soldier comes back. And I'm going to wear mine until my soldier does the same. I have faith in the Lord—and in you."

* * *

"Remember that, Jonathon? What we said when you were leaving?"

"Of course, I do."

"No matter what happens, I'll always have faith in you."

Silently, from under the bed, the cat moved out of the partially open door where Deliverance stood in the shadows of the hallway, watching and listening.

CHAPTER 10

That night, inside a shed on the Hobbses' property, shadows of tall, slender figures of animals were outlined against the wall of the candlelit room.

The cat sat on a workbench watching.

The shadows were from unlit candles fashioned in the shapes of owls—cats—snakes—along with other candles rather elaborately decorated.

Also, on the bench were several lumps of paraffin wax, kettles, and other accoutrements necessary in the art of candle making.

Deliverance sat on a chair by the workbench.

Bethia stood close by, holding an article of clothing in her hand. She smiled and placed the article into Deliverance's outstretched palm, then turned and walked toward the door.

Deliverance reached with her other hand and picked up a large pair of scissors from the table.

She began cutting off a small piece of the skirt that Lorna had worn on the desert trip.

CHAPTER 11

Keyes came out of the Hobbses' house, took a deep breath, and saw Joseph, Jacob, and a couple of other men of the town approaching, carrying a trunk and other articles they had retrieved from the wagon.

He waited until the men were closer, but Joseph spoke first.

"Morning, Reverend."

"Morning, Joseph, gentlemen."

Joseph and the gentlemen set their burdens on the ground.

"We thought you might be in need"—Joseph pointed to what they were delivering—"in need of some of these things while you were with us."

"That's very kind of you, all of you. Lorna and I appreciate what you've done—and are doing."

"Work of the Lord, Reverend, 'cast bread upon the waters.'"

"That 'bread' is awfully heavy." Keyes smiled.

"Good morning, one and all."

It was William Bryant and his young son who waddled in on crutches.

"Morning," they all returned Bryant's greeting.

"It *is* a good morning." Ethan smiled. "My dad and I are on our way to work."

"Ethan's my best helper now that school is out." Bryant tousled his son's hair.

"I'm sure he is." Keyes grinned.

"Well, son, let's get a get on," Bryant said, "we're burning daylight."

"Yes, sir." Ethan was on his way ahead of his father.

Keyes watched as Bryant and the boy made their way toward the store, then he noticed his Henry rifle that one of the men had placed on the trunk.

"We found this among your possessions in the wagon, Reverend." Joseph reached down, picked up the rifle, and extended it toward Keyes. "Thought it best to bring it along."

"Thank you, Joseph." Keyes paused a moment, then almost reluctantly took hold of the weapon just as Deliverance came out of the front door and walked toward them with a smile as fresh as a spring garden.

She motioned in the direction of the rising sun, and her smile broadened.

"Yes," Keyes nodded, "it is a beautiful day."

Deliverance's glance settled on the rifle in his hand.

Her eyes suddenly turned dark, her face sullen, tense, as she looked in a far-off distance.

Keyes and the other men quickly realized what she was looking at on the high slope of the street.

A figure on a horse, backlit by the circle of sun—but distinguishable.

Moon.

As still as a painting.

But daunting. Even at that distance.

They waited for him to advance. Not sure of what they would do—or of what he would do.

Time seemed tethered.

Then it happened.

As suddenly as he had appeared—he was gone, swallowed into the shimmering rays of the sun.

There was a shudder of relief through all of them.

Deliverance managed to smile again, but her face was no longer as fresh as a spring garden.

CHAPTER 12

"The way cats play with mice before they kill them," Caleb said when they told him of Moon's appearance. "Unfortunately, in this case, Moon's the cat . . . and we are the mice."

"But mice can't fight back . . . You can," Keyes said.

"With that rifle in your hand, Reverend?"

Keyes lowered the Henry he still held.

"There are other ways, Caleb."

"If you think of a good one, please let us know. In the meantime, we are all looking forward to your Sunday sermon. Have you been thinking about that, Reverend?"

"Yes, I have. I'm referring to the Bible you retrieved from the desert."

"Maybe the answer is in the Book, Reverend," Joseph said.

"There are many answers in the Good Book, Joseph, but I'm not sure the answer to Moon is among them."

"Maybe not," Caleb lit his pipe, "but the Bible does speak of evil, doesn't it?"

"Yes, of course."

"Well, right now I can't think of anything more evil than Moon," Caleb puffed from the pipe, "at least around San Melas." He pointed to the trunk on the floor. "But for the time being we'd better get you settled. Joseph."

"Right away, Caleb." Joseph motioned to Jacob and the other men.

Deliverance made certain that Caleb could see her as she proceeded to motion with her arms and hands.

"What is she saying?" Keyes asked.

"She'll join you in a few minutes. She has something to attend to."

"Very good." Keyes smiled and nodded to Deliverance, then started toward the stairway, still carrying the rifle.

Bethia sat on a straight-back chair next to the bed where Lorna was propped up with the feather pillows. Lorna's appearance and spirit were visibly improved as her husband and the other men entered.

"Mornin', ma'am," Joseph greeted, and the other men entered and set their burdens in the middle of the room.

"Where would you like us to put these belongings?" Joseph indicated, "There's a nice, roomy armoire . . ."

"Just leave them there, Joseph," Keyes smiled, "I'll put them away."

"I'd be happy to help." Bethia rose from her chair.

"That won't be necessary, Bethia, but thank you." Keyes placed the rifle on top of the trunk and turned to his wife. "Well, darling, you certainly do look much improved this morning."

But Keyes couldn't help noticing a slight look of uneasiness shading Lorna's face since they had entered.

Deliverance came through the open doorway holding a large new candle. She walked to the burnt-out taper on the bed stand and replaced it with the new one.

"Good morning, Deliverance," Lorna said. "That certainly is a beautiful candle."

Deliverance smiled.

"Almost seems a shame to burn it," Lorna added.

"Deliverance makes those candles herself," Joseph said.

"She does?" Lorna admired. "Beautiful."

"Yes, ma'am." Joseph pointed toward the window. "Out in the shed. Is there anything else we can get you, Reverend?"

"No, thank you, Joseph," Lorna replied. "We won't be here that long." She looked at Deliverance with the burnt-out taper in her hand. "And thank you for the beautiful candle, Deliverance."

As they left the room, Keyes went to the bed and sat beside his wife, who was gazing at the candle.

"Beautiful," Lorna said.

"The candle . . ."

"Yes . . . and the lady who brought it."

"Deliverance . . . and I'm sure you noticed her affliction. She can't speak."

"Yes, I noticed." Lorna paused. "Jonathon . . ."

"What is it, dear?"

"The trunk and all of these belongings . . . I thought we would be moving on."

"We will, just as soon as you get your strength back, but in the meanwhile, I'm sure our friends want us to be as comfortable as possible." He pointed to the open Bible on the desk, "And I'd better get back to that sermon."

"Sermon?"

"Don't you remember? I told you that they've asked me to give a service this Sunday . . . remember?"

Lorna nodded.

"And I want you to be there if at all possible."

"I'll be there. And Jonathon . . ."

"Yes?"

She pointed to the rifle atop the trunk.

"Are you going to go hunting while we're here in this house?"

"No," he smiled and kissed her forehead. "They just happened to bring it along with the other things."

"You always were very adept with a rifle, even before the army. I was so proud when you won that marksmanship contest back in Monroe."

"That's because most of the good marksmen were already at war . . . men like Custer . . . except there were no other men like Custer, at least none that I came across."

"I think you would have won first prize anyhow."

"First prize," Keyes smiled, "a silver plate, just what a farm boy—would-be-lawyer needed."

"I still have that silver plate, Jonathon," she pointed. "It's in that trunk . . . along with your medals."

"Instead of a law degree . . ."

"You are what you were meant to be, Jonathon. I wouldn't have it any other way."

"Are you sure, Lorna? We haven't very much . . . we could have had much more."

"We have each other, Jonathon. That's more than enough. And now you'd better get to work on that sermon."

Into the night he sat at the desk leafing through the Bible he had carried since the war, making notes and thinking about what had happened since . . . but . . . mostly since their rescue and arrival in the benighted village of San Melas. The good people and the misfortunes they had endured. Their church burned. Their minister dead. Their leader, Caleb Hobbs, not knowing how to cope with their plight. The brave Bryant family with their young, sunny-faced son struggling to walk on crutches. Joseph and his faith in the word of the Lord. The insolvent mine, and worst of all the imminent threat of the man called Moon. Keyes had witnessed the grim determination in hardened soldiers on both sides; men who had killed and would kill again, each with graveyard eyes intent on killing—but always in those same eyes—hidden, but never completely able to be hidden—the fear of being killed themselves. But that element was absent in the look of Moon. Only complete certainty. No fear. But something else. The wanton look in Moon's eyes as he viewed the beautiful, silent face of Deliverance.

He tried to push that thought out of his mind.

Reverend Jonathon Keyes began to make notes as to what he would say at the Sunday sermon.

CHAPTER 13

It was a Sunday like no other in San Melas. Even though there was no newspaper in town, word had spread to its citizens that this would be a special Sunday.

Men, women, and children, whom Keyes had met, and others he would meet for the first time, gathered at the grassy knoll to listen to a stranger, a minister, speak words they had not heard since their church had burned into a heap of smoldering ashes.

Some came more than an hour before the service was scheduled to begin. They sat murmuring in rapt anticipation.

Rows of benches were placed on either side of a makeshift aisle on the shady portion of the knoll.

Lorna had been helped from her bed and was seated in the front row near the temporary pulpit. Her face and body seemed the worse for having left the bedroom, but she had insisted on being present— as were the others from the Hobbs household—

Bethia, Caleb, and Deliverance. And, of course, Joseph.

William and Pricilla Bryant sat on the last bench, with Ethan closest to the aisle holding his crutches and near Jacob Brahmwell.

In front of the Bryants were Sam Hawkins, the burly blacksmith with a cabbage face, his wife Cassandra, a thin woman with a thinner face and their two children, Grace, a plump eight, and Brian, a string-thin seven.

A reverent silence swept over the congregation as Jon Keyes approached the pulpit carrying only his Bible.

"Thank all of you for coming here today to listen to the words of a stranger in your community.

"I spent hours making notes and doing my best to prepare something to say to you on this occasion. But as you can see I have no notes, no prepared sermon with me now. I threw it all away. I have only this."

Keyes held up the Bible.

"What is in my heart is contained in the words written here."

Keyes paused and looked at the Sunday faces of all who had gathered—the faces that were familiar; most familiar, Lorna, then Caleb and Deliverance Hobbs, Bethia, Joseph, Jacob, the Bryants and their son, Ethan, the other faces, some of whom he recognized from the street when Moon came—and the others . . . the troubled citizens of San Melas.

Then he held out the Bible with one hand and with the other pointed toward the top of a nearby hillock—and began to speak.

"'. . . and he opened his mouth and taught them

saying . . . Blessed are the poor in spirit: for theirs is the kingdom of heaven.'"

His hand with the Bible swept slowly across the congregation.

"'Blessed are they that mourn: for they shall be comforted. Blessed are the meek: for they shall inherit the earth.'"

The Bible hand paused at Caleb and Deliverance.

"'Blessed are they which do hunger after righteousness: for they shall be fulfilled. Blessed are the pure in heart: for they shall see God.'"

Then at Joseph and Bethia.

"'Blessed are the merciful: for they shall obtain mercy.'"

His other hand moved across to the opposite aisle.

"'Blessed are they which are persecuted for righteousness sake: for theirs is the kingdom of heaven.'"

Then to four children, ages six to nine, all towheads, blue-eyed, paying heed to the sermon.

"'Blessed are the peacemakers: for they shall be called the children of God.'"

His gaze went to Lorna, whose hand trembled noticeably as she ran it across her brow, but did her best to conceal her condition.

With the Bible still closed, he went on.

"'Blessed are ye, when men shall revile you and persecute you, and shall say all manner of evil against you . . . falsely, for my sake.'"

Then to all of the assembled.

"'Rejoice and be exceedingly glad . . . for great is your reward in heaven.'"

It was as if the entire congregation had taken a deep breath of consolation.

Keyes went on. His voice stronger.

"'For so persecuted they the prophets which were before you. Ask and it shall be given to you . . .'"

Deliverance's eyes were fixed on Keyes as they understood what Keyes was saying.

"'. . . seek, and ye shall find; knock and it shall be opened to you . . . for everyone that asketh receiveth; and he that seeketh findeth.'"

Keyes set the Bible on the pulpit . . . paused and spoke slowly but with mounting emotion.

"My friends, you have done me a great honor by asking me to come and speak to you this day. I know that this is not the best of times for you. You have been visited by misfortunes hard as a piece of the nether millstone . . ."

The citizens of San Melas looked at each other and reflexively nodded.

"There is 'darkness at noon' . . . But you must not lose hope. You must not give up. You are not forgotten. You are not lost."

Keyes motioned toward Lorna.

"I know. For only a short time ago it seemed that my wife and I were lost, hopeless, and abandoned . . . our bodies too weak to move . . . our spirits shattered. But there is strength within you if only you will summon up that strength."

But Lorna seemed even more uneasy.

"For there is hope in the midst of despair."

For only a moment Keyes's gaze fixed on Deliverance.

"There is a candle in the darkness."

Then swept across the assemblage.

"There is drink in the barren desert. And there is balm in bitterness."

Keyes became more fervent.

"'Your old men shall dream dreams . . .'"

He looked far out to where the Bryants sat.

"'. . . your young men shall see visions . . . And walk with faith.'"

Ethan, mesmerized by the words, seemed to be struggling.

"Draw upon the spirit within. 'Lift up your eyes unto the hills.' Arise and 'renew your strength.'"

Ethan rose to his feet with his crutches and began to hobble into the aisle and make his way toward the distant pulpit as Keyes's voice gained drive.

"'You shall mount up with wings of eagles.'"

Ethan let one of the crutches drop but kept walking toward the pulpit.

Keyes lifted the Bible and held it up to the congregation . . . but especially to Ethan.

"'Hearken to the voice of my cry. Behold and rejoice.'"

Another step by Ethan . . . and another.

"'You shall run and not be weary.'"

Ethan let the other crutch drop. There was a vocal reaction from the townspeople as Ethan stumbled . . . then kept walking . . . his eyes glaring directly at Keyes in a silent supplication for the minister to go on . . . to give him the power to continue.

Keyes responded, looked up to the sky . . . then back to the youth, his voice strong and charged with emotion . . . a command.

"You shall walk . . . 'walk and not be faint.'"

Ethan nodded, and with effort kept moving ahead.

Keyes set down the Bible and came from behind the pulpit, extended both his hands toward Ethan . . . giving the boy a goal to reach.

"'For darkness shall be lifted. And the crooked . . . shall be straight.'"

Keyes stood, waiting. Hands outstretched as . . .

Ethan's hands, also outstretched . . . toward Keyes, until . . . they touched his.

Keyes embraced the boy, who had tears in his eyes, as everyone in the congregation rose, smiling, laughing, and cheering while William and Pricilla Bryant rushed down the aisle toward their son.

Unseen, atop the hillock, outlined against the sky, mounted on a black stallion partially hidden by a tree . . . an ominous figure.

Moon's deathwatch face. His right hand moved slowly and touched the handle of his holstered gun . . . then again took hold of the reins. The stallion turned and moved away.

CHAPTER 14

Caleb was doing his best to usher the last dozen or so townspeople, all of them happy and smiling, from the parlor. Joseph sat in his rocker. Keyes, at a chair, his face pensive.

". . . Well, thank you all again for coming by, but it *is* getting late and it's been a very . . . trying day for Reverend Keyes. He'll see you all again tomorrow."

There were scattered "good nights" and "thank-yous" and the word "miracle" was audible more than once as Caleb managed to direct the crowd out the door and close it.

"It is a miracle, Reverend," Joseph rocked. "Like the Book says, 'you gave feet to the lame.'"

"No," Keyes shrugged in a self-effacive effort, "I didn't do anything. It was . . ."

"You're too modest, m'boy." Caleb lit his pipe. "You've given us hope. Maybe it's the beginning of more good to come. I'll tell you one thing, the whole town wishes you were staying."

"Well, thank you, but that's impossible."

"Nothing's impossible," Joseph said. "Not after today."

Keyes rose.

"I'd better go to Lorna. She seemed to be feeling poorly again."

"Too much excitement," Caleb proffered. "Probably should have stayed in bed a few more days."

"Yes. Well, good night."

"Good night," both Caleb and Joseph chorused.

"Oh . . . uh . . ." Keyes paused at the stairway. "I haven't seen Deliverance this evening."

"She must be working with her candles," Caleb conjectured.

"Yes. Well, please tell her I said good night."

"We'll do that." Caleb nodded.

Bethia sat in the straight-back chair next to the bedside as Lorna rested, her shadow-rimmed eyes looking at a letter she held in her hand. The room was illuminated by the candle Deliverance brought earlier.

"Well, hello." Keyes smiled as he came into the room.

"Jonathon," Lorna said, then looked toward Bethia. "Thank you, Bethia, for all your help."

"Yes, ma'am." She rose and walked toward the door. "You'll feel better in the morning after you've rested, I'm sure."

Keyes waited until she left the room, then went to the bed and sat next to Lorna.

"It's been a long day, but you look . . . fine, just fine."

"A little tired and weak, Jonathon. And there's that throbbing inside my head again."

"Mr. Hobbs was right."

"About what?"

"He said you got out of bed too soon."

"Didn't want to miss your sermon."

He moved closer and kissed his wife.

"Jonathon." Her face and voice uncertain. "That boy . . ."

"Ethan?"

"Yes. How . . . how did it happen?"

"I . . . don't know."

"I think I do. I think it was your strength that went out to him . . . when you spoke."

He took her hand and kissed it tenderly. The hand that held a letter.

"What's this?"

"One of your letters. I asked Bethia to get them from the trunk. You know I saved them all, every one. They meant so much."

"Lorna. I . . ."

"This one's about the first time you met General Custer after you enlisted. You said he called you 'Sport.'"

Keyes nodded and smiled.

"Your first battle. You never did write much about that part."

"The important thing I wrote was that I loved you."

"I had to hear about your field promotion from Libbie. No one's more in love than those two . . . except . . . the two of us."

"That's right, Lorna . . . and always will be."

He kissed her again, took the letter from her hand

"Go to sleep, dear."

He blew the flame out from the candle.

Moonlight flowed through the window into the room.

He sat beside her until she was asleep. It didn't take long.

Keyes, himself, was too restive to try to sleep.

He decided to go outside and think about what had happened that day, but after Lorna had reminded him of the letter his thoughts filtered back to his meeting Custer and that first battle.

It was at Hunterstown.

Keyes followed the adjutant as they both stepped into the tent where General George Armstrong Custer sat at his desk studying a map.

"Last of the new recruits, sir," the adjutant said. "Just arrived."

Custer looked up from his desk and smiled. "Well, Sport. I see you made it."

"Yes, sir. Thanks to your recommendation it didn't take long."

Custer looked at the adjutant.

"Another Wolverine, Jason. This one sidetracked from the courtroom to the cavalry." Then to Keyes. "That's a smart new uniform you're wearing. By the way, private, can you ride?"

"Yes, sir."

"Well, you're going to have to. We attack at first light. You have a horse?"

"No, sir."

"Well, pick one out. We've lost more men than horses. And Jason . . ."

"Yes, sir."

"See that he gets a red scarf."

While he was picking out a horse, Keyes noticed a tall, lean man, probably in his fifties, carrying a Bible and talking to the troopers.

Just before Keyes started to mount, the man with the Bible approached.

"You're new here aren't you?"

"Yes, sir."

"No need to 'sir.' I have no uniform or weapon . . . except this." He held out the Bible. "Reverend James Mason. Good luck, Private. God be with you."

"Thank you, Reverend."

"Ride, you Wolverines! Charge!" Custer shouted. "Follow me!"

And charge they did. Custer in the lead, into the eruption of Rebel rifles across the swamp, with flashes of smoke and a fusillade of bullets out of the brush.

Keyes, red scarf fluttering, found himself just behind Custer as one of the bullets crashed into the general's horse. Animal and rider toppled into the murky water. Custer fell face-first clutching his saber, as hooves thundered and splashed about him. Some of the Wolverine riders circled in confusion.

Keyes swirled his horse near the fallen man, reached out, and down, and grabbed hold of the dazed and muddied Custer by his uplifted arm. Custer, still gripping his saber, swung on behind Keyes.

"Charge, you Wolverines!" he cried again.

Out of the churning chaos and confusion, the Michigan Brigade regrouped and rallied behind their general, hatless and wet-haired, thrusting his saber toward the retreating Rebels.

But one of the Rebel troopers turned and aimed at

the double riders. Keyes maneuvered his mount and fired with his gun hand.

The Rebel's shot missed, but Keyes's didn't.

The Confederate retreat had turned into a rout.

That afternoon Custer, in his tent, sent for Keyes.

"I'm not going to make a speech, Sport. But you've earned that scarf. You're as good a cavalryman as we've got . . . and a damn good shot for a half-lawyer."

"Forgot one thing, sir."

"What's that?"

"I'm a full-fledged farm boy from Monroe, sir." Keyes smiled.

"That's where you learned to ride and shoot?"

"Yes, sir."

"You haven't got any more to learn before being a lieutenant."

"Sir?"

"I'm issuing a field order, Lieutenant Keyes. Ride to the left of me."

As he sat on a log outside the Hobbses' house that night, Keyes remembered Custer's words—and something else.

That was his first kill. But not his last.

Then Keyes noticed something else.

CHAPTER 15

There was a flicker of light from the shed in the not too far distance.

Inside, the cat sat next to a tall, red candle burning on the bench. Deliverance was covering an object in front of her with a damp cloth. She walked to the stove where two small cauldrons were boiling, picked up a long ladle, and stirred the contents of one of the cauldrons, then the other.

As Deliverance turned and started back toward the bench, there was a knock on the door.

She paused.

The knock again, slightly louder.

She had a curious smile on her lips as she moved with supple strides, the grace of a cat, toward the door and opened it, revealing Keyes.

He stood, his manner somewhat embarrassed, not quite certain how to begin.

"I . . . don't mean to disturb you, Deliverance, but . . . I . . ."

She opened the door wider, her eyes an invitation to come in.

He accepted the invitation.

Keyes looked around with genuine wonder.

"It's quite a . . . workshop you have here."

She was obviously pleased with his reaction.

He continued to take in the contents of the room.

"I haven't seen candles made since I was a little boy." He picked up one of the figures from the bench.

The cat did not move.

"This is more like a sculpture." He looked at the figure, then at Deliverance, awkwardly set the figure down again. "Well, as I said I didn't mean to disturb you. Just thought I'd say good night."

He started to walk off, but Deliverance touched his arm.

She looked at him a moment, then described a pattern with her expressive fingers. It became evident to Keyes that she was referring to Ethan, who now walked without the use of crutches. She nodded and smiled.

Keyes returned the smile.

"Yes. He's a wonderful boy. I'm glad that he was healed."

Deliverance pointed to Keyes, barely touching him.

Keyes shook his head.

"No. He healed himself."

She motioned her head in disagreement—"No"—then pointed to Keyes again. None of her movements were abrupt or exaggerated. Deliverance gestured with subtle, simplistic elegance, and attraction. She reached for his hand—took it and guided it to her face near her lips . . . and held it there for a moment.

She let go of his hand. He held his fingers to her face a moment more . . . then withdrew them.

Her eyes expressed an evocative supplication. Keyes recognized her entreaty.

"You're asking if I can help you?"

She nodded in anticipation.

"I only wish I could."

Her eyes became impelling, sensuous.

He thought for a moment.

"Deliverance, were you born . . . could you ever speak?"

She nodded again.

"I'll find out more from Caleb."

Deliverance was obviously pleased with his answer.

"Well," Keyes smiled, "I'd better . . . say good night." He walked to the door. "Don't work too late."

He left, closing the door.

Deliverance moved back to the bench and uncovered the object there. A partially finished wax figure that somewhat resembled Lorna.

It did, in fact, have wrapped around it, the cut-off material from Lorna's skirt.

Deliverance gazed at the wax figure. Her eyes no longer doleful.

CHAPTER 16

As silently as he could, Keyes closed the door to their bedroom and entered.

Lorna was asleep. He walked to the side of the bed, reached out and gently touched her bare shoulder, careful not to awaken her.

He walked to the window and looked out.

A flickering light still shone from Deliverance's shed.

He turned and made his way through the moon-bathed room, to the dresser, and looked at his dim reflection in the mirror. He removed his watch and chain from his vest, wound the watch, and placed it near the Bible.

His eyes went to the mirror again as he began to unbutton his shirt.

But he stopped abruptly.

The reflection was not of Keyes.

Instead, looking out at him was the face and torso of another man, about the same age . . . stripped to the waist . . . the face and body, bruised and bleeding, with a look of anguish, of supplication, in his expression.

Stunned, Keyes's hand wiped at his eyes, then covered them with both his hands.

When he uncovered his eyes they went first to the Bible . . . then to the mirror . . .

The reflection was of himself.

In a shivering sweat he started for the bed. His left foot kicked the rifle that was leaning against the trunk—knocking the weapon to the floor.

He looked to see if the noise had awakened his wife.

No.

Keyes almost staggered to the bed without undressing and lay there next to Lorna.

But sleep did not come for a long, long time, a fitful sleep in the battlefield of his mind.

CHAPTER 17

Ethan and a half-dozen other blue-eyed, towhead boys were playing near the entrance of the abandoned mine. Ethan just as active and agile as the rest.

When Keyes came out of the front door of the Hobbses' house, Caleb and Joseph were already sitting on the porch, Caleb smoking his pipe and Joseph enjoying the motion of a rocking chair.

"Good morning, Reverend," both men simultaneously greeted him.

"Morning."

"Well, Reverend," Caleb said, "you slept through most of the morning. Must've had a good rest."

"On and off."

"Have you had breakfast yet?" Caleb asked.

Keyes shook his head.

"Well, then," Caleb started to rise, "we'll have Bethia fix you a nice hearty midmorning meal."

"Thank you, but first I'd like to ask you something."

"Go ahead." Caleb smiled and sat back in his chair.

"It's about Deliverance . . . this affliction of hers. How . . ."

"Caleb! Joseph! Mr. Keyes! Please, you've got to help!"

William Bryant, followed by Jacob, several men, and one of the towhead boys, ran toward the Hobbses' house. Bryant shook with anxiety as he stammered for words.

"What is it, William?" Caleb asked. "Take a breath and tell us what happened."

"It's . . . It's Ethan . . . he asked this morning if he could go . . . go play with his friends . . . I said 'of course' . . . and . . . now . . ."

"Now what?" Caleb took a step forward.

"Now he's . . . trapped in the mine . . . some timbers collapsed . . . but they can still hear his voice . . . we need . . . help . . . all the help we can get . . . before . . . He's trapped . . . hurt . . . he . . ."

"We'll get there right away," Caleb assured him, "with all the help we can muster!"

"Caleb . . ."

"Yes, Reverend?"

"I want to go with you."

CHAPTER 18

More than half of the townsmen had gathered at the mine entrance, along with some of the women, including Ethan's mother and Deliverance, who was doing her best to comfort the nearly hysterical woman.

"How did it happen?" Caleb asked one of the young boys.

"We were playing . . . playing 'hide-and-seek.' Ethan, he was 'it,' and then after we hid we heard a crash . . . and then we heard him . . . hollering from inside . . . and crying . . ."

"Oh, William," Pricilla Bryant sobbed to her husband, "why did you let him do this? Just a short time ago he couldn't even walk."

"He wanted to play with the other boys . . . he seemed so happy . . . you saw how he was this morning . . ."

"Well, he's not happy now . . . if he's still alive . . . and you could have . . ."

"William, Pricilla," Caleb intoned. "Please . . . talking to each other that way won't help get him out. If you . . ."

"Is there," Keyes interrupted, "is there another way into the mine?"

"No," one of the men who had worked there replied. "The way in is the only way out . . ."

"So says the book," Joseph added. "'This is the way . . . walk ye into it' . . . Isaiah thirty, twenty-one."

Two of the other miners who had previously entered came out, their faces dirty and sweating.

"He's stopped calling for help . . . At least we can't hear him anymore. There's timber and rocks . . . maybe he's . . . he's . . ."

"Dead!" Pricilla Bryant cried out.

"And maybe he's not," Keyes said.

"With all that timber and rubble that fell," one of the miners shrugged.

"We're not doing any good out here," Keyes's voice was calm but strong. "Get shovels, pick axes, anything that can dig and hack through timbers . . . we're going in there."

"More's liable to come down anytime," a miner warned.

"All the more reason to get a move on," Keyes said, leading the way into the entrance. Sam Hawkins went in with the others.

For over half an hour they worked inside the shaft, clearing debris—stone, shale, planks, and crossbeams that had collapsed, edging inch-by-inch, foot-by-foot, inward. Bryant was desperately calling out his son's name.

"Ethan! Ethan!! Ethan!!! It's your dad . . . please son . . . can you hear me?!"

Finally there came an answer, faint and shallow.

"Dad . . . dad . . . back here . . . I'm hurt . . . I'm scared . . . I'm . . ."

"Ethan . . . It's Reverend Keyes. We're all here to help you. I've helped you before, didn't I?"

"Yes, sir. But I'm going to die. I'm going to die here . . . I know it."

"You're going to live, Ethan. Your father's right beside me, and your mother's just outside waiting for you . . . have faith . . ."

"But I hurt . . . there's a big post on top of me . . . I can't move . . . and I hurt . . ."

"Faith, Ethan . . . we're getting closer—can you hear what I'm saying?"

"Yes . . . sir," his voice faltered.

"Ethan, remember the words that helped you before . . . 'There is hope in the midst of despair' . . . 'Your young men shall see visions' . . . 'draw upon the spirit within' . . . remember?"

"Yes, sir."

"We're almost there."

The men renewed their labor, as if a new set of reflexes and mounting strength had empowered them, lifting rocks that were too heavy, timbers too weighty.

"Ethan, 'There is a candle in the darkness' . . . we can see you—'for darkness shall be lifted' . . . and so will that timber."

Keyes motioned to the other men and to the timber now in sight.

"Reach out to me, Ethan . . . as you did before . . ."

"I . . . I can't . . . I hurt . . ."

"Yes you can. Reach out. Take my hand . . . take it . . . they're lifting that timber . . . one side of it . . .

help us help you . . . give me your hand. I'll get you out . . . that's it . . . I've almost . . . Faith, Ethan."

Keyes strained . . . he touched the boy's outstretched fingers . . . then grasped his hand.

One side of the timber rose inches higher.

"'Wings of eagles,' Ethan . . ."

Keyes pulled slowly, but with all the will at his command.

"You're free."

William Bryant carried his son outside, followed by Keyes and the other grime-covered men.

There were cheers of joy and relief as Pricilla ran to take the boy in her arms, then turned to her husband.

"William! You saved him! You saved our little boy!"

Bryant shook his head . . . then pointed to Jon Keyes.

Deliverance looked at Keyes and smiled.

CHAPTER 19

"I'll ride ahead and tell the folks the good news," Joseph announced. "The Lord has shown His glory."

And he galloped toward San Melas, as Caleb, Deliverance, and Keyes followed in the buckboard.

"We'll have a celebration in your honor," Caleb said to Keyes, "for what you've done for Ethan . . . this time saving his life." Deliverance nodded in agreement.

"No. Please. I did no more than the rest of those men in the mine. Just so he recovers."

"Whatever you say, m'boy. But you saw that he already took a few steps before we left."

"Yes. That's wonderful."

"We'll have the mine sealed so nothing like that can happen again," Caleb added.

"That's a good idea," Keyes agreed.

"But, you've got to promise one thing, Reverend."

"What's that?"

"That you'll go easy on yourself. Get some rest.

Pardon my saying it, but you look a little the worse for wear. You need to take care of yourself."

Once again Deliverance nodded in agreement. She hadn't taken her eyes away from Keyes since they started back.

But there was another pair of eyes, atop the spine of a crest—looking down from his stallion.

Moon's eyes were fixed on Deliverance.

"I'll put the buckboard away," Joseph said as they pulled up by the porch.

"Thank you," Caleb nodded.

Keyes helped Deliverance off of the wagon. There was appreciation on her face, then she turned and walked toward her workshop.

"Your daughter is quite a . . ."

"Yes, she's quite a lady. And brave. I'm very proud of her."

"I wanted to ask you . . ."

"Let's go inside. I've a bottle of brandy for just such occasions . . . unless you'd rather have something to eat."

No, the brandy sounds better."

"What is it, m'boy?" Caleb asked as both men sipped their brandies. "What's on your mind?"

"Caleb," Keyes paused, "this affliction of Deliverance's . . . how did it happen?"

A veil of sadness came over Caleb's face. He set the snifter on the table and spoke slowly, painfully.

"When she was a child she had a series of bad dreams. Evidently, they were horrible nightmares. She'd wake up terrified . . . but wouldn't . . . or couldn't tell us what she'd dreamed. One night she woke up screaming. That was the last sound she ever uttered."

"I see."

"Reverend, you've already done so much . . . but, do you think you could . . . help her?"

"I don't know."

"She has so much faith in you." His voice quavered, "If you could, m'boy, I'd be . . . well, she's everything I have."

"I understand. But . . ."

Bethia was at the staircase.

"Pardon me, Mr. Keyes. Joseph told us what happened at the mine. Your wife . . . she's been asking . . ."

"Thank you, Bethia. I'll go right up."

"Lorna, I was coming right up to see you."

"It took long enough," her voice was hollow.

"We were at the mine . . ." He moved toward the bed.

"Yes, Joseph told us all about it. You've become quite a hero, haven't you?"

He sat on the edge of the bed and leaned closer.

"I did no more than the other men. The boy's all right, that's the important thing."

Her manner softened.

"Yes, Jonathon, that is important . . . and I'm glad you could help, and Joseph said you did more, much more. But you haven't forgotten . . . there's something else that's important."

Keyes said nothing, but waited for Lorna to go on.

"Saguaro. The promise you made to Reverend Mason. He's waiting for us. You haven't forgotten that, have you?"

"No, of course not."

"You seem so . . . settled, so comfortable here . . ."

"I'm only settled and comfortable until you're well. You're not ready yet. You know what happened when you went out to the sermon . . ."

"Jonathon, I'll make you a promise if you want to hear it."

"What is it, Lorna?"

"I'll get well soon. I promise."

CHAPTER 20

The streets of San Melas were silent. After sundown the boardwalks were unpopulated. Only the whisper of a vagrant desert wind wafted through the village structures. The light of oil lamps filtering through the curtained windows disclosed the silhouettes of citizens at supper.

Inside the Hobbses' house, in the dining room adjacent to the parlor, sat Caleb, Deliverance, and Joseph, at a table illuminated by two ornate candles.

Bethia, carrying a tray, made her way down the stairs, followed by Keyes, voicing his thanks.

"Bethia, Lorna and I do appreciate your bringing supper upstairs. The boiled New England meal was delicious . . . and we did want to be together."

"More than happy to oblige, Reverend," she acknowledged and walked toward the kitchen.

"And thank you, Caleb."

"Of course, m'boy. But we did miss you." Caleb was lighting his pipe. "Won't you sit with us for a while?"

He pointed to an empty chair next to Deliverance. "It's early yet."

"Thank you." Keyes nodded, pulled out the chair, and took a place at the table. "I did want to come down and say good night. I see you had supper by candlelight."

"Yes," Caleb blew out a perfect smoke ring. "Thanks to Deliverance. And aren't they beautiful?"

"Beautiful," Keyes repeated. He looked at Deliverance. It was not easy to determine whether he was referring to the candles, or the candle maker.

Deliverance's serene face was aglow, her silver-blue eyes reflecting the glimmer of the candle's flame.

There was a moment of silence.

"Mr. Bryant came by to express his thanks to you," Caleb broke the silence, "but we didn't want to disturb you and Lorna at supper. We told him we'd convey his message."

"How is Ethan doing?"

"Quite well, considering. Jon, how about another sip of brandy, a . . . what is it called . . . a nightcap?"

"No, thank you . . . but it is a beautiful night. The desert can be . . . enchanting, after the sun goes down."

"Yes," Caleb said, "and it's been a long day and very rewarding, thanks to you."

"How is the missus feeling?" Joseph asked.

"As well as could be expected." Keyes took a breath. "She . . . she's anxious to . . ."

"To leave San Melas?" Caleb finished.

"To get settled in Saguaro."

"Of course," Caleb nodded, "but your wagon is

still being repaired . . . wheels and the axle . . . and Mrs. Keyes is still in some need of repair. We wouldn't want her to go through what happened before . . . in her weakened condition. She's got to gain strength."

"I did mention that to her."

"'Therefore, shall the strong glorify thee,' the Book says," Joseph quoted.

"Yes, well, I'd better be getting upstairs. Lorna will be waiting." He rose. "Good night . . . and thanks again for that supper." His glance went again to Deliverance as he touched her shoulder, "Good night, Deliverance."

Lorna's hands held the open Bible. She placed it on the bed beside her as Keyes entered.

"Did you say your good nights, Jonathon?"

He nodded, then looked at the open Bible.

"My favorite passage." She spoke without looking down at it. "'The voice of my beloved! Behold he cometh . . . leaping upon mountains . . . skipping upon the hills.' Remember? The Song of Solomon . . . our song."

"Yes, I remember," he said softly.

"Jonathon, last night you tossed and talked in your sleep . . . I couldn't understand what you were saying. Was it the war again? Shenandoah? Was it what happened there?"

"I . . . I don't remember."

"I had hoped those dreams were over. Is there anything I can do to help?"

"Yes, there is, Lorna. Sleep. Rest and get well. I'll sit beside you until you fall asleep."

Inside the candlelit shed, the thumb and fore-finger of Deliverance applied pressure to the temples of the wax image of Lorna Keyes. The cat purred as Deliverance smiled.

Lorna had fallen into the pit of a deep sleep.

Keyes started to undress but stopped. He took the Bible from the bed and placed it on the dresser.

With cautious footsteps he started for the door.

CHAPTER 21

He sat on the stump of a tree and thought . . . and wondered . . . and remembered.

The journey toward Saguaro—his dream of the burning church with an image that could have been Deliverance. The wagon breakdown. Near death in the desert. The rescue. Caleb, Joseph, and Deliverance. Lorna, "recovering," wanting to get to Saguaro. The misfortunes of San Melas. Without a church. Deliverance's affliction. Young Ethan on crutches for the rest of his life. The mine run dry of gold. Moon, evil incarnate . . . his hell sport and promise to return. The Sunday service and Ethan's miraculous walk to him. Then the young boy trapped in the mine. His vision of the man in the mirror, bruised and burned. The battlefield of his mind . . . and the bloody battles riding with Custer.

Shenandoah.

Shenandoah.

Shenandoah.

Had it all started with Shenandoah?

He remembered.

Shenandoah. It began at Shenandoah.

"Shenandoah?" Sheridan asked rhetorically. "I'll tell you the answer. The answer is the Carthaginian solution, without salt . . . but with gunpowder, fire, and dynamite. Leave nothing standing. Homes, bridges, barns, crops, rail yards. What it took generations to build . . . blow it all apart, burn it, destroy it . . . structures and soldiers. Leave nothing or no one in enemy uniform standing."

The Shenandoah Valley. Geography and fate destined the Shenandoah Valley to be among the bloodiest of battlefields. The valley, more than one hundred fifty miles long and ten to twenty miles wide, nourished by the Shenandoah River, was rich in farmlands, orchards, and pastures. Between the Blue Ridge Mountains on the east and the Alleghenies on the west, the region was one of varied scenery and natural wonders.

Unfortunately for the valley, it was, also, the ideal avenue of approach between the forces of the North and South. Both sides considered it the passport to victory or defeat.

Philip A. Sheridan had chosen George Armstrong Custer to lead the North to that victory.

Ironically, the opposing commander, General J.E.B. Stuart, was a West Point friend of Custer's. Together, they had led the Yankee forces that defeated John Brown at Harper's Ferry. But since the war, the two had taken divergent paths to glory except when they crossed each other in the fields of battle.

"Jeb" Stuart, the charismatic Rebel general, was the military and spiritual inspiration of the South with victory after victory by his Invincibles, also known as the Black Horse Raiders. Never defeated—except by Custer—first at Brandy Station, where the reckless twenty-two-year-old Captain Custer led the First Michigan on what everybody thought was an impossible charge—and at Gettysburg where General Custer prevented Stuart from hooking up with Pickett, dooming Pickett's valiant charge.

And in the Shenandoah carnage Captain Jon Keyes rode with Custer in the midst of slaughter and devastation.

But with them, someone who Keyes could not help but notice, respect, and admire, Reverend James Mason, who carried no rifle, pistol, or saber—only a Bible, and who even during the crossfire gave words of solace and hope, before, during, and after the bloody conflicts.

During one of the respites from battle Keyes had asked the minister why he risked his life to be with the wounded and dying.

"To help heal the wounds."

"Isn't that a doctor's duty?"

"My friend, there are different kinds of wounds. Some visible, horribly visible, others are not, but just as deep. Sometimes deeper and more horrible. I can try to help, the only way I know how."

It was inevitable that there would be more deaths and more wounds, when Custer and Stuart would converge for a third time and Captain Jon Keyes would be there . . . at Yellow Tavern.

Keyes sat on that log at San Melas, quivering, with the fingers of his right hand stroking the side of his head just behind his ear where he could at times recall, and feel the effects of the wound, and then he felt other fingers, soft and soothing, between his own, gently brushing the same area.

He turned, the figure of Deliverance now stood near him, bathed in moonlight, as beguiling a figure as he had ever seen—or any man could hope to see.

She reached across and touched his face with cool, consoling fingers for just a moment and with a questioning look in her eyes.

"Oh, Deliverance . . . I . . . was just thinking of something . . . something about the war . . . it's over now . . . it seems so far away . . . especially now that you're here." He smiled. "I'm all right."

Her questioning look was still unanswered. She persisted as best she could without benefit of speech.

She pointed at him, then opened both palms close together.

"Something about me . . . and a book?"

She indexed her forefingers as if in prayer.

"The book . . . a Bible?"

Deliverance nodded and pointed at him again.

"A minister?"

Her lips formed a *yes*. Then she stood stiff-back straight and simulated shooting a gun.

"A soldier? Yes. Before I became a minister I was a soldier."

She touched the area of his head where he had been brushing. Her questioning eyes widened.

He nodded.

"A wound from the war . . . sometimes I can feel . . . part of the cartridge is . . . still there . . . and sometimes . . . well, I become aware of it"—he smiled—"but not now. You asked if I could help you, but now it seems you've helped me. Thank you."

He looked toward the shed.

"You're working late with the candles."

She smiled and nodded. Then motioned toward the trees and the star-studded sky.

"Yes, it is a beautiful night." He looked upward. "The moon is almost full . . ."

This time it was Deliverance who trembled, and her eyes were disquieted.

He rose and came close to her.

"When I mentioned the moon . . . you thought of . . . him . . . you're frightened. Isn't that it?"

She did her best to cloak her anxiety but couldn't completely mask her apprehension.

Keyes put his arms around her.

"Don't worry, Deliverance. I'll . . ."—he almost said *I'll take care of you* . . . but said instead—"Things will be all right."

He held her for just a moment more, then let his hands fall free.

"I'd better get upstairs now . . . Lorna . . . I'd better see how she is."

He thought Deliverance was motioning her thanks to him, but didn't want to think more about it . . . or her.

He turned and walked away leaving Deliverance outlined in the moon gloss.

With just as silent footsteps as he left, Keyes entered the bedroom and moved toward Lorna.

He needn't have been so silent. She had submerged into a deep cavernous sleep. Her jaws clenched tight.

He made his way to the dresser, took off his shirt, then noticed the Bible was now open.

Even in the darkness of the room there was enough moonlight to make out a passage his eyes fell upon.

". . . for judgment is toward you, because ye have been a snare . . . they have dealt treacherously against the Lord."

Then to the mirror and his own reflection which became—

The black-clad Moon, eyes of lust, thin lips twisted into a silent jeer.

He turned away but was compelled to turn back, this time to see *the prior reflection of the man, bruised, bloodied, and burned, now even more severely than the first time—a desperate plea in his hollow, tortured eyes. Both arms were outstretched to his sides as if affixed to an invisible cross.*

Keyes's hands tilted the mirror sharply upward on its hinges until he could no longer see any reflection at all.

Deliverance was at her workbench, a sublime look on her face as she manipulated the wax figure of Lorna, distorting the image with an uneven pressure of her fingers.

* * *

Keyes was at the bedside. He leaned closer to kiss Lorna's forehead. But she bolted up, her eyes wide in pain and horror, almost crashing into her husband's face.

"Lorna!"

"Oh, Jon! I . . ." She trembled and wiped at her eyes. "That pain . . . in my brain . . . as if it was being split with an . . ."

"Lorna, it was a dream . . ."

"The pain was no dream . . . it was real . . . worse than the sun in the . . ."

"Lorna. I'm here now. We're together."

"Yes . . . and it is subsiding . . . the pain . . . but, Jonathon, there's something about this place . . . these people . . ."

"It's your imagination . . ."

"No! It's real . . . don't you feel it, too . . . something?"

He looked toward the tilted mirror now reflecting the moon in the sky.

"No, Lorna . . ."

"Jonathon, as soon as the wagon is fixed . . . let's get away from this place."

"Yes," he nodded, "I'll see to it tomorrow."

"It'll be better for both of us."

Deliverance covered the wax image of Lorna Keyes with a damp cloth, blew out the candle, rose, and walked toward the door of the shed . . . followed in the darkness by the purring cat.

CHAPTER 22

The next morning the dresser mirror remained tilted upward.

While Lorna still slept he had dressed himself with no intention of looking into the mirror, even though the alien reflections had occurred only at night.

Before leaving the room Keyes walked back to the bed and looked down at his wife. Lorna had grown up as one of the most beautiful young ladies in Monroe, with only Libbie Bacon, now Mrs. Custer, as attractive. But, here, more than a little of that beauty seemed to have drained from her features. Even closed her eyes seemed sunken, her cheeks depressed, and her face uneasy.

As he moved toward the door he took note of the rifle, showing the effects of sun and sand, leaning against the wall. He wondered if the rifle was in operative condition, then went downstairs.

Keyes joined Caleb, Deliverance, and Joseph, who were about to begin breakfast.

"You're just in time, Jon," Caleb greeted, "We've just finished breakfast prayer, and we're ready for a hearty morning meal. Sit down," he pointed to the empty chair next to Deliverance, "and join us."

"Thank you," Keyes nodded, "and good morning."

"It is a good morning." Joseph nodded, "The Lord had made his face to shine upon us."

Deliverance handed Keyes a napkin from the table as he sat.

"Thank you, Deliverance. You look absolutely radiant this morning."

"I don't know how she does it," Caleb smiled, "works till all hours every night and rises with the sun fresh as a morning flower."

"Yes," Keyes agreed.

Bethia entered from the kitchen carrying a tray and moved toward the stairs.

"I thought I'd take the missus some breakfast."

"She's fast asleep," Keyes said.

"Well, she'll have to wake up sometime . . . and need some nourishment." Bethia was already on the stairway.

"Is Mrs. Keyes making progress toward her recovery?" Caleb asked as he sipped his tea.

"Not as much as I had hoped," Keyes said, "but she's anxious to start toward Saguaro. She asked about the wagon. I told her I'd go down this morning and see what shape it's in. Have you heard, Caleb?"

"No. But I'll be glad to go with you and find out."

"Mind if I go along?" Joseph asked.

"Of course not," Keyes said.

"After breakfast," Joseph added and forked another mouthful of scrambled eggs.

* * *

The Conestoga's back end rested on the floor of the repair shop with only the front suspended by wheels.

"I'm sorry," Sam Hawkins shrugged, "I thought the rear axle could be repaired, but it can't, not well enough to make it across that desert. I'll have to fashion a new one . . ."

"You're sure?" a disappointed Keyes asked.

"Very sure. I couldn't in good conscience let you even try. I'm working on a new axle," Hawkins pointed to his workbench, "as you can see."

"How long will it take you, Mr. Hawkins?"

"I'll do it as fast as possible . . . a few days."

"I appreciate that."

"After all you've done, Mr. Keyes, it's the least I can do."

Keyes thought for a moment.

"Caleb, is there another wagon in town that could make the journey? I'd be glad to pay the difference, if . . ."

"No. I'm sorry, m'boy."

"But you must have gotten here, all the way from Connecticut with sturdy wagons?"

"We did. But when we decided to stay in San Melas, we dismantled all of them, so no one would get a notion to abandon the community. We took a vote and decided to use the wagon wood and parts to help build what you see out there."

"'The Lord helps those who help themselves,'" Joseph said.

"Yes, well thanks again, Mr. Hawkins, I'll check back with you from time to time."

"Fine, Reverend. You do that."

As the three men walked back along the main street they heard a familiar voice.

"Good morning, Reverend . . . Mr. Hobbs, Joseph. Good morning."

"Good morning, Ethan," the three responded.

The young boy walked toward them.

"Well, Ethan, m'lad," Caleb said, "I see you're up and at 'em already."

"Yes, sir. Going to give my dad a hand today . . . thanks once more to Reverend Keyes. Thank you, sir."

Keyes nodded and smiled as the boy started across the street and the men moved on.

After a short silence, Caleb took the pipe from his pocket, but instead of lighting it, looked at Keyes, hesitated, then spoke.

"Reverend, this morning, before you came down . . . Deliverance told me, in her own way, that you were a great comfort to her last night."

"I didn't do much . . ."

"She's so concerned . . . worried about Moon."

"There's not much I can do . . . if anything."

Keyes stopped and looked down the street where Moon had ridden in.

"I know what you're thinking. Yes, he'll come back," Caleb said.

"Maybe . . ."

"There is no maybe. He'll come back just as sure as the earth turns. Have you forgotten what he did to Joseph . . . and you . . . that he dragged you down this same street? Have you forgotten the look on his face when he stared at Deliverance? Have you forgotten that he's evil?"

Keyes made no answer.

"Reverend, you said that you made a vow regarding the use of guns . . . of weapons. Was it something to do with the war?"

"Yes. That I would not kill any man again . . . unless my life depended on it."

"Or your wife's . . . or someone you love?"

Still Keyes did not answer.

CHAPTER 23

All that day Lorna had not touched anything on Bethia's breakfast tray.

Several times Keyes had looked in, once or twice thought about waking and urging her to take some nourishment, but thought that sleep would be a better balm for her condition.

He, himself, had noon meal and supper with Caleb and Joseph. Both times Deliverance was not at the table.

During the noon meal, he mentioned her absence to Caleb.

"It's not unusual for her to be at work out there all day long, as well as at night. She makes candles for our people in the village, and before it burned down, for our church."

"Without having anything to eat?"

"Oh, Bethia takes good care of her in that department. Don't you, Bethia?"

"Yes, sir," Bethia nodded on her way to the kitchen.

"But lately, the poor dear hasn't had much of an appetite."

When Bethia left the room, Caleb leaned closer to Keyes. "Not since that last visit from him."

"Moon?"

Caleb nodded.

"'Therefore I went about to cause my heart to despair of all the labor I took under the sun,'" Joseph quoted.

That afternoon Keyes did catch a glimpse of Deliverance walking in the nearby woods as she held the cat in her arms. Her face, what he could see of it, meditative, her eyes distant but frightened.

Was she thinking of what would happen when Moon returned? Keyes wondered.

He thought of approaching her, started to move toward her, but she turned, saw him, smiled a forced smile, then proceeded back toward the shed.

That evening Keyes had brought up a bowl of broth and entered the bedroom. In spite of a long sleep, Lorna had not improved; if anything, it was just the opposite. She seemed lethargic, enervated, indifferent, somewhat confused, and silent, with more than a glint of suspicion in her voice when she did speak.

"Well, what did you do today, Jonathon?"

"I'll tell you all about it as soon as you finish this broth." He sat on the bed beside her and spoon-fed the soup to his wife until the bowl was empty.

After that, her spirit seemed to rise somewhat.

"Well, the first thing I did was to see about the wagon. Caleb and Joseph went with me."

"And Deliverance?"

"And Deliverance, what?"

"Go with you?"

"No. Just Caleb and Joseph."

"Then you didn't see her today?"

"Only at breakfast," Keyes said, without mentioning that afternoon by the woods.

"How was she?"

"Just like she always is."

"Beautiful."

"Well, yes . . . and a little . . . plaintive."

"Being unable to speak?"

"Yes."

"But she has other ways to . . . communicate."

"Yes, but it's not the same . . . still an affliction."

"In some ways."

"I don't know what you mean, Lorna."

"What about the wagon?" Lorna changed the subject. "When can we start for Saguaro? Is it ready?"

"No, it's not, not yet. Mr. Hawkins says he has to make a new axle."

"How long will that take Mr. Hawkins?"

"Not very long."

"You told him we were anxious to leave?"

"Yes, Lorna. I told everybody."

"Everybody?"

"Lorna, you seem . . ."

She pressed her hand against her forehead. "I just feel . . . Jonathon, I think I'll close my eyes for a little bit . . . I think that broth made me . . . drowsy."

"You do that, Lorna. You'll feel better."

Deliverance, her eyes now bright by candlelight, her supple fingers at the wax image of Lorna, pressed against the forehead.

* * *

Keyes sat at a chair near the half-empty trunk. He reached in, searching for a moment or two, then lifted the object of his search.

The red scarf.

The red scarf he had worn around his neck, streaked with sweat and faded from rack of sun and rain, stained with dried-out blood long ago turned brown against the once bright crimson cloth that had been each trooper's flowing guidon in General George Armstrong Custer's charging Wolverine Brigade in the Shenandoah Valley, at Fort Royal, Winchester, Waynesboro, Falls Church, and Yellow Tavern.

Yellow Tavern. Keyes gripped the red scarf, looked at the rifle leaning against the wall, and thought of that evening before the charge at Yellow Tavern . . . with Keyes in Custer's tent.

"You sent for me, sir?"

"Yes. Sit down Jon. I just wanted to tell you that no matter what happens tomorrow, you've been a good soldier. The best. I appreciate all you've done for the brigade . . . and me. I've written your fiancée about you, and to Libbie, of course . . . and in truth, about someone we're going to meet tomorrow . . ."

"Jeb Stuart."

Custer nodded and said nothing.

"You've beaten him before. At Brandy Station and Gettysburg. No one else has."

"But this has to be the last time for both of us. He's a good man—a good friend—and a great general."

"So are you, sir."

"We were on the same side at Harper's Ferry—saved one another's lives . . . we both raced to capture Brown."

"The way I heard it, sir, it was you who saved his life when one of Brown's men aimed a pistol at Stuart, point-blank, but you shot first."

"Jeb and I were together at Brown's hanging. I'll never forget what he said. 'I, John Brown, am now quite convinced that the crimes of this guilty land can never be purged away except with blood.' I've faced officers and friends from West Point before, but at Yellow Tavern, it'll be my best friend—and I've got a feeling it'll be the last time for one of us."

"Sir, you've come far being what you were meant to be. You mustn't change—any time or place—including Yellow Tavern."

"I know that, Jon. But I'm glad we had this talk . . ."

"Excuse me, gentlemen." Reverend James Mason entered the tent holding his Bible.

"I've just come from the others, and I wanted to give both of you a blessing for what you're doing for our country."

Minutes later, just outside Custer's tent Keyes spoke to Reverand Mason.

"Reverend, may I ask you a question?"

"Of course. What is it, my son?"

"At this same time do you think that there is someone like you giving a blessing to the soldiers on the other side?"

"I hope so." The minister said.

* * *

Deliverance smiled, then relieved the pressure from the forehead of the wax image of Lorna, looked at the wax figure, and then at the cat hunched on the workbench. She reached for the damp cloth.

Keyes looked at the red scarf still in his hand, then at the rifle against the wall. He started to rise and heard her voice.

"Jonathan . . ."

"Yes, Lorna, what is it?"

"I'm . . . I'm sorry . . . if earlier I seemed somewhat . . . abrupt . . ."

"Not at all."

"I woke up thinking about something we talked about before leaving Monroe . . . I wonder if you remember?"

"We talked about a lot of things." He smiled.

"Including having a family, a baby. Remember that?"

"Yes, of course."

"Do you still want . . . ?"

"More than anything. As soon as we're settled in Saguaro."

"Thank you, Jonathon. That makes me feel much better."

"Go to sleep, my dear."

"I will, now."

Keyes walked to the dresser, stood for a moment, and started to adjust the mirror from its upturned position, then hesitated. He looked at the Bible on top of the dresser.

Then moved away without touching the mirror.

CHAPTER 24

The next day was the most pleasant since their arrival in San Melas.

At least it began that way.

Both Lorna and he slept peaceably through the night.

In the morning, Bethia brought up breakfast enough for both of them, and they partook together and even recalled good times in Monroe before the war—including the first occasion they spent time together.

It began with the Fourth of July shooting contest.

Five of the most attractive—and eligible young ladies had prepared picnic baskets. Libbie Bacon had excused herself since she was unofficially engaged to George Custer, who was away at West Point.

Mayor Claude Markham made the announcement concerning the contest.

"A dozen contestants with their rifles will compete against each other—and the best five shooters will take their pick of the five beautiful ladies and their baskets—in the order that the shooters finish."

Reggie Harris, the richest and most favored of the contestants, sidled up to Lorna Benton, smiled, patted the barrel of his rifle, and whispered, "Lorna, looks like you and I are going to picnic together."

And throughout most of the contest, it did look that way.

It came down to a tie for first place between Harris and Jon Keyes.

Each had one last shot at the target.

Harris shot first and made a direct bull's eye.

"Seems like Mr. Harris is the winner," the Mayor proclaimed, "but go ahead and shoot, Mr. Keyes."

Jon Keyes took aim and fired.

It looked like he missed the target altogether.

"Sorry, Mr. Keyes," the Mayor said, "but it appears you're in second place."

"Take another look, sir." Keyes said.

They did.

Keyes's shot had split Harris's lead right down the middle.

He walked directly to Lorna Benton.

"May I have the pleasure of picnicking with you, Miss Benton?"

"You may indeed, Mr. Keyes."

They managed to find an isolated, shady spot along the Raisin River.

"You're a good cook, Miss Benton."

"I'm glad you enjoyed the chicken, Jon, and please call me Lorna."

"It wasn't because of the chicken that I chose you . . . Lorna."

"No? Then why? You've hardly ever even spoken to me in all these years. Why?"

"Because we were on different sides of the tracks, but . . ."

"But?"

"I've always had my eye on you, matter of fact both eyes—like Reggie Harris . . ."

"Those tracks don't make any difference to me . . . and Mr. Harris might as well be in China."

"Well, I won't be in China . . . but there's law school . . . and even though you say it doesn't make a difference, it'll be easier for a lawyer to cross those tracks and have a better . . . outlook."

"Look out for yourself, Jon . . . and in the meantime . . ."

"In the meantime?"

"You won't have to win anymore shooting contests if you want to go picnicking . . . or . . ."

"Or?"

"Cross those tracks and come a'calling."

"But the war changed all that, for everybody, including us," Keyes said.

"Changed for the better. You came back. We're together . . . and we'll be together in Saguaro."

"Speaking of Saguaro, there's something I have to do."

"What?"

"Clean that rifle." He pointed. "Make sure it's in working order. We might need it along the way to hunt with."

An hour later Keyes walked down the stairs into the parlor carrying the rifle.

There was an obvious reaction from Caleb, Deliverance, and Joseph.

"Well, Reverend," Caleb noted, "looks like you're loaded for bear," Caleb observed.

"I've cleaned and oiled it, just in case we need it for hunting when we leave San Melas."

"We'll provide you with plenty of supplies," Caleb said.

"Appreciate that, Caleb, but you never can tell. Thought I'd go outside, shoot a couple rounds, make sure it's in working order."

"Not a good idea, Jon. Not in town . . . might scare the parishioners. They're not used to the rifle shots."

"You're right, I didn't think of that."

He turned to go up the stairs.

"Wait a minute, Reverend. Deliverance was just about to go riding . . ."

Keyes noticed that she was dressed in riding apparel.

"Why don't you join her?" Caleb suggested. "Do your shooting far out of town. You do ride don't you?"

"I have done a little riding," Keyes smiled. "But," he looked at Deliverance, "will it be safe . . . I mean . . ."

"Oh, she knows a safe place. Rides there often. It'll be perfectly safe."

CHAPTER 25

She on her pinto, he on a buckskin, they had not ridden far, but it might as well have been to another part of the world—or even to another world.

The narrow fold of the entrance through craggy rock-shell was nearly invisible except when the sun had angled at a precise aspect above.

The two riders paused just inside the scanty passageway, and Keyes's eyes were widened in disbelief.

In startling contrast to the raw beige and barren terrain they had traveled, Keyes beheld a verdant valley, ripe with variegated foliage: grass, fern, cypress, and butternut—a vale in thirty shades of green—and in the distance even a lily pond reflecting the gleam of sunlight.

Keyes gazed at Deliverance, then waved his hand across the horizon.

"Deliverance, this is miraculous. A virtual oasis. I've never seen anything quite like it, and in the middle of . . . nowhere."

She smiled and nudged her mount toward the pond. Keyes watched for just a beat, then followed.

She dismounted at the edge of the pond and stood waiting. She didn't have to wait long.

He was at her side, still under a spell of where he was and what he was seeing.

Deliverance picked up a fallen branch and with the point wrote something in the damp ground.

My Secret Garden.

"It *is* a Secret Garden," he nodded, "Caleb said you ride here often."

She smiled and began to motion with her hand and fingers, pointing to him and then around to the pond and the environs.

"I don't understand what you're trying to say . . ."

She touched his shoulder and motioned again.

"Something about . . . me?"

Her lips formed the word *yes.*

"About me . . . here?"

Again, the *yes*—and then shook her head as she motioned to him.

"Are you saying that I'm the only one you've ever brought here?"

Her eyes widened as she nodded, and her smile broadened.

"Well, Deliverance," he took her hand, "I'm . . . flattered . . . and, well, thank you."

With both hands she simulated shooting a rifle, then pointed to the rifle on his mount.

"Oh, yes. That's why we came here, isn't it?"

He moved to the horse, removed the rifle, and walked back and looked around.

She pointed to a tree with low hanging branches.

"Oh, the branches," he said. "Well, there's nobody

around to hear the shots. Let's see if it works and how accurate."

Keyes took a quick aim and fired twice.

Two branches split and fell to the ground.

Deliverance clapped her hands in approval.

"That's enough," he smiled, "don't want to waste cartridges."

But she reached out, tapped the rifle, then pointed to herself.

"You want to take a shot?"

Deliverance nodded.

"Well, go ahead. I guess we can spare a couple more cartridges." He handed her the rifle. "Be careful," he smiled again, "it's loaded."

Without hesitation, she aimed and fired twice.

Two more branches split and fell.

"Say, you're full of surprises. Must've had a lot of practice."

No, she shook her head and held up one finger.

"First time?"

Yes, she indicated, and handed back the weapon, then pointed to the ground near the pond.

"You want to sit for a while and rest?"

She had already begun to lower her body.

"Well, why not? It's as good a spot as any," he looked at her, ". . . better than I've seen in a long time."

Her lithe body, narrow of waist, and blossoming in the right places, settled softly onto the bank, and Keyes, still holding the rifle, sat next to her, close enough to be aware of the exotic oils and wax she used in making the candles.

"You're an extraordinary young lady, Deliverance.

Delicate, but strong, artistic hands, and excellent shot, and you sit a horse smartly."

She shrugged, took his hand, and guided it to her lips, his fingers barely touching them.

"But you can't speak. Is that it?"

She nodded.

"Well, these things sometimes come and go. Maybe in time . . ."

Deliverance pointed to him.

"'Can I help you?'"

Another nod.

"As I said, I wish I knew how. But in the meantime, you should be content with what you *do* have. Just look in this pond."

They both leaned closer to the clear water reflecting their images.

He smiled at her, then looked back into the pond and his reflection instantly became that *of the man in the mirror, bruised, bleeding, burned, and pleading—or warning.*

He took the rifle and splashed the butt into the pond despoiling the grotesque image.

She seemed stunned, with a quizzical look in her eyes.

He labored for control.

"I'm . . . I'm sorry, Deliverance . . . I thought I saw . . . some kind of . . . lizard, or . . . I'm sorry." He started to rise. "We'd better get back. Lorna will be . . . we'd better get back."

She followed him to where the horses stood.

"Can I help you up?"

She shook her head and began to mount holding the reins loosely.

A sinister hissing sound.

The snake struck but missed the nervous pinto's foreleg. The horse bolted with Deliverance barely holding onto the saddle and both reins dangling on either side and both her boots out of the stirrups.

Even as he mounted the buckskin, galloped, and gave chase, he thought to himself that anybody else would have already fallen, but though the reins flopped on either side of the animal, she managed to stay on as the frenzied pinto raced on. Her body slipped and swayed in the saddle.

He spurred and whipped his reins across the racing buckskin, with all four hoofs sometimes galloping off the ground, until he caught up, horses flank to flank. He reached out with his right arm, circled her waist, and lifted her alongside of his horse. He held her tight, and as she exhaled breath after breath, he could feel the pulsing of her heart.

Keyes reined in the buckskin and dismounted with her still in his arms.

"Deliverance, you . . . are you all right?"

She smiled and touched his face while he still held her.

"Seems like that snake scared but just missed your horse." Keyes pointed. "Look, he's coming back to you—as if he's sorry about what happened."

Her arms were yet around him, seeming to draw him closer.

"Well, Deliverance, I'll say one thing. I'll never forget your secret garden. We'd better get back."

Only after he loosed his hands from her body did she lower her arms from him.

When they came back to San Melas, Caleb puffed on his pipe and smiled.

"How did it go?" he asked.

"Yes," Joseph rocked in his chair. "Tell us, how did it go?"

Deliverance began anxiously to answer, signing with her hands.

But Keyes answered instead.

"The rifle worked," Keyes replied and looked toward Deliverance. "No need to make more of it."

It was obvious to Keyes, if not to the men in the room that a shadow of disappointment had fallen across Deliverance's face. Disappointment that he had not given a more detailed account of what had happened at her Secret Garden—his awed impression of the environs, his and her marksmanship, the pond, his rescue of her on the runaway pinto—but Keyes was content to say that the "rifle worked" and "no need to make more if it."

For a moment it appeared that Deliverance was about to tell Caleb her version of the events. She even began to motion with her hands, but instead, she turned abruptly and strode out of the room—presumably toward her shed.

Caleb continued to puff on his pipe, Joseph to rock in his chair, and Keyes started up the stairs, still holding the rifle.

CHAPTER 26

Lorna lay propped against her pillows, with Bethia sitting in the straight-back chair near the bed as Keyes came into the room.

"Lorna. Bethia."

"Oh, Jon," Lorna said and looked toward Bethia.

Bethia rose and moved toward the door.

"Excuse me," she said, "I'll bring up a supper tray for both of you." And closed the door behind her.

Lorna pointed at the rifle.

"You were gone a long time. Something wrong with the rifle?"

"No," Keyes smiled. "You know what they say about these Henrys, 'load it on Sunday and shoot all week.' But Caleb thought it best not to shoot here in town, so I had to go some distance away."

He decided it was best to make no further explanation and set the rifle against the wall.

"Well, Jon, I hope you never have to use it on the way to Saguaro—or after we get there."

"So do I, Lorna. So do I, unless I have to," he added and sat on the chair.

"Jon, how long do you think it will take us? From here to Saguaro?"

"Just as fast as fresh horses will take us." He grinned.

That night after supper, Keyes and Lorna lay in their bed, Lorna asleep, but Keyes awake, rubbing his fingers through the back of his head where he had suffered that wound at his last battle—Yellow Tavern.

In her shed, Deliverance, with an enigmatic smile, sat holding the cat with one hand and with the fingers of the other hand plying a wax figure of . . . Jonathon Keyes.

"Yellow Tavern," Keyes uttered more comatose than conscious. "Yellow Tavern."

For Custer and Keyes the fiery path to Yellow Tavern was strewn with the devastating advance of the Union forces in the Shenandoah, as the reputation of General George Armstrong Custer grew to legendary proportions. His fame spread, then soared with each victory—at Chancellorsville, where in the coarse darkness, Stonewall Jackson lay mortally wounded, and at Cedar Creek, where what was left of General Jubal A. Early's army was overwhelmed and broken by Custer's charges.

The fabled Wolverines had made rubble of Shenandoah's principle towns—Winchester, Front Royal, Luray, Stanton, Waynesboro, and Lexington—and laid waste to the once fertile countryside.

The last impediment stood between them and complete victory.

Yellow Tavern loomed as the third, fateful, and

final encounter of the two most dramatic and daring cavalry generals of the North and South. Custer was also known as "Cinnamon," "Curly Top," "Boy General," and "Yellow Hair." Stuart—"Knight of the Golden Spurs," "Flower of Cavaliers," and "Chevalier Bayard."

Yellow Tavern—and General Jeb Stuart. Jonathon Keyes recalled Custer's words to him before the battle began.

"Jon, I'll never forget what Jeb said to me just after John Brown's hanging.

"Well, George, that's the end of that."

"No, Jeb. That's the prelude, the overture—there's already talk of succession, more than just talk. The Union will never countenance succession—and where will you stand— you and the other Southerners at the Point?"

"We won't just stand. We'll fight for States' Rights."

"You were born in the United States of America."

"But those states have the right to become un-united."

"I don't think so—neither does the Constitution."

"The Constitution? That's just a piece of paper that can be torn."

"As Brown said, 'Not without blood,'—including yours and mine, my friend."

"Let's hope it doesn't come to that, George."

"But it has, Jon—or will—in just a few minutes."

Custer galloped at the head of his troops.

"Ride you Wolverines! Follow me! Ride! Charge! Ride to the sound of guns!"

The earth shuddered under the din of hoofbeats. The striking of sword blades, the barking of rifles— through foaming streams, across flaming farmlands and battle-scarred forests—against the cacophonous chorus of gray-clad troopers screaming their Rebel

Yells, trying and dying in vain to hold the advance of the Michigan brigades led by Custer with Keyes to his left, close behind.

The Boy General noted a slightly vulnerable line in Stuart's left flank and tore at it in the lead of his red-scarf command, charging ahead into the gray line of defense.

General Jeb Stuart was everywhere trying to rally his exposed left flank, firing at everything blue, but still his left flank fell back from the effect of the Wolverines' repeating carbines.

Gun smoke smeared the air; riders on both sides fell, and the battlefield became hell incarnate—with Stuart himself riding into the thick of it to seal the bending, then broken flank.

Both Custer and Keyes spotted General Jeb Stuart at the same time.

"General!" Keyes shouted.

"I see him!"

Both fired at the same time—one shot just missed, the other found its mark—General Jeb Stuart's chest.

Stuart fell from his horse.

Custer had lost a friend—and won the day.

At the sight of their beloved commander on the ground the die was cast—but not quite.

One of the retreating Rebels turned and fired a final shot.

Captain Jonathon Keyes grabbed at the back of his head, then fell to the ground.

* * *

Keyes, still in bed, stirred fitfully, next to Lorna who was in a deep sleep.

Even asleep his face was disturbed, sweating, and faintly mumbling, with the flameless candle nearby in the room illuminated only by moonlight.

Deliverance, with a satisfied smile curled on her lips, gazed at the wax image of Keyes.

In his unconscious mind he envisioned their honeymoon night, he and Lorna, their bodies entwined, their lips sealed together—until Lorna became the face and figure of Deliverance, her eyes locked in ecstasy—but not for long as Keyes turned and twisted in bed to dispel the image.

But almost immediately there appeared another image against a velvety black background.

Keyes was running, but in a torturous, slithering, sated motion—struggling to move faster—away from something or someone in pursuit—but each step agonizing, as if his muscles were stretching and screaming with pain—his face sweating, eyes terrified, wanting to look back, but afraid to . . . finally he did and saw . . .

The bruised and bleeding man from the mirror, pursuing him.

The man, too, was running in slow motion—arms outstretched—desperately trying to reach Keyes—but pursuing in vain—not quite able to overtake him. A marathon, seemingly endless, infinite, both men near exhaustion, legs leaden, lungs drained, until . . .

Keyes looked ahead and saw Deliverance.

Dressed in a diaphanous white gown, revealing every curve and dip of her shimmering outline—standing just inside of a doorway—her arms outstretched, beckoning.

Keyes nodded, pumped anodizing air into his lungs, and called on every fiber of his being in an effort to run faster toward her, with the half-naked man in pursuit.

In a final burst, Keyes crossed the threshold as Deliverance closed the heavy door behind him, shutting out the pursuer. The door slammed with a resounding clang.

And Keyes found himself once more with his arms locked around the body of Deliverance.

His face bolted upward, awake but trembling. He breathed heavily and did his best to compose himself, not quite knowing at that moment where he was.

Keyes stroked the back of his head as he had just before he fell at Yellow Tavern.

But he knew that this was not Yellow Tavern.

Lorna was now awake and in bed next to him, upright on her elbows.

"What is it, Jonathon?"

Unsteadily, he wiped at his perspiring face.

"Nothing, honey. It was just . . . a dream."

"More like a nightmare again . . . you're ringing wet . . . the war?"

"Yes . . ." he nodded. "I lay down a minute and fell asleep."

Keyes rose with effort and went to the bowl and pitcher on the dresser. He dipped his unsteady hands into the bowl of water and wet his face, covering it with both hands.

He held his hands, blanketing his face, as he realized he was in front of the tilted mirror again.

Lorna sensed that her husband was more than just upset from a dream. He was afraid.

"Jonathon"—she rose, made her way to the dresser, stood beside him, and placed her hand on his shoulder—"is there something I can do?"

Slowly he withdrew both his hands from his face, tilted down the mirror, looked into it, and saw—his own reflection with Lorna near him.

He savored the moment in relief.

"You already have, Lorna."

He took her face in his hands and kissed her tenderly.

"You're the one who has to take care of himself," she smiled, "if we're going to get to Saguaro."

"Yes. I know," he said and kissed her again.

Deliverance covered the wax image of Jonathon Keyes with a damp cloth and smiled as the cat leaped from the floor next to her on the table.

CHAPTER 27

The next day Keyes, as he had promised Lorna, suggested to Caleb and Joseph that they pay a visit to Sam Hawkins and see what progress he was making in the repair of the Conestoga.

They readily agreed and proceeded to accompany him to the stable.

On the way they passed William Bryant's grocery-hardware store where young Ethan was brooming the boardwalk.

"Good day, Mr. Keyes, Mr. Hobbs, Joseph," the lad greeted, then rested his chin on the slanting broom-stick.

"Good day," Keyes responded, "are you sure you're up to such hard work?"

"The boy's a one-man work machine," Bryant grinned as he stepped out of the doorway, "next thing you know I'll have to make him a full-fledged partner. I'll have to get a new sign made 'William Bryant and Son' . . . after he finishes school."

"You couldn't do any better," Caleb smiled.

"How are you doing in school, Ethan?" Keyes asked.

"I can do my sums, sir, and read and write as good as anybody . . . except for Maggie Blythe. She's real smart."

"Don't neglect to read from the Book, boy," Joseph said, "'give thy heart to know wisdom.'"

"Yes, sir, I do that every night before bedtime."

"Time well spent," Joseph added, as the three men proceeded toward the blacksmith's.

"I've put everything else aside," Hawkins said as he pointed to Keyes's wagon, "except what absolutely has to be done and am concentrating on the Conestoga. Coming right along . . . that axle's quite a challenge, but I'll get her done and done right."

"Very good, Mr. Hawkins . . . how long do you think . . . ?"

"Sooner than later, Reverend."

"I'm much obliged . . . and so is Lorna."

"How's she doing?"

"Better every day it seems . . . Well, we'll leave you to your work."

"Fine," Hawkins pointed to the fire pit. "I have to strike while the iron's hot," he smiled.

On the way back to the Hobbses' house, Caleb managed to light his pipe as they walked along.

"Caleb," Keyes said, "there's something else I'd like to ask you about."

"Certainly, Reverend, but can it wait until we reach the shade of our porch and relax a bit?"

"Of course."

As the two men sat on chairs and Joseph rocked in his chair in the shade of the porch, Caleb relit his pipe and turned to Keyes.

"Before you ask about whatever is on your mind,

there's something I'd like to say to you . . . it'll just take a minute or two, if you don't mind?"

"Please, go ahead."

"Well, this morning Deliverance, in her own way, told me about what happened to you and her at her Secret Garden."

"Told you . . . what?" Keyes seemed more than a little apprehensive.

"About the snake and her runaway pinto. How you rode to her rescue and saved her from . . ."

"Oh, that," Keyes smiled with relief. "I'm sure she exaggerated a bit. Deliverance is an excellent rider. She would've been all right. As I said, she's an extraordinary young lady . . ."

The extraordinary young lady stood at the doorway of the porch carrying a tray with a pitcher of lemonade and several empty glasses.

"And now she's come to our rescue," Keyes said. "I could use a little . . . libation."

"So could we all," Caleb agreed.

Deliverance poured, then took a seat near Keyes.

"Now, m'boy, what was it you wanted to ask?"

"Well, sir, you said that after you got here you dismantled your wagons and used them to help build the village."

"That's correct."

"You also said that your people don't believe in weapons . . ."

"That's also correct."

"But what I wondered was . . . how could you make that long, perilous journey through what must have been hostile territory without guns and rifles to protect yourselves?"

Caleb, Joseph, and Deliverance looked at each other for just a moment, then Caleb spoke.

"A very pertinent question . . . part of a long story . . . but I'll tell you as briefly as possible . . . if you care to hear."

"I certainly do . . . and take your time, sir."

"You've heard of Brigham Young and his Mormon followers who were persecuted and decided to come west, then founded a place for themselves. Well, we, too, had been persecuted and decided to follow their example—with all our worldly possessions—except for guns, which we had none of.

"But we had determination . . . and faith in finding a place of our own. So we began our journey, and somehow without incident, until we reached the great desert.

"Desolate landscape, and an unforgiving furnace during the day—and at night a devil wind thrashing our faces—like you—we lost track of time and place— and with little food left and empty canteens, we lost more—members of our congregation, including my wife, Deliverance's mother. We buried them with crosses to mark the desert's doing.

"The animals were spent and so were we—bone weary and dry—tongues thick with no sign of water— and desert sand caking our faces and bodies.

"But just before the desert could claim us, it appeared that another fate, just as final, would be our destiny.

"They rode in from all directions, yelping and

firing flaming arrows and blazing rifles—first in a wide circle, then circling closer around our wagons.

"They seemed in no hurry, relishing their certain victory. We could see their painted faces and bodies racing against the bald sky.

"Many of us knelt to pray—our final but futile prayers. Others sought useless cover inside or beneath the wagons.

"All but one of us.

"Deliverance. Just a little girl, not yet seven, but she stood on a wagon seat in plain sight, her long flaxen hair glistening in the sun, her arms upraised toward the heavens, lips quivering, unable to speak but in supplication.

"The astonished eyes of the circling riders seemed riveted on the strange little figure—even more astonished at the sudden sound of what seemed to be gunfire from above.

"But not gunfire.

"Thunder.

"Repeating, relentless thunder.

"Then lightning.

"Bolts of crooked lightning, flashing down from the heavens—one bolt spearing into the ground amidst the startled riders—then rain. A torrent of rain poured from the melting sky.

"One of the riders who carried the coup stick of a chief pointed with it to the rain-burst sky, reared his frightened mount, and rode toward the distant mountains.

"The rest of them followed.

"Soaking wet, we rushed to fill our canteens and whatever buckets we could find.

"All but Deliverance, who still stood on the wagon bench and lowered her rain-splattered face."

Everyone on the porch sat in silence as Caleb finished with his answer to Reverend Jonathon Keyes's question.

Then Keyes looked at Deliverance.

"Yes," he said just above a whisper, "she is a remarkable young lady."

CHAPTER 28

"I'm really not sure, Jonathon . . ." Lorna responded to her husband's question.

". . . there *are* times when I do feel somewhat better, even stronger and in better spirit, but then . . ."

". . . Then what, Lorna?"

"It's as if we're out there on the desert again . . . The sun, or something . . . pressing against . . . or into my brain . . . sapping that strength . . . everything becomes hazy . . . I lose all sense of time and place . . . drained, as if my body were on some distant sphere . . . struggling to break out . . . struggling against I don't know what . . . and then, then it seems to pass . . . and I'm here with you again . . . Oh, Jonathon, sometimes I wonder if I'll ever be well again . . ."

"Of course you will . . . and I have some idea of how you feel. There was a time after . . ."

"Yellow Tavern?"

He nodded.

"It was a terrible wound," she said. "I'll never forget General Custer's letter doing his best to ease my worry . . . when things looked so . . . dark."

* * *

For hundreds of thousands of fighting men, Blue and Gray, the war was not yet over, but tens of thousands of them would fight no more.

In the aftermath of some battles it seemed that there was not enough land to bury them all, but buried they were.

They had come from streets of cities, from narrow sidewalks of villages, from fields and farms, rich and poor, from plantations and backwoods shacks, across the flowing waters of the Mississippi, the Missouri, the Red, the Ohio, and the Shenandoah, to heed the call of the Confederacy or the Union, the trumpets of triumph, or the dirge of defeat—and for the dead to hear no more.

But in the aftermath of those same battles, some of the men, thousands, lay in battlefield hospitals like the one at Yellow Tavern.

Lined with stretchers and beds of wounded, bleeding, and blinded, and some already near death, with not enough doctors to tend the bitter harvest of war, for some in victory, for others in defeat.

Murmurs, moans, and gasping outcries rang through the tented triage.

And a voice, calm but concerned.

"Doctor Clemmins, I know you and your staff have more than you can handle—with the wounded on both sides."

"General, I've been with you since Culpeper where you were wounded . . ."

"And thanks to you, I . . ."

"Don't thank me, General. You have your duty, and I have mine."

"And nobody's better at it. Tell me the truth, doctor, what are Keyes's chances?"

Before the doctor could answer, Reverend James Mason left a stretcher and came closer to the bedside holding his Bible and listened.

Doctor Clemmins paused, then answered.

"He has no chance, none at all, unless we operate. And very little, if, and when, we do."

"You've *got* to operate."

"And I'm going to, but you ought to know, if you want the truth . . ."

"Go ahead."

"What's left of the shattered cartridge, from what I can determine, is extremely close to a nerve center in his brain. A very delicate and risky operation under the best of circumstances—which here, they are not. I'm doubtful that I can remove all of what's necessary for survival . . ."

"Yes you can, Doctor . . . and you will."

"I'll do my best."

"And so will I," Reverend Mason said and held on to his Bible.

"Lorna, I have no recollection of anything that happened after I was hit and falling . . . falling it seemed into the sleep of death—only, occasionally I seemed to hear the sounds of voices—some familiar, Custer and Reverend Mason, other voices, strange and from where, I've never known. If there is a place between two worlds . . . that's where I was."

"But thank God, Jonathon, you're here and we're together . . . even though, at times . . . you wake up remembering . . ."

". . . Remembering those I killed, and those who tried to kill me."

Keyes looked at the rifle across the room.

". . . That's why I'll only use that rifle if . . ."

"Jonathon, don't even think about that. Things will be different in Saguaro. Saguaro will help you forget. Now you've got to get some sleep and think about better tomorrows."

"It's strange, Lorna, I asked how you were feeling . . . and we ended up talking about me."

"Well, I feel better after our talk, my dear, so let's both get some sleep."

They did.

But Deliverance was not asleep. She was in the candlelit shed with her fingers working on the two wax images of Jonathon and Lorna as the cat purred softly.

CHAPTER 29

It was deep into the bleakness of night where even the moon was mostly shrouded by a motionless cloud. A Walpurgis night as the poet had written:

> *"Much of madness, and more of sin . . ."*
> *"Primitive impulses of the human heart . . ."*
> *"All that we see or seem*
> *Is but a dream within a dream . . ."*
> *"Silence! and Desolation! and dim Night! . . ."*
> *"Death looks gigantically down . . ."*
> *"Shadowy and vague . . ."*
> *"In the ghoul-haunted woodland of Weir."*

But this was another woodland, where only the yellow eyes of owls pierced the gloom, where a soft wind whispered through curled branches of leafless trees rising as if not of this earth, from another time and space, from some malevolent nether land, with untold secrets, veiled in an unholy sable-vested night.

A world within a world.

Deliverance's world.

Keyes lay as if in a drugged sleep.

Lorna awake, stared into nothingness, until—

Suddenly, she squeezed her eyes shut as her face became a basilisk of pain. Her hands flew to her temples trying to rub away the torment within.

She rose and did all she could to keep from crying out and waking Keyes.

She managed to walk to the open window and open it even more, breathed deeply, then noticed far off in the yard below . . . three or four indefinable figures holding large candles flickering through the darkness—her eyes drawn by whatever was unfolding below.

She seemed to be in a trancelike state. The pain was gone, superseded by something else—a call— a command—a hypnotic force—a summons to which she was compelled to respond.

The next thing she realized was that she was no longer in the bedroom but on the ground below, moving mesmerized as if led by some mystic force.

She paused and listened, at first to the faint, filtered sound of the night wind and then to something else . . . voices.

Young voices, chanting voices, voices as she'd never heard before, young voices delivering a strange incantation, with illusory words in an alien language, invading the darkness of the night and her brain.

> *Go blat . . . som blat . . . carradon . . .*
> *go loos. Com blat . . . go blat . . .*
> *go loos . . . carradon . . .*

Then again:

> *Go blat . . . som blat . . . carradon . . .*
> *go loos. Com blat . . . go blat . . .*
> *go loos . . . carradon . . .*

She took one, two, three steps toward those voices and saw in the distance . . .

Four figures varying in size . . . three to five feet tall . . . figures dressed in white robes and their faces covered by masks of animals . . . a wolf . . . an owl . . . a goat . . . a sheep.

Each of the four figures held a large lit candle before it . . . sending an eerie glow wavering upward toward the mask.

They stood close to something wrapped in an oilskin on the stump of a tree as they continued their chant.

> *Go blat . . . som blat . . . carradon . . .*

Drawing Lorna toward the hypnotic ceremony, but as she moved forward, suddenly her foot landed on something other than the ground.

Something that quivered, jerked, and then screeched.

Lorna stumbled.

The cat screeched again, eyes burning at Lorna, then leaped and disappeared into the night.

Lorna's trance was broken.

She regained her balance.

The chanting had ceased.

Now fully conscious, Lorna turned toward whence it had come.

The figures had vanished. Only the oilcloth with whatever was wrapped inside remained on the stump.

She walked slowly toward it and stopped in front of the dead tree.

She mustered all her courage and commenced carefully to loosen the cloth . . . then looked down.

Her face shook.

Her hands trembled as she slowly continued to unwrap the oilcloth. She paused wondering if it were best not to find out, to leave whatever was enclosed to stay that way until daylight when there would be others to witness the contents. But no, some impulse drove her to do it now.

As she did a dead owl rolled off the stump at her feet.

She could bear no more.

Lorna screamed a soul-searing shriek and fainted into a labyrinthine tunnel of oblivion.

CHAPTER 30

Out of the dimmest recesses of her mind, out of an indigo haze and into nebulous conscious, Lorna's eyes tried to focus, and when they did, she became aware, first of her husband and then the others.

She was on the ground not far from the stump. Keyes held her head, doing his best to soothe her, while Caleb, Joseph, Bethia, and Deliverance stood nearby.

This time the voices she heard were familiar.

"She must 'a been walking in her sleep, Reverend," said Joseph.

"No . . . No," she responded. "I wasn't asleep. I was awake, and I saw them . . ."

"Lorna, it's my fault. You were disturbed by my dream . . . then you fell asleep . . . you . . ."

"No! I tell you, I saw them . . ."

"Them?" Caleb questioned. "What was it you think you saw?"

"There were four of them . . . with candles and robes . . . with masks like animals . . . a wolf, a goat . . ."

"My dear," there was compassion in Caleb's voice, "you're still suffering the effects from the sun . . . playing tricks on your mind."

"No. There was the dead body of . . . by the stump. Look by the stump and you'll see," she pointed.

They all moved closer to the stump, including Lorna. All but Deliverance.

Nothing there.

Not even the oilcloth.

The group looked at each other, then at Lorna.

Silence.

Until Caleb took a step.

"Mrs. Keyes, it's been a trying day for all of us."

"Lorna . . ." Keyes whispered.

"Don't look at me like that! I saw it. Just as sure as I'm standing here now . . .

"Jonathon," Lorna pleaded, "I swear to you . . . I did see it . . . it wasn't a dream. Say that you believe me."

"All right, dear," he nodded slightly, "I believe you. Now, let's get you away from here."

Keyes lifted her up in his arms and started to carry her.

"Yes," Caleb said, "everything will look brighter in the morning."

"That's so," Joseph quoted, "'we shall awake to righteousness.'"

As Keyes carried Lorna toward the house, Caleb glanced at Deliverance, her face cool, calm . . . cryptic.

CHAPTER 31

Midmorning the next day, while Lorna was still asleep, Keyes walked outside onto the porch where Caleb and Joseph were standing.

Even before he could greet them, Keyes noticed that both men had a concerned look on their faces as they stared at something or someone in the distance.

Keyes immediately determined the object of their anxiety.

Moon, on horseback at the rim of the hill on the edge of town.

"How long has he been there?" Keyes asked.

"Don't know," Caleb replied, "we just came out here . . . and there he was, but the others must have seen him. The street is deserted."

"Yes," Keyes nodded. "Do you think he'll come in?"

"Don't know, Jon. But that rifle of yours . . . don't you think you ought to . . ."

"No, Caleb. If he saw the rifle it would be a challenge to him . . . an invitation to dare me to use it."

"But . . ." Before Caleb continued, Moon had turned

with his horse and disappeared over the other side of the rise.

"Still the cat with the mice," Caleb took a deep breath and wiped at his face. "But how long before he? . . . I don't know what."

There was a momentary silence as the three men continued to look toward the rise to make sure that Moon hadn't changed his mind and decided to come back.

"Well," Caleb said, "it appears that we've gotten a reprieve, at least for the time being." He pointed to the chairs on the porch. "Why don't we sit down and breathe easy for a while?"

"Good idea, Caleb," Joseph nodded and moved to his rocker.

Keyes and Caleb went to two of the other chairs.

"Caleb," Keyes said, "I want to ask you . . ."

"Something about what happened last night? Caleb was lighting his pipe.

"No. Not right now . . . about what we just saw."

"Moon?"

"That's right, Moon. I've been wondering about a few things . . ."

"Such as?"

"When did you first see Moon? How did he come to grip the town in terror? Has he killed? Where does he live? Does he take supplies? Food? Anything else?"

"I can answer some of those questions, Jon, not necessarily in that order . . ."

"The order doesn't matter. Just tell me what you know about him."

"Well," Caleb took a deep draw from his pipe,

"sometime ago he was first seen watching the men working the mine—watching from a distance.

"He appears from out of the desert and disappears back into it.

"Never has he asked for food or supplies of any kind. Not even a drink of water. Only for gold. Where, or how, he spends it we don't know . . . only that he rides into town on that same horse, with those same guns . . . and that same look . . . often directed at Deliverance.

"It began at a church service when Reverend Joyner was still our minister. In the midst of that service there was gunfire . . . Three times—gunfire that shot the flames out of three of the candles on the altar.

"Everyone recoiled and turned to see Moon striding down the aisle with a smoking gun in one hand, and, of all things, a rusty horseshoe in the other.

"He stopped near the altar and turned to face the congregation. Without speaking at first, he holstered the gun, then with both hands, unbent the horseshoe with little effort . . . straightened it out, then let it drop on the altar.

"'My name is Moon,' he hissed, 'and you've just seen a small sample of what I can do. What no one else among you can.'

"He paused and waited for a reaction.

"It came from Sam Hawkins, who was the biggest and strongest among us. Sam rose from his pew and approached the altar . . . and Moon. Without speaking, Sam took the horseshoe from the altar while Reverend Joyner, Moon, and the rest of us watched.

"The blacksmith squeezed with both hands and

bent the horseshoe until both ends were touching each other.

"Sam started to take a step toward Moon, but before he had barely moved Moon backhanded him a stunning blow to the face, then pounded a fist into Sam's chest and the other fist into the side of his jaw, knocking him to the floor. As Sam struggled to get up, a shot rang out and tore into Sam's sleeve.

"'The next one's in your chest, strong boy, if you try anything.'

"Moon faced the congregation.

"'Now, who's the Boss Man around here?'

"I could see and feel the eyes of the congregation turning toward me.

"I rose slowly and faced Moon.

"'I'm the mayor of San Melas,' I said.

"'All right, Mr. Boss Man, here's how it's going to be from now on. Listen, all of you because I'm only going to say it once.'

"The look on his face, and what he had done was more than enough to make us listen.

"'You've all heard of tithing. I suppose you even tithe to this church. From now on you're all going to do a little more tithing . . . to me. But instead of ten percent it's going to be fifty. Half of whatever you take out of that mine at the end of the month . . . from now on . . . every month.'

"Moon started to walk, not fast, not slow, down the aisle, but after a few steps he stopped where I was still standing.

"At first I thought he was looking at me. But his eyes were fixed on Deliverance, who sat beside me.

"'And as for you, Angel Face, they'd better keep that gold coming . . . and on time.'

"His meaning was clear . . . and it still is."

Caleb emptied the dead residue of his pipe against the palm of his hand and let it sprinkle to the porch floor.

"That's how it happened, Reverend," Joseph said, "every bit of it and right in our church . . ."

"Well," Keyes looked at Caleb, "I appreciate your telling me. I only wish . . ."

"You don't have to say anything more, m'boy. We know how you feel . . . and appreciate what you've already done. And now, how is Lorna this morning? Did she get over that dream last night?"

"She was still asleep. I'll go up and see her now."

"You do that, Jon . . . and let us know if there's anything we can do to help."

"Thank you, Caleb," Keyes rose, and as he did, he noticed that the citizens of San Melas, who had earlier taken cover, were beginning to come back onto the street.

CHAPTER 32

When Keyes entered the bedroom Lorna was still sleeping and intermittently murmuring words in a chant-like rhythm, indistinguishable words that Keyes had never heard before. He listened for a few seconds then gave up trying to decipher them.

Keyes thought it best to let her sleep. He moved to the dresser, looked at the Bible, picked it up, and randomly opened it.

His eyes fell on a passage from the Book of Samuel.

> Then said David to the Philistine, "Thou comest to me with a sword, and with a spear, and with a shield: but I come to thee in the name of the Lord of hosts . . ."

Then

> And David put his hand in his bag, and took thence a stone, and slang it, and smote the Philistine in his forehead; and he fell upon his face to the earth.

Keyes closed the worn Bible and wondered to himself . . . was it meant to be that he was David and Moon the Philistine? Was his rifle the stone . . . and he the defender of his hosts . . . in spite of his vow?

And what was real and what was delusion?

With mounting trepidation he straightened, looked into the mirror, and with sublime relief saw the reflection of himself.

But his eyes continued their gaze, as if he were trying to look beyond the mirror, back to the time he lay in the battlefield hospital, hearing familiar and strange voices, sometimes real and at other times unreal, while suspended between two worlds . . . from the effect of his wound.

And what about Lorna and last night? What had she heard and seen?

Was it all real . . . or an illusion?

A mirror of the mind.

In a way she had been wounded. Wounded by the effects of the desert and the scorching sun, without food and water, lying near death in a delirium . . . between two regions of the universe . . . perhaps it was like that last night . . . he didn't know—but he had to find out.

Maybe the answer was in the yard down below.

Then he heard her voice.

"Jonathon . . ."

"Yes, Lorna. I'm here."

He turned. Lorna was still in bed, sitting up.

"You do believe me, don't you, Jonathon?"

"What?"

"I said," she spoke slowly with a voice in need of reassurance, "you do believe that I saw something out there last night . . . that I wasn't dreaming?"

Keyes came across the room and sat on the edge of the bed. He took her hand and held it tenderly.

"Yes . . . I do."

"Thank you, Jonathon. That's very important to me."

"And you're very important to me—the most important thing in the world."

He kissed her.

"This morning . . . do you remember all that happened last night?"

"How could I forget? The sounds . . . the voices . . . the masked figures with candles . . . their chant . . . that cat . . . the dead owl . . . it was all there . . . it was. Jonathon, this is important too . . ."

"What?"

"We . . ." she touched his face . . . "we won't be here much longer, will we?"

"No."

"There *is* something about this town. These people. Don't you think so?"

He pulled back slightly.

"No. No, I don't. Why Caleb is as . . ."

"Not Caleb."

"Then who?"

She brought him closer again.

"Never mind. I just want to . . ."

Her words were interrupted by a knock on the door.

The door opened as Keyes pulled away, and Bethia entered carrying a tray.

"Oh, I'm sorry," Bethia said, "I didn't mean to intrude."

"That's all right, Bethia," Keyes motioned, "come in."

"I brought something for the missus, thought she

might need some nourishment after . . . her ordeal last night."

"That was very thoughtful of you, Bethia," Keyes said.

Bethia placed the tray in front of Lorna.

"Thank you," Lorna nodded, then turned to her husband. "Jonathon, would you bring me some paper and your pen from the desk?"

"What?"

"I want to write Reverend Mason a letter in Saguaro . . . to tell him that we'll be delayed just a little longer."

"Good idea," Keyes smiled. "He'll be glad to hear from us."

"I'll fetch 'em, ma'am," Bethia said.

"Thank you, Bethia," Keyes responded, then turned to Lorna. "I'm . . . I'm going out, dear. I'll be back soon."

"Very well, Jonathon . . . and please, do make it soon."

As he left the room, Bethia moved toward the desk.

"Feelin' better this mornin', ma'am?"

"I . . . I think so."

"Good. Eat your breakfast, ma'am. It'll give you strength . . . and I'll bring you what you need to write that letter."

CHAPTER 33

There were some doubts, some questions in Keyes's mind. Doubts that had to be dispelled, questions that had to be answered.

Last night in the darkness, the confusion, and with Lorna's condition, it was neither the time nor place to look for those answers.

In the light of day, and in reflection of those events, Keyes thought a closer look around the yard might bring to surface the truth about what did and did not happen; whether, as Caleb and the others presumed, Lorna was walking in her sleep and dreamed of voices, images, and a dead owl—or whether it was all something else—something strange, inexplicable, improbable, but possible.

For nearly half an hour Keyes had gone over the same ground that Lorna had walked last night, with no visible evidence to confirm Lorna's version of the events.

Once again he walked and looked around, surveying the area, then stopped. His eyes came to rest on the empty stump. He reflected for less than a minute, then proceeded toward it. About a yard from the stump he studied the ground, looked closer . . . noticed something, took another couple of steps . . . stooped to one knee . . . extended his hand and brought some substance up from the ground.

On his fingers there were definite traces of wax.

Then as he noticed something else, he turned and rose at the sound of Caleb's voice.

"Good morning, Jon."

"Morning, Caleb."

Caleb puffed from his pipe and glanced toward the shed.

"If you were going to pay Deliverance a visit, she's not here. Went to the Bryants' store to pick up another supply of wax."

"No, that's not why I came out here . . . It's about what happened last night . . ."

"Don't you believe she was sleepwalking?"

"If she was, so were some other people."

"What do you mean?"

Keyes held up his hand.

"Wax . . . from candles."

"Oh, that?" Caleb smiled, "Well, of course."

"Lorna said there were candles . . ."

"Jon, I know what Lorna said, but there's a simple explanation. I'm sure you'll find some of it around the yard."

Caleb pointed toward the shed.

"You can see that Deliverance's shed is close by."

"Yes," Keyes nodded, "I know."

"She often gives the children wax to play with."

"Then maybe they were playing right here last night, maybe . . ."

Caleb shrugged good-naturedly.

"No, Jon. We're very strict about our young ones. They all say their prayers and go to sleep in their beds very early every night."

"There was something else I noticed just as you came up."

"Something else?"

Keyes reached close to the stump and lifted two flossy objects.

"Feathers," he said.

"Of course," Caleb pointed to the sky. "Birds fly around here all the time."

"Maybe this bird was an owl . . . a dead owl."

"And maybe you're letting your imagination run a little wild. As I said, all of this can be explained."

"Maybe . . . and by the way, where's Joseph? Usually he's right by your side."

"Joseph is helping Deliverance with the wax and other supplies from the Bryants' store—and Jon, Deliverance was close by, in the shed last night. If anything was going on out here she would have been aware of it—voices, lit candles."

"Evidently, she wasn't aware of Lorna."

"Jon, you've got to relax some while you can. I think a great deal of Lorna. She's a fine girl. But I honestly think she's still affected by that terrible ordeal in the desert. And in some ways, maybe you are, too."

"Maybe," Keyes nodded, then looked at the wax and feathers in his hand.

* * *

"Do you feel better, Lorna?" Keyes asked after entering the bedroom.

"I feel better," she smiled, "now that you're back. Where did you go, Jon?"

"Not far, just out to the yard where you . . . where we were last night."

"By the shed?"

"Yes."

"Was Deliverance there? Did you see her?"

"No. Only Caleb," Keyes paused, then walked closer and sat on the edge of the bed. "About what you said happened last night . . ."

"*Said!* . . . *Said!* It did happen! A little while ago you *said* you believed me. Now, after your visit down there with Caleb, have you changed your mind? Do you think it was a mad dream, my husband? Is that what you're going to tell me now?"

"No, Lorna, anything but . . ."

"It began with those voices . . ."

"I know about voices . . . That's what I was going to say—when I was in that hospital after Yellow Tavern, but not knowing where I was, from time to time I heard voices, strange and unfamiliar, until out of that battlefield haze the voices became familiar . . . I could definitely distinguish the voices of Reverend Mason and General Custer, voices that lifted me out of a void and into this world, and I could understand what they were saying . . . I, I remember every word . . ."

"*Reverend, you've got to get some rest.*"

"*And what about you, General? You've ridden all the way*"

from Beaver Dam. You look like you could use some rest yourself."

"Maybe, but what about Keyes? And you? They tell me you've been up three days and nights and after finishing with the other wounded, you've been here with Jon all night, soothing his brow and speaking words of encouragement even though he can't hear them."

"I hear his words, General—and yours."

"That was the first time I spoke since I fell off that horse.

"Well Reverend, it seems like the sleeping beauty is no longer sleeping."

"So it seems, General, and it looks like Dr. Clemmins got enough of that cartridge out of his head to make a difference."

"General . . ."

"What's on your mind, Captain?"

"What're you doing here? I thought our next strike is at Beaver Dam?"

"We've already struck. I just rode back to . . ."

"He rode back to see for himself how you're doing and write a letter to your fiancée . . ."

"And a letter to the War Department about a medal for a certain captain at Yellow Tavern."

"Those are the voices I heard, Lorna . . . and not in a dream. Now listen to my voice . . . listen to what I'm going to say. I was out there a few minutes ago and I believe you. With all my heart and mind, I believe what you say you heard and saw did happen. I don't know how—or why it happened. Yes, in a way you, too, were wounded—by that desert—but I believe, like me, you came out of your haze. Last night you were yourself again and helped me when I needed help. So I want you to know that's why I went down there, and since I did, I'm more convinced that you weren't sleepwalking—that, as Caleb said, 'there is an easy explanation.' I saw traces of wax from candles and feathers that could have come from that owl— but most of all, I believe it because you say it's so— and the day, no the hour, the minute you feel strong enough we're going to make for Saguaro."

"Jonathon, what you've just said is the best possible medicine any doctor could have given me."

But now Deliverance was in her shed, working with a wax figure, while her cat watched and purred.

CHAPTER 34

From the bedroom window Keyes had seen Deliverance walking toward, then into the shed carrying the cat.

"Lorna, do you mind if I go out and get a little fresh air?"

"Of course not, Jon. There's no reason why you should stay cooped up all the time because I have to stay here a little longer . . . and I mean just a *little* longer. I feel much better since that 'medicine' Doctor Keyes gave me this morning. I'll be ready to pack up and leave just as soon as that wagon of ours is ready."

"So will 'Doctor Keyes,'" he smiled, "good and ready."

As Keyes was leaving the Hobbses' house he saw Caleb sitting on the porch puffing on his ubiquitous pipe.

"Hello again, Jon."

"Hello, Caleb. For a time I thought you two were joined at the hip."

"How's that?"

"This is the second time I've seen you without Joseph at your side."

"Oh, he and some of the other men are at the mine. They're going to seal it up. We wouldn't want another accident out there now that the vein's run out, would we?"

"No, of course not. I see that Deliverance is in her workshop. Did she get the wax and other supplies from the Bryants' store?"

"Oh, yes. And she's back at work with her candles again."

"Do you think she'd mind if I interrupted for a minute or two?"

"I think she'd be very pleased to see you, and m'boy, you will do all you can to help her with her affliction, won't you?"

"I'll do anything I can, Caleb, while I'm here."

As she heard the knock on the door of the shed, Deliverance carefully covered the two wax figures on the workbench with the damp cloth, rose, and walked toward the entrance. The cat leaped from the workbench and followed.

Deliverance opened the door and smiled at Keyes.

"Deliverance, is it all right if I come in?"

She nodded and with an invitational motion pointed inside.

"I see you got the wax and what you needed from Mr. Bryant."

Again she nodded and smiled even more.

Keyes looked at the workbench and the wet cloth.

"What is it you're working on now? More candles?"

Her lips formed a *yes.*

"I'd like to see them when you're finished."

Without hesitation she nodded.

"All these hours out here, day and night, with only your cat, you must get . . . lonely."

A slight shrug and an enigmatic look in her eyes.

"Among the congregation, isn't there some young fellow . . . ?"

Deliverance shook her head and her hair bobbed loosely over her shoulders. Her fingers went to her crimson lips.

"The fact that you can't speak? I shouldn't think that would be any deterrent."

As she had before, she pointed to him and then to her mouth.

"You're asking if I can help you."

She answered with an eager look in her eyes.

"I just told Caleb I'd do whatever I could. But, Deliverance, it might help if I asked you about last night."

There was the hint of disappointment in her aspect, but she did her best not to show it.

"The night was so quiet, not even a trace of wind, and you're so perceptive . . . didn't you hear, or through the window see anything out of the ordinary? Didn't you see Lorna?"

She shook her head deliberately, then pointed to the workbench.

"You're saying that you were concentrating on your work?"

Once more her lips formed a *yes*.

"Then the first time you were aware of anything or anyone outside was when you heard Lorna's scream?"

Deliverance nodded.

"I can understand that. Sometimes when I'm working on a sermon, I'm oblivious to anything or anyone else . . . I only wish that my sermons were as good as the work you do with wax . . . and speaking of that, I've taken up enough of your time. I'll let you get back to your candles, but don't work too hard and too long."

He started toward the door, but turned back and pointed to the wet cloth.

"And I *would* like to see what you're working on when you're finished."

After he left, Deliverance, just as carefully, removed the wet cloth that covered the wax figures of Jonathon and Lorna Keyes.

The cat leaped back onto the workbench.

Keyes stopped by the stable to check on Hawkins's progress with the wagon repairs, but the stable doors were just slightly ajar, and there was no response when he stepped inside and called out Sam Hawkins's name. Keyes noticed that the fire pit had not been used recently.

As he proceeded toward the Hobbses' house he was greeted by a number of townsfolk . . . all women, except for a few of the older men and young boys and girls.

In front of the Bryants' store Ethan and three of his young friends were playing a game of what might have been hopscotch.

"Hello, gentlemen."

"Hello, Reverend," Ethan replied and so did his friends.

"Good day, Reverend," William Bryant said as he came out of the store. "See you're out for a stroll."

"Yes, I stopped by Sam Hawkins's stable to see about the wagon, but he was out."

"Oh, yes," Bryant smiled, "he and most of the other men are out at the mine."

"Right," Keyes nodded, "Caleb told me about sealing it up."

"Wouldn't want these kids going back in there to play after what happened. I told Ethan he could take a break from work so he and his friends could play out here."

Keyes watched as the youngsters were back at their game.

"Mr. Bryant, how has Ethan been sleeping since the accident? Any trouble? Any dreams about what happened out there?"

"Not at all. After supper, just says his prayers and sleeps the whole night through . . . thanks to you, sir."

"I'm glad to hear that, sometimes . . . well, I'm glad to hear that. Good day, Mr. Bryant."

It seemed that everything was back to normal in San Melas . . . except for the prospect of Moon's promise to return.

CHAPTER 35

Lorna sat up in bed addressing a letter.

Reverend James Mason
Saguaro

As Keyes entered the room she put the envelope aside.

"Well, Jonathon," she smiled, "did you get a good stretch of the legs?"

"I did." He looked at the letter on the bed. "To Reverend Mason?"

She nodded.

"You know, Jonathon, it's strange, I'm writing a letter to a man I've never met, but somehow I feel close to him from what you said about him . . . what he did for you and the other patients in the hospital . . ."

"And on the battlefields at the risk of his own life. He's the reason we're going to Saguaro . . . but there's one thing that happened I've never told you about . . ."

"Tell me now, Jonathon. I want to know as much

about him as you can tell me. He seems to have done so much for you."

"He did."

"Then tell me."

A look of solemn remembrance came across Keyes's face as he recalled.

"It was at the hospital as I was still recovering and still thinking of what he had already done for me and all the other patients, Union and Confederate . . .

"One morning while Dr. Clemmins was making his rounds after all night in the operating room . . . he was so exhausted he could barely stand on his feet . . . suddenly we heard a rebel yell and the breaking of a bottle . . . and all of us who were able turned toward the direction of the yell and broken glass.

"There was a Confederate soldier, named Jed Rawlins, a musician in civilian life, whose left hand had been amputated at the wrist—he held Dr. Clemmins from behind, held him fast, with the stump of his forearm, and in his right hand he held the jagged edge of a medicine bottle at the doctor's throat.

"Rawlins's eyes were twin torches of flaming fury.

"'I want you all to watch,' he screeched, 'This butcher who cut off my hand because I'm a Southerner . . . so instead of tending to it . . . it was easier to cut it off . . . and now I'm going to do some cutting on him . . . I'm going to cut his throat from Yankee ear to Yankee ear.'

"Rawlins jerked the sharp edge of the bottle closer to the doctor's face.

"Reverend James Mason took a step forward with the Bible in his hand.

"'Jed, you know me . . . '

"'Sure I do . . . you're that Bible-thumper. Well, don't waste your time with any holy-blown words . . . my mind's set and if you try to stop me I'll kill you, too—maybe first . . . I swear to God!'

"'God?! Who's God, Jed?'

"'The God who said, 'an eye for an eye.' He didn't say 'turn the other hand.' Did you ever hear of a one-armed pianist?!'

"The reverend looked for just a second at the closed Bible in his hand.

"'No, but I did hear God's command: "turn your swords into plowshares . . ." "vengeance is mine; saith the Lord" and you're no Lord . . . and what vengeance are you talking about? Jed, gangrene had set in. Dr. Clemmins saved your life . . . stop and think a minute . . . and how many other lives can he still save if you kill him? Union and Confederate? Look around you . . . There are as many Confederates, your comrades, in this room as there are Union soldiers . . . '

"'Words! Words! Words!'

"'That's right, and listen to these words . . . I know you have a wife, Jed . . . do you think she'll think any different toward you if you come home from the war having lost a hand fighting for the cause? And how will she feel if you kill the doctor who saved your life so you *could* come home? . . . The War Between the States will soon be over . . . but will yours? . . . your wife and the South will need you even with one good hand . . . you're a musician . . . there's a lot you can do besides killing the man who saved your life . . . and that of most of the people in this room . . . if it weren't for Dr. Clemmins you'd be in a battlefield grave instead of this hospital . . . you're a musician . . . you can't play music, but you can still write it, compose it, and teach it . . . not use it to take his life, and your own, because if you kill him you'll never get out of here alive . . . Jed, there is no good war, except what we can learn from it . . . and we don't learn by killing.

"'I'm coming to you, Jed, and you will have to kill me first. You're a brave Southerner . . . act like one. Put that bottle down. Son, it's your last chance to end your own war . . . and win it.'

"Rawlins trembled as if feeling the pain in the hand that was no longer on his body. With a barely perceptible nod, and softened eyes, his shoulders slumped. He lowered his right hand and the bottle dropped onto the floor. The stump of his left arm loosened from Dr. Clemmins's chest, and Reverend Mason moved to help the doctor step away, as a couple patients who were able, were at the doctor's side.

"Rawlins stood frozen for just a couple of seconds, then slumped, first to one knee, then to the other, on the side of the bed, his head buried in both arms.

"Reverend Mason moved close behind him and gently placed a hand on Rawlins's shoulder."

Lorna looked at her husband, took a deep breath, and managed to smile.

"Jonathon, I'm glad that you told me. I feel as if I know Reverend Mason much better now."

"He is as brave as any soldier I ever met. I'd be proud to take his place anywhere, even though I know I couldn't come close."

"You will take his place in Saguaro, Jonathon . . . and I'm sure he'll be proud of you . . . as I am."

CHAPTER 36

Keyes walked out of the house onto the porch. Joseph's rocking chair was empty and so were the other chairs.

Caleb Hobbs was not in the house, nor on the porch. As he looked around Bethia stepped out through the doorway.

"Is there anything I can do for you, Reverend?"

"No, thank you, Bethia, but I was just wondering about Caleb. I don't see him around here. Did he decide to go out to the mine?"

"No, sir. He's just up the street at the burned-out church site. He goes there sometimes . . . when he's feeling . . . melancholy."

"I understand."

"Sir, if you don't mind my saying, I think it might be of comfort to him if you went over there. He does feel much better when you're with him . . . after all you've done."

"Well, thank you for letting me know, Bethia. I'll go over and visit with him."

"Very good, Reverend, and I'll go up and see if there's anything I can do to help the missus."

"Thank you," Keyes smiled. "We appreciate all you've done, Bethia."

Caleb sat on a large stone in front of the charred church gazing at the skeletal ruins.

The pipe still in his mouth was smokeless, but he didn't seem to notice, or care, as he looked straight ahead.

And he didn't notice Keyes's approach until Keyes spoke.

"Hello, Caleb."

"Oh, hello, Reverend," there *was* a melancholy look in his eyes as he turned.

"I'm sure it was a fine-looking church, Caleb."

"It was an exact replica of the one we left behind in Connecticut. Small, but well suited to our needs, and it helped keep us together, and now it's gone, and so is the mine . . ."

"But you're all still here . . . and together."

"For how long? What happens when Moon comes back? Will we still be together? Or will he want to take something . . . or someone else?"

"You're thinking about Deliverance?"

"Yes."

"Couldn't she leave? Go someplace else?"

"Where, Jonathon? In her condition, where could she settle? Here she can be understood, by me at least, and she's content with her work. But anyplace else she'd just be a muted stranger, looked upon almost like . . . a freak."

"Not a beautiful girl like Deliverance."

"You're right about one thing, she is beautiful . . . and Moon's noticed that, too."

"*Moon! Moon!*" Keyes said. "It always comes down to Moon."

"So it seems, m'boy," Caleb looked back at the remnants of the church. "But maybe the Lord will show us the way. He's done it before. He sent you here, didn't He? We must have faith."

"Well, as I said before, I wouldn't count on the Lord to strike down Moon with a bolt of lightning before he comes back."

"Oh, I don't know, Reverend," Caleb smiled, "as Joseph would say 'the Lord works in mysterious ways.'"

"Not *that* mysterious," Keyes smiled back, "otherwise there'd be a lot less evil in this world."

"Then what do you think brought you here?"

"Who knows what to call it? Fate? Destiny? Chance?"

"You call it what you will," Hobbs nodded toward the church site, "but I think His hand is upon us, otherwise you wouldn't be in San Melas."

"Right now it seems you're more the minister than I am. Maybe you should be up there on that pulpit when you do rebuild the church."

"Jon, I don't have your gift . . . I could never have done what you did for Ethan . . . at the service . . . and at the mine, and for Deliverance on that runaway horse. You have the calling."

"Well, it's good of you to talk that way, but . . ."

"Jon, I'm going to ask you something that I'd never ask of anyone else in this world. Do you mind?"

"Go ahead, Caleb."

"You're going to Saguaro with your wife . . ." he paused. His voice took on the tone of quiet last resort.

"If Moon doesn't come back here before you leave, would you take Deliverance with you and Lorna . . . take her to Saguaro with you and save her from . . ."

From a distance, on the street, sounds of a strident voice, hoofbeats pounding. Joseph, Jacob, and Sam Hawkins were riding into town as if their saddles were on fire. Joseph held up a canvas sack, and his horse leaped over a water trough as he hollered with all the might of his lungs.

"Where's Caleb! Got go find Caleb and tell him! It's a miracle . . . purely a miracle! Where's Caleb?"

Keyes and Caleb reacted to the commotion and hoofbeats and quickly moved toward the sounds and the riders, along with dozens of townspeople doing their best to keep up with the horsemen.

Joseph, when he spotted the two men, leaped off his mount as if he were seventeen, still holding the canvas sack.

"Caleb, it's a miracle!" Without pausing for breath, he went on. "Purely a miracle! Just look here . . . a miracle, Caleb. Looks like the Reverend's done it again!"

"What is it, Joseph?" Caleb said. "What's happened?"

Deliverance had come out of the shed, the cat in her arms, and waited with the rest of them for Joseph's answer.

Joseph made no attempt to subdue his excitement. Neither did Jacob and Sam Hawkins, who were now beside him. Hawkins started to speak, but Joseph interrupted.

"Let me tell it, Sam!"

"Well, go ahead and tell it," Caleb said.

"We was out at the mine . . . to board it up like you

said, so the children wouldn't go in there and get lost . . . but before we did, some of us went inside to make sure there wasn't anything left that we could use . . . then it happened!"

"What!?"

"One of the old shafts collapsed . . . 'mightier than the noise of many waters' . . . nobody was hurt, but Caleb, there it was . . . the richest vein I ever seen . . . the mother lode. Just look!"

Joseph reached into the canvas sack and pulled out some small rocks.

"Look at these!" He handed Caleb one of the rocks and passed some of the other samples to those nearest in the crowd.

Caleb's eyes were aglow as he studied the nugget in his palm.

"There's more like these?"

"A whole mountain more, more than ever before." He turned toward Keyes. "Yes, sir, Reverend, once again you brought us good fortune . . . Hallelujah!"

The rest of the crowd joined in with cheers of celebration and unabashed relief.

Caleb placed the glittering stone in Keyes's left hand, then grasped his right in a hearty handshake.

"Jon, 'Fate?' 'Destiny?' 'Chance?' I don't think so . . . the hand of the Lord . . . and yours."

Keyes looked at the stone in his palm, then at the people of San Melas, still celebrating . . . everybody except Deliverance as she gazed silently at Jonathon Keyes.

Lorna had finished the letter to Reverend Mason in Saguaro. Bethia was still in the room and had the wedding portrait of Keyes and Lorna in her hand, dusting it.

Lorna turned toward the open window and listened to the sounds of voices from outside.

"Bethia."

"Yes, ma'am."

"What's all the excitement out there?"

Bethia went to the window and looked down.

"I don't know, ma'am. I'll find out."

"And would you do me a favor, please?"

"Yes, ma'am," she returned to the desk and placed the wedding portrait on it.

Lorna held out the envelope.

"Would you see that this gets sent with the next mail?"

"Of course, ma'am. I'd be glad to."

CHAPTER 37

"Well, Jonathon, in return for saving our lives, it seems that your being here has been of quite some benefit to the people who did the saving."

"How's that?"

"I'm told they call it another miracle. First, what you did for that little boy, Ethan, at the service and then at the mine, and now that new vein of gold."

"Lorna, I had nothing to do with the gold."

"The people here think otherwise . . . and maybe they have a right to."

"Never mind that, the important thing is how are you feeling? You seem much improved."

"I guess so, and sending that letter to Reverend Mason made me feel even better. If it weren't for him . . ."

"If it weren't for him our lives would be much different."

"How did he feel when you told him?"

"I'll never forget. It was at the hospital just as I was about to leave."

"Well, Captain, you're as good as ever. The war's over, and you're ready to resume your law studies."

"No, sir, I'm not."

"What do you mean?"

"I mean I've changed my mind."

"About what?"

"About being a lawyer. I'd like to be something else."

"Like what? A soldier?"

"No. I've had enough of soldiering. Something like you . . . if that's possible."

"A minister?"

"A minister, who helps others, like you helped me and the rest of the people you've come across. I feel I was spared for some purpose . . . and that's it."

"It's not an easy life, my son . . . and not monetarily very rewarding."

"There are other rewards, sir . . . you know that."

"Have you told your fiancée?"

"Not yet. I didn't want to put it in a letter. Will you help me?"

"To tell her?"

"No, sir. To become a minister."

"Why don't you think it over, after you go back?"

"I've already thought it over. Will you help me?"

"I'll do all I can . . . and start right now."

"How?"

"By giving you this Bible."

"Your Bible? No, sir, I can't take it."

"You can, and you will. It's helped me along many a thorny path. Maybe it can do the same for you."

"I . . . I don't know what to say . . ."

"Don't say anything. Just do what you must do."

"I've carried his Bible since then, Lorna. In a way we both have. It's been with us all the way."

"All the way to Saguaro, Jonathon . . . and beyond . . . I'm so glad we sent that letter."

The letter in the envelope addressed to Reverend James Mason was now in the hand of Deliverance at her workbench.

Her eyes glistened by candlelight as she looked at the envelope for a moment . . . then to the cat on the table . . . then to the wax figure of Lorna.

Deliverance moved the envelope closer to the flame of the candle and held it there as the flame consumed the contents.

CHAPTER 38

Caleb Hobbs pointed with his pipe to the burned-out church.

"Well, Reverend, less than twenty-four hours ago we stood here on the same spot. How things have changed since then. And soon this site will be filled with the lumber and tools it takes to rebuild, and most of the people of San Melas will be using those tools while some are at the mine . . . Yes, m'boy, San Melas is once more a bustling, prosperous community . . . thanks in good measure to you."

"That's enough of that, Caleb," Keyes said with an effacing smile.

"All right, Jon," Caleb relit his pipe, "but seriously . . . on behalf of the people of San Melas, I'm going to ask you to do one more thing . . . for all of us . . . and in a way for yourself, too."

"What's that?"

"Stay with us just a little while longer . . . not necessarily until the church is finished . . . at least until the framework is up and we can go inside and listen to you give the first sermon."

"I'd like to, Caleb," Keyes hesitated, "but Lorna is feeling better, and she's . . ."

"All the more reason to stay! It'll do her good to gain even more strength and at the same time see you up there doing what you were meant to do."

"Well," Keyes shrugged, "I'll talk to her . . ."

"I'm sure she'll agree . . . and one more thing we won't have to worry about, when Moon comes back, and I'm sure he will . . ."

"So am I."

"We'll have gold to give him, even more than before."

"Yes, Caleb, I've thought about that, too."

"And, Jon, when you do leave, we'll see to it that you have some of that gold to take with you."

"No. No. I don't want . . ."

". . . To help you and Lorna get started in Saguaro. Now don't argue with me m'boy. The trip all the way out here has cost you a lot, and ministers don't exactly swim in money . . . so let us give you a little boost."

Lorna looked out of the window and stared at the light flickering from Deliverance's shed. There was a renewed weariness in her shoulders, and the rest of her body slumped noticeably as her hands leaned against the sill for support.

"How long do you think it will take before you can give that first sermon . . . even if the church isn't finished?"

"Not very long. They're going to work as fast as they can . . . but, Lorna, I won't . . . we won't stay if you're . . ." he rose from the desk, ". . . Lorna, are you all right? You seem . . ."

"Just a little dizzy, I . . . think I'll lie down . . . it'll pass."

"I'm sure it will."

She moved unsteadily to the bed and lay against the pillows.

He took her hand and held it tenderly. Lorna looked at both of their hands entwined.

"Jonathon . . . our rings . . . remember what you said after you came back . . ."

He nodded.

"It was at the same secluded spot along the Raisin Riverbank where Libbie and General Custer had interrupted us during the war. But now the war was over."

"Jonathon, I know there's something on your mind. I can tell by the look on your face, the way you've been acting since you've come home."

"Lorna, I didn't want to write and tell you this, but . . ."

"What is it, my dear? Is it about the wound? Something I should know?"

"Not exactly the wound, but, yes, something you should know . . . and if you change your mind . . ."

"About what?"

"About what I'm going to do, or rather, not do."

"Then tell me, Jonathon."

"I'm not going to go back and finish law school."

"Is that all?"

"No. That's what I'm *not* going to do. But . . . I've

decided to become a minister. Reverend Mason's written me a letter. He's getting old, and the war's taken a lot out of him. He's going to retire soon, and he's asked me to come to Saguaro and take his place when he does. It's not an easy life . . . and not much money . . . or prospect . . ."

"Are you finished telling me?"

"No, Lorna . . . what I wanted to say is that . . . well, I asked you once before, when I was leaving for the army—and now that I've told you about this—if you want to take off that ring I gave you . . . the engagement ring . . . I'll understand."

"Oh, Jonathon, you sweet, darling fool. Do you think I wanted to marry a lawyer? I wanted to marry *you*. I still do . . . and always will."

"I remember, Jonathon. How could I ever forget," she held up her left hand. "And I remember saying that I'll always wear this ring, even after I die."

"So will I, Lorna." He leaned closer and kissed her.

"I can understand why they'd want you to give the first sermon . . . and a few extra days won't make that much difference, as long as we're together . . . I . . . I'm a little tired . . . I . . ."

"Go to sleep, Lorna. I'll be beside you in just a few minutes."

Keyes rose and walked across the room toward the dresser.

A sublime look of satisfaction came across the face of Deliverance as her fingers moved from the wax figure of Keyes to that of Lorna.

* * *

Keyes finished dampening his face from the dresser washbowl and reached for a towel but stopped abruptly as he glanced at the mirror.

He was there.

The agonized image of the half-naked man, seared and tortured, arms outstretched, his blemished mouth trying to convey a message, but voiceless, hollow eyes imploring in desperation. His trembling fingers stretched out trying to reach him but could not break through the barrier of the mirror.

Keyes instinctively drew back, then slammed the damp towel against the mirror and turned away as Lorna bolted upward from the bed in a harried quake.

"Jonathon!"

"What is it, Lorna?"

She recoiled with a deep breath.

"It . . . must have been a bad dream . . . I felt I was falling . . . I . . . Oh, Jonathon, come put your arms around me . . . hold me."

CHAPTER 39

Lorna was still in a deep sleep, and Keyes had hardly slept at all.

He decided to go outside and think things over but was surprised to see Caleb, Joseph, and Deliverance having an early breakfast served by Bethia.

"Good morning, m'boy," Caleb puffed between sips of coffee. "Just enjoying a brief repast before another day's work. Please join us." He pointed to the empty chair next to Deliverance. "Have some breakfast."

"Just some coffee, thank you," Keyes sat and was already aware of the exotic mixture of fragrances and wax that was ever present when he was near her.

"Did you have that little talk with your wife?"

"What?"

"About the first sermon . . ."

"Oh, yes . . . it looks like we'll be staying just until then."

"Very good. I was sure she'd agree. How is Lorna feeling?"

"She, uh, has her ups and downs, but," Keyes was hesitant about saying more.

"Well, I've got an idea about what will make her feel better."

"What's that, Caleb?"

"Why don't you, the two of you come by the church site later on? She can get some fresh air—and the sight of what you've done, and what we're doing, I'm sure, will have a salubrious effect on her."

"I'm not sure . . ."

"Well, I am . . . and we'll have food and refreshment to whet her appetite . . . and yours, too, something besides coffee."

Caleb pointed with his pipe at Keyes's cup as Bethia poured.

Overnight Keyes had begun to have ambivalent feelings about many things . . . about what had happened . . . and what might happen.

He did his utmost not to reveal to Caleb, Joseph, and Deliverance the shadow of doubt that had slowly crept into his thinking about this place . . . and these people—people who had saved his life and Lorna's, and since then, had been so helpful . . . gentle people . . . devout . . . caring . . . concerned . . . ingenuous . . . and so burdened with near calamity— until his arrival . . . and what a difference that had made in San Melas and its citizens . . . and what a difference it all had made on him. But at the same time, he thought of Reverend Mason, how tirelessly he had endeavored to do what he could among those who were facing death on battlefields, without concern for his own safety . . . and later, in hospitals among the maimed, day after day and night after night, at their bedside . . . at his bedside, with words of comfort and hope . . . this man who had changed him from a would-be lawyer, then soldier . . . and then gave motive for him to become as much like that minister as was possible . . . and here at San Melas he had been given, heaven knows how, or why, the spark to bring them light in their darkest hour . . . as Caleb had reminded him, with the "miracle" of young Ethan, the rescue of Deliverance from that snake-frenzied pinto, and the resurgence of an abandoned mine . . . was it all a coincidence . . . or was there now some of the goodness and strength inside him, borrowed from Reverend Mason, that helped him reach out and be of remedy to those in distress . . . and yet, there was a shadow . . . the image in the mirror and at the lake, unseen by anyone else, and meant only for him . . . an image of dismay . . . and was it some unexplainable warning of danger here in San Melas . . . and what about the chanting, candlelit masked figures, the dead owl near Deliverance's shed that Lorna had seen? Keyes had said he believed her. Didn't he still believe her?

For all their goodness, piety, and virtue, there, somehow, seemed to be a gossamer veil beyond which he could not see or understand.

Yes, somehow there was an ambivalence.

Deliverance passed him the sugar.

CHAPTER 40

"You didn't eat much of your breakfast, Lorna."

"I didn't feel very hungry."

"Well, maybe Caleb is right."

"About what?"

"You know they've started to rebuild the church. The whole town's pitching in."

"Yes, I know."

"Caleb says they're going to take a little time off out there at the site, with food and refreshment . . . a sort of picnic, and he thinks it would be a good idea if we, both you and I, come out for a little while . . . we'll find you a nice shady spot . . . you can enjoy the fresh air and as he says, maybe it'll whet your appetite."

"A picnic?"

"Sort of."

She smiled.

"Remember the last picnic we were on, Jonathon . . ."

"With General Custer and Libbie . . . he was feeling a little out of sorts."

"A little? He was ready to fight the war all over again . . . or any other war."

"Damn it, Captain, I envy you . . ."

"General . . ."

"I'm not a general anymore. I'm a lieutenant colonel without a command . . . rotting away."

"Yes, George," Libbie smiled, *"you'll be twenty-eight on your next birthday, and besides, you've had offers . . ."*

"Hell, yes. Offers to run for mayor, for governor, maybe even president, but I'm no politician . . . offers to use my good name and front for corporations that have nothing to sell except my good name. Well, I won't do that . . . ever. That's why I envy you, Jon. You've found your calling, and you're going to practice it. Well, I found mine a long time ago, and they won't let me. They've sent other ex-generals out west, but not the Boy General. There are politicians and general officers jealous of that 'glory-grabbing Custer' who don't want his reputation to grow too much—in fact, they prefer that he just lie fallow and be forgot."

"This country will never forget," Libbie said, *"what you've done for it, Autie."*

"Seems like it's been forgot already . . . if it weren't for you, Libbie, I'd go crazy. I might just go crazy anyhow. Excuse me. I'm lousy company. I'm going to go for a walk along the river . . . and if I couldn't swim, I think I'd jump in."

"General, do you mind if I walk with you a ways?"

"Not if you don't mind lousy company . . . Reverend . . . and don't bring your Bible."

"Some picnic," Lorna smiled as Keyes sat at the side of the bed.

"What did you talk about, Jonathon, you and George Custer?"

"He did all the talking, about his favorite subject . . . war. What did you and Libbie talk about?"

"She did most of the talking," Lorna smiled, "about her favorite subject, General George Armstrong Custer. Did you know, Jonathon, that General Philip Sheridan bought the table that generals Grant and Lee signed the surrender on at Appomattox? Well, he did and presented it to Libbie with a note saying, and I remember every word of it . . . Libbie repeated it to me:

> *My dear Madam,*
>   *I respectfully present to you the small writing-table on which the conditions for the surrender of the Confederate Army of Northern Virginia was written by Lt.-Gen'l. Grant; and permit me to say, madam, that there is scarcely an individual who has contributed more to bring about this desirable result than your very gallant husband.*
>
> > *Very Respectfully,*
> > *Phil. H. Sheridan*
> > *Maj.-Gen'l.*

"Well, Libbie told me that she had just sent a letter to Sheridan virtually begging him to cut through the bureaucratic red tape, and whatever else it took, on behalf of her husband. But she hadn't told him in case Sheridan couldn't help . . . and Custer would be even more despondent and 'out of sorts.'"

"What a woman!" Keyes laughed. "There aren't many like her . . . and like you, Lorna."

"And the same could be said about Custer . . . and you, my husband."

"That could only be said," Keyes smiled, "by you . . . my wife."

"I'll say this Jonathon . . . let's go on that picnic."

Moon, dressed in his satanic black, with that impenetrable look on his face, outlined against a gunpowder sky, rode slowly toward his destination.

CHAPTER 41

A rough-hewn cross marked the site of the new church being constructed—but there was more evidence than that—living evidence.

Townspeople, Joseph, William Bryant, Sam Hawkins, Jacob, and all the rest—hammering, carrying lumber as some of the framework was already taking shape. Children were doing their share of the lighter work. Even Caleb was at it in his supervisory capacity, with his ever-present pipe still stuck in his mouth.

More than a dozen of the ladies, including Deliverance and Bethia were preparing food and liquid refreshment at a nearby table. A covey of cooked chickens, baked potatoes, varied other vegetables, salads, pies and cakes were on display.

Lorna sat in a chair under a shady spot sipping lemonade, but her face was somewhat drawn and now almost colorless.

Keyes approached carrying a saw, his sleeves rolled

up, as he wiped a patina of perspiration from his brow.

"Lorna, would you like me to bring you a fresh glass of lemonade?"

"No thanks, I'm fine."

She didn't exactly look fine to Keyes, and he did his best to cheer her up.

"At the rate they're going," he pointed with the saw toward the activity, "the church will be ready for that first sermon in short order."

"I hope so, Jonathon, but . . . to tell you the truth, I'm not sure how much longer I should stay out here."

He leaned close and kissed her forehead.

"Lorna, please, you've got to stay a little longer . . . until you have something to eat. It'll do you good. Just look at that table and the fare those ladies are preparing."

"All right, Jonathon, I'll stay for a while."

"Reverend."

Ethan and one of the other boys approached.

"Yes, Ethan?"

"I just wanted . . . wanted to say . . ." there was a broad smile on his sweaty face, ". . . that I'm glad you're still with us . . . and we all look forward to your next sermon."

"Thank you, Ethan . . . and how are those legs of yours coming along?"

"Great, sir. Just great," he grinned, "doing my share of the work here."

"Yes, well, don't overdo it, Ethan."

"No, sir, I won't."

Ethan was already on his way back to work.

Keyes watched after him as the young lad practically skipped along as he moved out.

"What a change in that little fellow since we've been here."

"Yes, Jon, there've been a lot of changes."

"And things usually change for the better."

"Usually," Lorna replied. There was a trace of doubt in her eyes . . . a trace that Keyes noticed, but tried to ignore.

"Are you sure?"

"What?"

"About the lemonade?"

"I'm sure, Jonathon . . . about the lemonade."

"I'll be back soon." He smiled.

"Very good." Lorna did not smile, but continued to look as he walked away—and noticed that he did not take the shortest route toward his destination, but deviated, walking toward the food-laden table . . . and Deliverance.

Lorna could not see her husband's face, but couldn't help noticing the avid smile on Deliverance's face and radiant, sun-reflected look in her eyes.

Both Lorna and Deliverance continued their gaze toward Keyes in the work area as he commenced to saw one of the planks. Lorna's look occasionally shifted to Deliverance, but Deliverance's gaze never deviated from the minister.

"Reverend," Joseph appeared carrying a hammer and removed a six-penny nail from between his lips, "the Book says that 'there is a time for all things.'"

"So it does, Joseph . . . and what time is it now," he smiled, "according to that Good Book of yours?"

"Reverend, the sun has passed its zenith and is journeying into the west."

"Does that mean you're getting hungry?"

"'All the labor of man is for his mouth, and yet the appetite is not filled.'"

Keyes put down the saw.

"Well, let's fill it."

"Amen, Reverend."

"I couldn't help overhearing the conversation of you two gentlemen because I was doing my best to listen, so I'll just second . . . or is it third the motion. These old joints of mine are beginning to creak and not just from old age but from lack of nourishment," Caleb's voice grew louder. "Somebody ring the dinner bell."

"Don't have a dinner bell, Mr. Mayor," Sam Hawkins hollered back.

"Then ring the church bell, we still have one, even though we haven't got a church yet."

The church bell rang out . . . and as it did the sun passed into a cloud and spread a layer of darkness across the area. A chill wind snapped through the framework of the church, and workers and women who were sweating just a moment ago, now were trying to rub warmth into their shivering bodies.

But their bodies were not shivering only from the chill wind . . . it was from his sudden, almost mystical, appearance.

MOON.

A vision of darkness where a moment ago there was sunlight.

MOON.

Mounted on his stallion as if lord and master viewing his domain.

MOON.

Silently commanding all that he surveyed . . . and beyond.

He sat there full height in the saddle so they could all get a good look.

But this time he dismounted, slowly, in perfect balance, in every movement with the grace of a ballet dancer . . . even with the twin pistols strapped on either side of his narrow waist.

Moon walked slowly, then stopped in front of the cross stuck into the ground.

He smiled. Not out of respect.

Still he said nothing.

He looked at the food on the table and moved toward it.

"Looks good enough to eat."

He stopped directly in front of Deliverance, reached out . . .

"Moon . . ." Caleb took a step forward.

"Shut up!" Moon took a sliced carrot from a plate and bit off the end.

"Moon," Caleb persisted, "we've been waiting for you."

"You have?" Moon's look went from Deliverance to Caleb. Then around all those gathered, watching and listening to what he had to say next. "Well, then you won't have to wait any more."

"Moon . . ."

Moon waved a hand in the direction of the food . . . and Deliverance.

"All this feast just for me!" His smile broadened, then quickly narrowed. "You went to all this trouble

just for me? Very hospitable . . . but not hospitable
enough . . ."

"Moon, listen to me . . ."

"I'll listen, when I'm ready . . ."

He picked up another carrot stick and took a bite.

"Armies travel on their stomachs," he smiled again,
"and so do snakes"—the smile disappeared—"but I
don't."

The cat was still playing with the mice, but this
time the cat seemed a mite more playful, but at the
same time, a mite more grim.

On other occasions Moon had doled out words in
dollops; this time his word count was more prolific,
his gestures, a mite more sweeping. He almost seemed
like an actor enjoying performing to an audience—
particularly one member of that audience. More often
than not his glance singled out Deliverance.

This time Moon picked up a pickle, turned and
pointed it at Caleb. There was an unmistakable shade
of malevolence in his voice.

"I'm ready, Mr. Mayor, to listen . . . for just a little
while."

"Moon," Caleb spoke quickly, eagerly, persuasively,
"we've had some good fortune . . . good for all of us.
Listen! We've found a new vein of gold in the mine.
It's rich! I tell you there'll be gold . . . more than ever
before. You'll get your share!"

Moon took a bite, consuming more than half of
the pickle and tossed the rest of it on the ground. He
reached onto the table, grabbed a chicken, rented it
in half, and commenced to eat while some of the
juices leaked down his chin.

And all the time he was looking at Deliverance.

Caleb took another step forward.

"You'll be rich, Moon. Come back in a couple of weeks . . . give us a chance to work the mine."

Moon continued to eat and to look at Deliverance.

"I'll give you a chance. And I'll come back . . ."

His hand lunged out and grabbed Deliverance . . . roughly drew her close.

Nobody moved.

Not Caleb. Not Joseph. Not Sam Hawkins. Not Jacob. Not William Bryant. Not Reverend Jonathon Keyes, nor did any of the women or children.

As still as a painted desert. And as silent.

Moon dropped the chicken bone and with the palm of his hand on the back of her neck, forced Deliverance's face closer.

A fierce kiss with his food-smeared lips, a kiss that twisted her face in horror. Terrified, she tried to tear away, but Moon's hawser-like hand was on her . . . pulling, ripping away part of the dress that covered her shoulder and more, much more. Her hair fell undone and splashed onto her shoulders.

Deliverance's cat ran from under the table and disappeared into the framework of the church.

As Moon again drew Deliverance's body closer, pressing against his, leaning in to kiss her once more, Reverend Jonathon Keyes stepped out.

"Moon!" Keyes stood legs spread, right hand held out.

Moon stopped but still held Deliverance in the grasp of his left hand.

"Well, if it isn't the Preacher Man."

"Moon, in the name of decency . . ."

"Never heard of it," Moon smiled.

"Then listen . . ."

"If you're gonna spout some sort of sermon, save your breath to cool your soup . . . and your soul . . . cause I ain't got one . . . 'sides, what's she to you and you to her?"

Lorna was staring at them. She did her best to rise, but fell back onto the chair.

Keyes looked to his wife then back to Moon and Deliverance.

"Now listen to me Preacher Man. I let you off easy the first time. But don't push . . . or I'll push back hard. She's my little plaything, till I get the gold."

Moon shoved her rudely ahead but held onto her wrist. She did her utmost to scream as her mouth widened in dread, but there came no sound.

Caleb moved as quickly as he could, clutching at Moon.

"I won't let you take her . . ."

In a swift terrible stroke Moon backhanded Caleb who fell in a half-conscious heap.

There were gasps all around from the men and women who covered their children's eyes. But nobody moved to stop Moon.

"Anybody else want to try!?! Just go ahead . . ."

He paused, then drew the gun from his left holster and threw it to the ground. Then laughed . . . an ugly, lascivious laugh . . . a taunting challenge.

". . . Try it."

Moon's chainlike fist still gripped fully around Deliverance's slender wrist, he pulled her alongside of him.

"You spunkless pack of craven milksops . . . and

don't try to follow. You won't want to see her when I get through with that lily-white . . ."

Moon laughed again and pulled Deliverance with him.

". . . you won't want . . ."

Keyes leaped to the gun on the ground, grabbed it, and with a quick aim fired.

Moon's back bent; he twisted, drew with his right hand . . . and as Keyes fired again, Moon staggered, pitched forward a step, tried to lift and aim, but there was another shot, and Moon collapsed.

In Keyes's trembling hand the gun was still smoking. He covered his eyes with the palm of his left hand but only for a beat. He lowered his palm to make sure Moon did not move.

But there was no movement in Moon's sprawled body.

None.

Caleb rose to his feet and absorbed what had happened.

The rest of the congregation was too stunned to do anything but stand still and stare.

All except Joseph, who went to the fallen Moon and stooped over him, then looked up.

"Dead."

Keyes let the gun drop to the ground, rose slowly, swayed slightly, and took an intense breath.

Both Caleb and Joseph approached, but Joseph spoke first.

"'Spite the wicked,' it's been said, and now it's been done . . . by you, Reverend."

"M'boy . . ."

It took every fiber of Keyes's being to gain control, but still not fully.

"I've killed. I've . . . taken a man's life."

"He wasn't a man," Caleb said.

"I've killed."

"You saved her . . . and the rest of us. Jon, he was an animal . . . a mad dog. Jon . . ."

But Keyes still struggled against the realization of what he had done . . . the vow he had broken . . . until—

Deliverance's hand touched his hands and took hold of one of them.

Slowly, he looked up into her grateful eyes.

Lorna's gaze was frozen on both her husband and the woman he had rescued.

Deliverance's lips quivered. She spoke for the first time Keyes ever heard her voice.

"Thank you . . . thank . . . you."

This time it was Keyes who remained silent but managed to nod an acknowledgment.

But while Keyes remained silent, the others who were assembled did not when they heard Deliverance speak those words of thanks.

Other words shot through the crowd—"miracle"—"killed Moon and gave her speech"—"phenomenon"—"wondrous"—"amazing"—"unbelievable"—words mixed with relief that Moon was no longer a threat and that Deliverance could at long last speak.

"Joseph. Sam," Caleb's voice broke the chatter of the crowd. He pointed to the crooked body of Moon on the ground not far from the rough-hewed cross.

Joseph and Hawkins responded by stepping closer to Caleb as he pointed with the stem of his pipe.

"Cover the body with something, and get it out of here."

The two men started to carry out his orders as Caleb looked around at the still mesmerized congregation.

"Then, let's all go home," he said, "this day's work is done."

CHAPTER 42

Lorna was in bed staring straight at the ceiling, and although Keyes sat next to her on a straight-back chair holding the Henry rifle in his hands, she heard nothing of what he was saying. Her mind, her thoughts, and maybe her spirit were adrift in some other sphere.

Although he didn't realize it at the time, Keyes was talking to himself and the rifle.

"It's ironic, Lorna, all this time, this rifle," he turned it over in his lap, "all this time making sure it was clean and accurate in case I needed it to hunt for food, or to save our lives if we were attacked out there in the desert or anyplace else.

"And here in San Melas, I killed a man, not with this rifle, but with his own gun . . . a despicable man, a man without conscience, without scruple . . . but a man, nevertheless . . . who am I to judge whether he should live or die, in spite of his malicious intent . . . who am I to judge and execute? Lorna . . ."

But by then, when Keyes did look from the rifle to her, Lorna's eyes as well as her mind were closed.

He rose, leaned the rifle against the wall, left the room, and walked into the darkened hallway. As he reached the stairs and started down, Bethia stepped out of the shadows.

In her hand she held a large pair of scissors. She looked toward the stairway to make sure Keyes was out of sight.

Then Bethia walked toward the bedroom where Lorna lay sleeping.

Both Caleb and Joseph looked up from their chairs as Keyes reached the bottom of the stairway. Caleb held his pipe, and Joseph, the handle of his teacup.

"She's sleeping," Keyes said.

"Good," Caleb nodded.

"Caleb, how is Deliverance?"

"She's in her room for a change, instead of out there in the shed."

"Is she . . . has she spoken since . . . since we left the church?"

"Spoken? M'boy, she's not exactly chattering away without taking a breath, but she's more than holding her own in the word department, and her voice is gaining strength with every word she speaks."

"Good."

"She does want to talk to you, Jon, to thank you properly . . . for what you . . . well, we are all beholden to you for ridding us of that monster . . ."

"Please, Caleb . . . no more of that."

"Just as you say."

"Except . . ."

"Except what?"

"What did you do with his . . . "

"Moon's body?"

Keyes nodded.

"Buried it by the cemetery pond, but not too close to the others."

"I'd like to go up there."

"What for?"

"Is there a marker?" Keyes did not answer the question.

"Yes, but not a cross. Just a wooden plaque with his name."

"I'll go up tomorrow."

"If you like."

"Reverend," Joseph set the cup of tea on the table, "would you want me to go over there with you?"

"No, thank you, Joseph, I'll go alone. Caleb, about Lorna . . ."

"Yes, m'boy?"

The long sharp scissors in Bethia's hand moved closer to the sleeping Lorna. Moonlight filtered through the open window and framed her face as the scissors traveled closer, much closer. Bethia's other hand reached down and carefully took up a long lock of Lorna's hair, and with the scissors, she clipped off the lock. Bethia paused a moment more, glanced down at Lorna, then looked across the yard where Deliverance was holding her cat and walking toward the unlit shed.

"Caleb, she's not getting any better, worse, if anything. I'm worried. I wish there were a doctor here . . . or near here."

Caleb silently shook his head before speaking.

"The best medicine in the world for her is you. If what you say is true, the worst thing would be for her to travel across that brutal desert in a bumpy wagon."

"If we traveled in the cool of the night . . ."

"You might end up even worse . . . without land-marks to guide you . . . get lost at night and end up heaven knows where?"

"Yes, I guess you're right."

"Caleb is a wise old party, Reverend, a wise old party," Joseph nodded.

"I'm sorry she was there today . . . to see what happened . . . it was just too much. She's never seen anyone killed before . . . and certainly not by her husband, a minister . . . too much."

"I know, m'boy."

Keyes held up his "gun hand."

It quivered.

"Even during the war . . . not like this . . . but then, it was my duty, my obligation to . . ."

"In a way this, too, was your obligation . . ."

"To Deliverance?"

"To decency . . . and against a godless monster who had to be destroyed. You did the only thing a man like you could do. The right thing. Jon, in spite of our belief, if anyone of us was that close to that gun we would have done the same thing . . . at least I hope so."

"So do I, Caleb."

"Reverend," Joseph lifted his cup, "would you like some tea?"

"Tea! Never mind the tea, Joseph," Caleb rose and went to the sideboard. "What he needs . . . what we all need is a jigger of brandy. A double jigger."

Caleb reached for the bottle.

Deliverance reached out and took the lock of Lorna's hair from Bethia's hand.

"Thank you, Bethia."

"You're welcome, Miss Deliverance."

Deliverance looked down on the table at the wax image of Lorna, then at the lock of her hair in her palm and smiled at Bethia.

"Yes . . . this will do nicely."

All three men sipped the brandy from their snifters.

"There is no bracer quite so bracing as a serene swallow of brandy. Care for a refill, Jon?"

"No, thank you."

"Jon, now that things are . . . different . . . here in San Melas. Different for all of us, we want you to reconsider making this your home. We will see that you are amply rewarded . . . in all ways, a house of your own, the new church. Without you we wouldn't have . . . well, will you, Jon?"

"I don't think so . . ."

Keyes noticed that Deliverance had entered and stood by the back door.

". . . I think it's best I . . . that we leave all this behind, as soon as possible. I know Lorna does."

"But you will stay until the church is in shape for you to preach the first sermon?"

Keyes hesitated.

Deliverance took a step forward.

"Please."

CHAPTER 43

Keyes entered the dark bedroom, silently walked to the bedside table, struck a match and lit the candle.

"Jonathon," she whispered.

"I . . . I thought you were asleep."

"I was, while you were . . . downstairs. Jonathon . . ."

"Yes, my dear?"

"They've asked you to stay."

Silence.

"Haven't they?"

"Yes," Keyes nodded.

"Do you want to stay?"

"We've promised Reverend Mason."

"I asked you, do you want to stay . . . and what else have they promised you?"

"What do you mean?"

"I mean you saved Deliverance's life. What other inducements did they offer you?"

"Lorna, have you forgotten? They saved *our* lives.

Caleb's opened his home to us . . . taken care of you . . ."

"Some care . . ." she turned her face toward the window and the yard.

"It's not their fault that there's not a doctor here, any more than there's not a minister . . ."

"Yes . . . no doctor, no minister . . ."

". . . and they've treated me like a son."

"I know."

"Then what is it?"

"I told you before. This . . . it's as if they were from another time . . . another world."

"Caleb explained that. Look, when settlers come from the old country they bring their language and customs with them. Well, these people are from New England. That's why they seem so strange out here."

"I suppose."

"And Lorna, I've been able to help them . . ."

"By killing Moon?"

"Lorna, you don't know how much I've suffered . . . and probably will for the rest of my life . . . for that. If I had to do it over, I don't know what, well . . . I just don't know . . . but it's done. I know that if he were coming after you . . . I know what I'd do."

"I know that, too, Jon," her face was uneasy. She did not look at her husband.

Keyes sat on the chair near the bed.

"They're really fond of me . . . of us . . . and they need us."

He leaned closer.

"Caleb said they'd build us a house . . . pay us more than we could ever hope to get in Saguaro."

"We weren't going to Saguaro for the money." It came out fast and harsh.

"I know, Lorna."

He paused.

"I'm sorry . . . and you're right about that."

"We've sent Reverend Mason a letter telling him we're on our way," another pause, "but are we, Jonathon?"

Keyes rubbed his palm across his face and looked around.

"You . . . don't want to stay here, do you?"

"'Wither thou goest, I will go, and where thou lodgest, I will lodge: thy people . . .'"

The look in Keyes's eyes changed, he smiled, then kissed her and finished the quotation.

"'. . . shall be my people.' Lorna, we're going to Saguaro. Just as soon as you're strong enough."

Her face brightened. She was much relieved.

She had won.

"I'm feeling better already."

"A week or so . . . I'll make sure Mr. Hawkins has the wagon ready. We've still got a stretch of desert to cross."

"Just thinking about it," Lorna smiled, "makes me thirsty."

"Would you like a nice drink of water?"

"You know, Jonathon, I think I would at that."

Keyes rose from the chair.

"Then my darling bride, your husband will get you a very nice drink of water."

He made his way to the dresser, picked up a glass from the tray, then poured from the pitcher into the glass until it was just more than half full. He glanced

toward the mirror. But it became more than a glance
as he stared at the image.

*The agonized man struggled to move his tortured body,
his racked arms outward toward Keyes . . . his hollow eyes
trying desperately to convey what he had no voice to say, his
bleeding body writhing, struggling to pitch forward.*

Keyes instinctively flung the glass out toward the
mirror splashing the image away, but striking the mirror
a hard blow.

But neither the glass, nor the mirror broke.

"Jonathon!" Lorna's head braced up from the pillow.
"What happened?"

Keyes inhaled and tried to regain his composure.
He managed to pour more water from the pitcher into
the glass. Barely managed.

"I . . . accidentally hit the mirror."

"Did it break?"

Keyes was afraid to look back into the mirror. He
turned toward Lorna and tried to smile.

"No. No, Lorna. The mirror's all right."

"Well," she smiled, "at least we're not in for seven
years bad luck."

Deliverance's fingers moved away from the wax
image of Lorna—the wax image now fitted with the
lock of Lorna's own hair.

The cat, poised nearby on the bench, purred.

Deliverance looked at the cat, smiled, and nodded,
then turned back and reached out with both hands
toward the wax replica of Lorna Keyes.

CHAPTER 44

The next morning Keyes tried several times in vain to awaken Lorna, but each time, without opening her eyes, she pushed his hands away and faced the other direction.

Keyes decided it was wiser to let her sleep; besides, he had little, or no other choice.

Her face, what he could see of it was anything but tranquil, as if struggling against some unseen enemy.

Also, he had something on his mind he wanted to attend to . . . and this was as good a time as any.

"Would you care for breakfast now, Reverend?"

"No, thank you, Bethia."

He looked at the dishes on the table.

"I see the others have already eaten."

"Yes, sir. Deliverance is working in the shed and Joseph and Mr. Hobbs are at the church site."

"Thank you . . . I'll go over and see . . . how the church is coming along."

"Very good, sir."

"And Bethia, would you please look in at Mrs. Keyes

from time to time, and see if she'll have something to eat. She's asleep now."

"Don't you worry, Reverend. I'll be glad to."

The construction activity at the church site had resumed full bore.

Measuring, marking, sawing, lifting, placing, and hammering.

Joseph, Jacob, Hawkins, Bryant, and all the other able-bodied men, some of the women, and even the young ones, contributed their share of the work. All but Caleb Hobbs, who had assumed an even more supervisory attitude aboard a tree-shaded chair and puffed contentedly on his pipe.

At the sight of Keyes all work ceased as the citizens clapped and cheered at his appearance but resumed as he held up a hand, smiled, and signaled for them to stop.

"Morning, m'boy. Did you get a good sleep?"

"On and off, Caleb, on and off."

Caleb leaned in a little closer and asked in a confidential tone, "Did you get a chance to talk to Mrs. Keyes about our conversation last night?"

"I did . . . and I . . . we are extremely grateful for your generous offer . . . but we've decided to fulfill our promise to Reverend Mason and continue to Saguaro."

"Well, I'm sorry for us, but if that's what you've decided, so be it."

"I hoped you'd understand."

"I can't say I'm not disappointed, deeply disappointed, but whatever you think is best for you . . . and maybe someday you'll change your mind and come back to us. Consider it an open invitation."

"Thank you, Caleb and there is just one more thing . . ."

"Name it."

"The cross."

"What cross?"

Keyes pointed to the cross in the ground in front of the construction site.

"What about it?"

"I'm going to the cemetery and, well, he was killed . . . he died practically in the shadow of that cross. You mentioned there was none . . . only a marker at his grave. Do you mind if I take it and place it there?"

"Not at all. You do what you think is right, m'boy."

Keyes stood among the mounds and markers in the sunbaked cemetery with the rough-hewn cross in his hands.

The day was as still and static as the mute inhabitants of this place of lasting slumber.

He moved, slowly walking through the rows of heaped earth, looking for one particular marker.

He saw it, some distance from the rest, near a lily pond. A wooden tablet with the lone legend:

MOON

Keyes approached and forced the sharp end of the cross into the ground at the base of the marker.

He stood silently looking at the cross, reached into the pocket of the light jacket he wore, started to slip out the Bible, but changed his mind and let it rest in the pocket.

He clasped his hands in front of him and spoke just above a whisper.

> The Lord is my shepherd; I shall not want.
> He maketh me to lie down in green pastures:
>   he leadeth me beside the still waters.
> He restoreth my soul: he leadeth me in the paths
>   of righteousness for his name's sake.
> Yea, though I walk through the valley of the
>   shadow of death, I will fear no evil: for thou
>   art with me; thy rod and thy staff they
>   comfort me.
> Thou preparest a table before me in the presence
>   of mine enemies: thou anointest my head
>   with oil; my cup runneth over.
> Surely goodness and mercy shall follow me all the
>   days of my life: and I will dwell in the house of
>   the Lord for ever.

Keyes raised his hand upward, then back toward the grave, his voice somewhat louder as he spoke to the man he had killed.

"There must be some good in every man. Maybe in that life to come we can all find, and live, the other side of the coin.

"In this life the wrong side of the coin came up, but in the next, you may get the chance to make up for what you've done . . . and after the final days of judgment, find forgiveness and atonement."

He paused and drew a breath.

"May we both—may we all make up for our trespasses and find the true path to forgiveness and righteousness.

"May the lion lie down with the sheep and find

peace from the valley of darkness into the green garden of goodness."

His throat was dry, his face and neck dry from the radiant heat of the sun. He turned from the grave and walked toward the pond as a frog leaped from the water onto the grass and disappeared into a thicket.

Keyes moved to the water's edge, sat alongside the pond, withdrew the red scarf from a pocket, and while the water was still wavering from the frog's departure, he dipped the cloth into the pond, let it soak, then applied it to his neck and face. He held it there for how long he did not know.

He turned and looked into the now stilled pond— saw his own reflection—and hers. He spoke her name.

"Deliverance."

"Yes, Jon," she smiled, "do you mind if I sit beside you? I wanted to talk to you."

"No, of course not. How did you know where to find me?"

In response, her voice was almost mystical.

"I have my ways."

"Yes. I guess you have."

She sat. Close.

A little too close, Keyes thought. He almost started to move away, but decided to stay and absorb the exotic fragrance of her nearby body.

As warm as the day was, she seemed as cool as an autumn breeze, as refreshing as a spring rain.

"I understand that you've decided against our invitation . . . that you're not going to stay."

"We'll be leaving just as soon as the wagon is ready. Lorna is anxious . . ."

"Lorna is sick, sicker than she'll admit."

"I know, but staying here doesn't seem to help . . . she doesn't want to stay any longer."

"Do you?"

He didn't answer. But there was no doubt about the conflict within, drawing him in opposite directions.

"But you will stay," her face came ever so slightly nearer to his, "at least for the first sermon? You promised, Jon."

"Yes, and I do think she'll agree to that."

"So do I," Deliverance smiled, "and maybe after that, she'll change her mind."

Keyes instinctively drew back.

"I don't think so, Deliverance."

CHAPTER 45

Keyes and Deliverance spent most of the rest of the day together—but not just the two of them alone.

They went back to the church site where the building activity was going nonstop and the construction itself, more evident.

Joseph, Bryant, and the rest, all working at a feverish pace, all except Caleb Hobbs, still in the shaded chair puffing contentedly on his pipe and casually issuing suggestions, which actually were commands.

As Keyes and Deliverance approached Caleb, Keyes looked around and noticed an absence.

"Good afternoon, Reverend, Deliverance."

Good afternoons were returned by both Keyes and Deliverance.

"I see you're still captain of the ship," Keyes smiled.

"Someone has to set the course and keep this vessel on schedule, m'boy."

"Well, Captain, it looks like you're even ahead of schedule . . ."

"That's due to superior seamanship and a steady hand at the wheel," Caleb held up his pipe.

"But I don't see Seaman Sam Hawkins around," Keyes said.

"I gave him shore leave to work on that wagon of yours, mate."

"Thank you, Caleb," Keyes grew serious, "I do appreciate that."

"Anything we can do to help, m'boy."

"Well, speaking of help, Bethia said she'd look in on Lorna, so why don't I pitch in here for a couple of hours or so? Permission to come aboard, Captain?"

Caleb inhaled from the pipe and nodded.

"Permission granted."

It was more than just a couple of hours later when Lorna managed to wobble to her feet, walk to the open window just before sundown, and breathe in the prenight breeze just in time to see her husband and Deliverance walking slowly toward the shed.

They stopped at the entrance . . . Deliverance opened the door.

Lorna could not hear what was being said, but it was obvious Deliverance was extending an invitation.

Keyes declined.

But he did reach up, touch her shoulder, smile, then reluctantly turn away and move toward the Hobbses' house.

Deliverance stood watching for a long time.

So did Lorna.

Lorna was back in bed when Keyes did enter carrying a tray full of food and drink.

"Well, Lorna, you and I are going to have breakfast."

"At sundown?" she said through thin lips.

"Bethia said that you haven't eaten all day . . . so we're going to have breakfast together . . . now!"

"Oh, Jonathon, I've felt worse today, weaker . . . and somehow even more despondent, even though we've decided to leave here."

"Well, cheer up, Lorna."

He set the tray on the bed, pulled up a chair, and sat.

"Remember the old saying . . . 'darkest before the dawn' . . . remember Custer and me at the White Horse Tavern in Monroe?

"I couldn't remember seeing Custer more despondent . . . even on the battlefield," Keyes recalled. "He was out of uniform and certainly out of patience."

"Jon, I don't know which of us fired the shot that killed Jeb Stuart, but sometimes I wish that it was I, not Stuart who died at Yellow Tavern."

"Autie . . ."

"At least I would have died a general in battle, not some forgotten colonel dying of dry rot without a command, without a cause to fight for . . . a forgotten footnote in some musty history book . . ."

Over Custer's lament we hadn't noticed, but a bulky man in a disheveled lieutenant's uniform and beetled eyebrows came into the White Horse, ordered a bottle of whiskey, took it and a glass over to the piano, drank a couple of stalwart drinks, and began banging on the piano and bellowing in a slightly off-key baritone:

> *Let Bacchus' sons be not dismayed,*
> *but join with me each jovial blade,*
> *come booze and sing and lend your aid,*
> *to help me with the chorus . . .*

It became impossible to carry on a conversation . . . but we tried.

"Autie, there's Libbie . . ."

"I've said it before, a hundred, a thousand times, if it weren't for Libbie, I'd blow my brains out, but I'm so rusty I'd probably miss. But there's one thing I'd like you to do, my friend . . ." And he sang:

> *Instead of spa we'll drink down ale*
> *and pay the reckoning on the nail,*
> *for debt no man shall go to jail;*
> *from Garry Owen in glory . . .*

"Just a minute, General, I can hardly hear you. I'll be right back."

I tapped the singing lieutenant on the shoulder.

"Excuse me . . ."

"You're excused, mate."

"No, lieutenant, I mean do you mind putting a mute on that singing so my friend and I can carry on a conversation?"

"I do mind, and you and your friend can go outside and talk. I'm just mustered out of the army, and I intend to celebrate."

"Could you kindly celebrate softer? I can't hear what my friend is saying."

"Is what he's saying more important than my song?"

"I can't judge that if I can't hear what he's saying. Can I?"

"Judge this!"

He whirled and threw a punch.

I ducked.

He started to swing again but Custer was in between us and shoved him hard against the piano.

"What's the matter? Can't your friend do his own fighting? I have."

"So has he . . . so have we all . . ."

"General Custer! I didn't recognize you without that uniform . . ."

"Colonel Custer now, and this is former Captain Jon Keyes, currently Reverend Keyes."

"Reverend! Sorry, Reverend. I'm Willie Cook, former lieutenant, United States and other armies. Glad to meet you both."

"Then sing that song some more—it's got a beat to it, like a cavalry charge."

"Sure, it's sung by the Queen's own regiments—the Irish from Limerick."

Lieutenant Cook took a sizable swallow directly from the bottle.

"It goes like this, sing along mates. Just follow me."

First Custer, then the rest of us did.

> Our hearts so stout have got us fame,
> for soon 'tis known from whence we came,
> where're we go they dread the name,
> of Garry Owen in glory.

Well, Lorna, you know just as we were finishing, Libbie and you rushed into the tavern. Libbie had one hand behind her back.

Custer was not surprised. He was astounded, and so was I, but Custer moved in close and asked just above a whisper . . .

"Libbie, what the devil are you doing here?"

"Well, I . . ."

"And you too, Lorna," I interrupted.

"I guess we thought that there's safety in numbers."

"What's wrong, Libbie?" Custer demanded.

"Wrong! You're wrong, Colonel Custer. I'm not Libbie! I'm a mail carrier . . . with an official dispatch."

That's when she brought a letter from her back and thrust it toward her husband.

"It's from the War Department, and I took the liberty of opening it. Read it, George, read it out loud."

We three, General Grant, General Sherman, and I, Philip Sheridan, and nearly all the officers of your regiment, have asked for you. Can you report at once? Eleven companies of your regiment, the Seventh Cavalry, will move soon against the hostile Indians.

> General Ulysses S. Grant
> General William Tecumseh Sherman
> General Philip H. Sheridan

"Can I report? Can I report! Well, Libbie, my sweet, can we report?!"

"You bet your spurs we can. We're practically packed."

Then Custer turned to me and grinned.

"Jon, Reverend, what I wanted to talk to you about . . ." He held up the letter.

"That won't be necessary anymore."

"Hold on mates, I suddenly feel like reenlisting, if you'll have me, sir."

"Have you? Why Queen's own, I want you and that song, both. It's our good luck tune, 'Garry Owen'!"

"Remember, Lorna?"

"How could I forget?"

"That was Custer at the darkest, just before the dawn. And now he's once again, in pursuit of glory."

"Yes, Jon, and now, what are we in pursuit of?"

"What else?" he smiled, "Saguaro, and a new life together."

Near the vibrating light of the candle, Deliverance's hand moved forward. Her thumb and forefinger squeezed into the lock of hair on the wax image of Lorna, as the cat leaped on the table and watched.

Deliverance's manipulation soon began to work on Lorna's mind . . . and on her husband's.

But in different ways.

Jonathon Keyes had fallen into a deep, but serene, sleep. An untroubled slumber.

Lorna was asleep, too, or was she?

She certainly was not awake or even semiconscious. She didn't know where she was, but she had to be someplace else. Without thinking more about it, she rose and something compelled her to go to the window and look out onto the dark yard.

This time there was no light emanating out of the window of Deliverance's shed.

But the yard was not completely dark. On the stump of the tree there was a large candle fashioned in the form of a hunched cat, with the flame wavering in the whispering wind of the night.

But more than that, even from that distance there wafted the aromatic fragrance of the candle reaching up to Lorna through the open window . . . a beckoning fragrance to which she must respond.

Still in a trancelike state, the next thing she realized was that she was outside walking on the ground in the backyard against a tree silhouetted semiluminous night sky, once again compelled to continue, until once again she heard the voices.

Young voices chanting . . . delivering that same strange incantation in an alien language:

> *Go blat . . . som blat . . . carradon . . .*
> *go loos. Com blat . . . go blat . . .*
> *go loos . . . carradon . . .*

Lorna took one step after another until the four figures once again came into focus.

Varied in size . . . three to five feet in height . . . dressed in white robes and their faces covered by masks of animals . . . a wolf—an owl—a goat—a sheep.

Each figure held a candle before it, transmitting an eerie light upward toward the mask.

The chanting was repeated.

> *Go blat . . . som blat . . . carradon . . .*
> *go loos. Com blat . . . go blat . . .*
> *go loos . . . carradon . . .*

Suddenly, as if on command, the chanting stopped. The flames from the candles disappeared—and so did the figures themselves.

It seemed the same as before, but somehow different.

And it was different.

On the tree stump. The same stump alongside the candle . . .

An owl.

But this time a living owl.

One eye open, the other hooded,

The wings fluttered slightly,

Then suddenly,

A screech.

From nowhere, Deliverance's cat leaped up and across, toward the stump, claws outstretched.

But the owl flew away leaving only a few fluttering feathers behind.

The cat screeched again, or was it the owl, or Lorna's soul-searing shriek that rent the night.

Just as before, once again she collapsed.

There remained no wax cat candle on the stump. No owl, nor Deliverance's cat.

Only Lorna's crumpled form on the ground near the empty stump.

CHAPTER 46

It was the same as last time.

Only it was different.

Lorna was on the same ground, on the same spot.

Keyes was bent over her, propping her head.

Caleb, Joseph, Bethia . . . and Deliverance holding her cat.

The same empty stump.

"Lorna. Lorna, can you hear me? It's Jon."

"Yes . . . Jonathon . . . I . . . can . . ." Her eyes opened slowly, "I can see you . . . but it's dark . . . Jonathon, where are we?"

"Don't talk, darling. We'll . . ."

"No . . . I want to know . . . where?"

"We're outside in the backyard. With Caleb, Joseph, Bethia, Deliverance."

"How did . . . I get here?"

"We don't know . . . but like the last time . . ."

"Yes, the same as the last time . . . only different . . ."

"The same? Different? How?"

"Same young voices . . . children . . . candles . . . masks . . . but different."

"How different, Lorna?"

She half-rose and looked around.

"On the stump a candle . . . a cat candle, and an . . . owl this time, alive . . ." She looked at Deliverance and the cat in her arms, "this time Deliverance's shed was dark but the cat . . ."

"What about the cat, Lorna?"

"Jumped . . . owl flew away . . . but this time I'm not sure."

"Of what?"

"Of . . . anything . . ."

"Mrs. Keyes," Caleb stood next to the stump, "the candle you saw on the stump . . . was it lit?"

"Yes . . . that's what drew . . . me here."

"Mrs. Keyes, there's no trace of wax on this stump."

"My cat was upstairs with me," Deliverance said.

"Last time," Joseph nodded, "the owl was dead . . . this time . . ."

"Yes, I know . . . and this time I'm not really sure of anything I saw . . . or heard . . . it's all a cloudy mist in my mind . . . a dusky dream . . . this time maybe I was walking in my . . . but it seems something was pulling me . . ."

"Well, dream or no," Keyes said, "we're not doing any good out here in the dead of night. Lorna, I'm going to carry you upstairs."

"No, Jon, just let me lean on you a little. I can walk."

"Shall I warm some milk for you ma'am?" Bethia volunteered.

"Or a snifter of brandy?" Caleb added.

"No, thank you. Jonathon, just put your arm around me."

As Keyes helped his wife walk toward the house, Caleb, Joseph, Bethia, and Deliverance, with the cat in her arms, stood watching, and from above, perched on the limb of a tree, with one hooded lid, an owl looked down on them.

In bed he kissed her good night.

"Lorna, from now on whenever you wake up at night, you know what's the first thing I want you to do?"

"What, Jon?"

"Wake me up, too. At night," he smiled, "we walk in double harness."

"I will, Jon, if I can help myself, but something drove me to do what I did. This time I'm not sure of anything. I don't know what's real and what isn't anymore. But I know that this place is . . . it's like an infection of some kind . . . and the only cure is to leave . . . or it'll get worse."

"We won't let it, Lorna, we just won't let it. We'll be far away, you and I together."

CHAPTER 47

The structure of the church was definitely taking on shape even to the outline of the steeple topped by a cross conformed against the sky.

It seemed as if each of the men, women, and children knew exactly what to do except for an occasional prompting from Caleb Hobbs on his "captain's chair."

"Morning, m'boy."

"Good morning, Caleb."

"How is Lorna this morning?"

"Caleb, she only has one thing in mind."

"Leaving San Melas?"

"Well, let's say going to Saguaro."

"That is a more . . . 'diplomatic' way of putting it," Caleb smiled.

Keyes pointed upward toward the steeple.

"I see you've got the cross in place."

"Those were my instructions. What's a church without a cross? And in just a few more days the place'll be ready for your sermon."

"I noticed something else?"

"What's that?"

"I should say 'someone' else."

Sam Hawkins, carrying an oversized hammer, was approaching the two men.

"Mornin', Mr. Keyes."

"Good morning, Mr. Hawkins. I see you're taking a little time off from fixing the wagon."

"The wagon doesn't need me anymore . . ." Hawkins smiled.

"How's that?"

"All fixed . . . as good as I can fix her."

"Will she make it to Saguaro?"

"And back," his smile broadened, "if you care to do that, Mr. Keyes."

"Well, we'll take it one step at a time . . . and Lorna and I are grateful to you . . ."

"Not as much as San Melas is grateful to you, sir."

But Keyes's attention now was directed toward Deliverance carrying a tray of biscuits, followed by Bethia holding a large pot of coffee.

Deliverance looked even fresher and more illusory than usual.

"Good morning, Jon," she smiled, "would you care for some coffee and a hot biscuit?"

"Don't mind if I do, Deliverance, don't mind at all."

"I was just going back to the house," Bethia said, "to look after Mrs. Keyes."

"Thank you, Bethia, and you, too, Deliverance, I'll have that coffee and biscuit, then earn my keep," Keyes pointed toward the construction, "by doing a little carpentry."

Keyes felt a tap on his shoulder from behind.

"You can use this saw, Reverend," Joseph smiled, "whenever you're ready."

Hours later Lorna managed to make one more trip from the bed to the window and look down at the yard . . . and once more wonder what it was that drew her there last night . . . and how much, if any, was real . . . the candle . . . the chanting voices . . . the masked children . . . the live owl . . . Deliverance's cat.

And how much a miasma of the mind that depletes, obscures, and corrupts the thought process?

During those first few days in San Melas, she believed that it was the effect of the sun, of the desert ordeal that had depleted and obscured, that had confused her thought process.

But, from time to time, that miasma had come and gone, and then come back again . . . affecting her mind and body both . . . as if pressured by an unseen force, a hypnotic conjuration to conform to some somniferous command.

But whose?

And why?

Or did all this presage madness?

It was her husband whose head had been wounded, who suffered the effects of that wound with nightmarish dreams and demons, while her mind had always been uncluttered and clear . . . until San Melas.

And in a strange way, too, her husband had been affected by this place and these people who considered him a "miracle worker," who, if not idolized him, were at least overly attracted to him: Caleb, Joseph, the Bryants, Ethan, the entire citizenry, and in particular . . . Deliverance.

Lorna was not unaware of the seemingly innocent, but inwardly wanton look in the eyes of Deliverance, even when she glanced at Jonathon Keyes. She was a beautiful young lady, with an exotic aura about her, not of her native New England, nor even of this country, but of some symmetrical blend of Scandinavian Valkyrie and august princess of Araby. Attractive, aloof, and yet inviting, especially when it came to Lorna's husband.

There were other women in other churches, where Jonathon Keyes had been invited to give guest sermons, where other ladies of the congregation were obviously attracted to him, but not in the sensuous way of Deliverance.

And Lorna couldn't help wondering, despite his piety, how much he couldn't help being drawn to her.

As she fought against the thought, she once again saw the two of them walking close together in harmonious step toward the shed.

Walking, she thought, like two lovers, as did she and Keyes years ago, from a Sunday picnic—not in any hurry to reach the place where they must part, but walking with lingering footsteps before arriving at their parting destination.

But was this the place where the two of them would part?

The shed.

Or . . .

This time when she opened the door and motioned toward the interior, with words that Lorna could not hear, this time would he, or would he not, accept her specious invitation to look at her latest handiwork with wax and savory scented perfumes?

She held her breath.

Watched and waited.

This time a little longer . . .

As Deliverance opened the door and went through the nearly identical procedure.

Once again Keyes reached up, this time touched her cheek, smiled, then took a step back, turned, and walked away.

Lorna breathed again as Deliverance closed the door of the shed.

"Jon, your shirt is wringing wet," she said from the bed, "it looks like you've been swimming in it."

"Not swimming," he smiled, "just sweating. Helping to build that church for the last few hours. The sooner it's in shape, the sooner the sermon, the sooner Saguaro. It's hotter today than it was yesterday, and I put in more hours."

Keyes had unbuttoned and was taking off his shirt.

"There's a nice clean shirt in the second drawer, Jon."

"Good. And speaking of good, do you know who else was working at the church today?"

Keyes sponged himself off and reached for a towel.

Lorna was reasonably certain he was about to bring up the presence of Deliverance but cleared her throat and inquired.

"Who, Jon?"

"Sam Hawkins."

A quizzical look came over her face.

"Sam Hawkins?"

"The blacksmith, Lorna."

"Yes, I know who he is . . ."

"The blacksmith who's been working on our wagon."

"Oh, yes, of course, and . . ."

"And he says it's fixed. It's ready to go, so we can leave anytime right after the sermon."

"Jon, that is good news," she nodded, "it's wonderful. Come over and sit here. Let me button that shirt."

"Lorna, I'm perfectly capable of buttoning this shirt," he grinned.

"So am I . . . and in the first place I want to do it . . . and in the second place . . ."

"In the second place . . . what?"

"In the second place," she smiled warmly, "I want to feel the touch of my fingers against your . . . nice, clean shirt."

"And . . . vice versa," he bantered, then moved and sat on the edge of the bed.

He kissed her.

"I love you, Lorna."

"And . . . vice versa," she bantered, then went to work on the shirt buttons.

"Say, did anyone ever tell you that you are a very good shirt-buttoner?"

"No, kind sir, because I've never buttoned anybody else's buttons before."

"Well, you better practice some more because we're going to have some boy babies and they'll need to have their shirts buttoned for them when they're young."

"Just boy babies, my husband?"

"You just watch the boy and girl population of Saguaro grow after we get there."

"Oh?"

"More than just watch, my wife."

"I intend to."

"So do I."

"He kissed her again. This time longer, more intensely."

"There," she said, "all done."

"What do you mean by that?"

"All done. The shirt's all buttoned."

"I hadn't noticed." He rose. "My mind was somewhere else."

"At the church that's being built?"

"No, but that's where I saw Bethia, and she said she was coming over to tend to you, and that's why I stayed to help out. Did she bring you something to eat?"

"She did."

"And did you?"

"Eat?"

"Yes, eat."

"I did . . ."

"But not enough. Lorna, you haven't eaten enough since we got here."

"I'll make up for it after we leave."

"Sure you will, they'll kill the fatted calf when we get to Saguaro."

"Jon, is it as hot in Saguaro as it is here?"

"Don't think so. There's a river that runs through it, and it's not in the middle of the desert."

"These people here don't seem to be affected too much by the heat . . . especially Deliverance. Was she at the church today?"

"She was."

"Even in this desert heat she always seems so . . . cool, calm, and composed, doesn't she?"

"What?"

"I said, doesn't she? Deliverance, seem so . . . decorous."

"I never thought about it," he shrugged, "but maybe after all those years of not being able to speak . . . she's acquired . . ."

"Acquired what?"

"A certain," he shrugged again, "I don't know . . . a certain composure."

"Jon," Lorna couldn't help smiling, "what's that got to do with sweating?"

"I don't know, Lorna . . . I honestly don't. You brought up the subject . . ."

". . . Of sweating?"

"Of Deliverance, my dear."

"You're right . . . and I'm going to change the subject."

"Good," he chuckled, "to what?"

She rubbed her chin in mock seriousness, furrowed her brow, and responded.

"How about that river that runs through Saguaro? What's the name of it?"

"I really don't know. Reverend Mason mentioned a river, but not by name."

"Do you think it'll be as beautiful as the Raisin in Monroe?"

"It will . . . if you're there."

"The Raisin River," she reflected, "that last picnic just before we left Monroe. The four of us at our favorite spot along the bank . . ."

". . . Custer, his eyes literally glowing with thoughts of glory . . ." Keyes said.

"Libbie, who could hardly take her eyes off of him. And you and me getting ready to pack for a new place and a new life."

"Yes," Keyes nodded, "and I remember, Custer and I were both in civilian clothes, but he asked that we both wear our red scarves for old-time's sake."

"Well, Sports, this is the last camp before our paths divide—mine and Libbie's—and yours and Lorna's . . . Libbie and I by rail to Duluth and by wagon to Fort Lincoln in the Dakotas . . . and you two damn fools, by steamboat to St. Louis, then Conestoga to some benighted flyspeck called . . . what's the name of that flyspeck, Reverend . . . Sedona . . . Sonora . . . Somalia . . ."

"It's Saguaro, General, and you know it."

"Sure I do, Reverend . . . but do you know . . . what you're in for?"

"General, nobody knows for certain . . . any more than we know if the four of us will ever be together again."

"What do you think, George, do you think you and I will ever meet Lorna and Jon . . . after Monroe?"

"Well, Libbie, there's an old saying, 'it's a creation-big country, but trails cross.' Ours just might do that, somewhere, sometime."

"It's a long way from Saguaro to the Dakotas."

"True, Lorna, and it was a long way from Monroe to Appomattox . . . and back. But here we are . . . the Reverend and I. And what were the odds of that after Winchester, Waynesboro, Falls Church, and Yellow Tavern? Thousands and thousands of dead men ago?"

"But that was war. We're at peace now. The war's over."

"Is it, Lorna? And even if it is, what does that mean? It only means that for the time being, we're between wars. But I'll tell you something, all of you, Jon, Lorna, Libbie—we picked the right time to be born, here and now . . ."

"You mean Monroe?"

"Hell no, I . . . oh, excuse me, Libbie, Lorna, Reverend—I gave up a lot of other ribald habits, but just can't quite quit that damn curs . . . see what I mean?"

"Yes, Autie, we see what you mean and hear it, too."

"Sorry, Libbie, I'll try to ease off, but what I really meant about time and place was the United States of America at the time of a new birth, with a whole new frontier. The land west of the one hundredth meridian to be surveyed and settled . . . there's gold, silver, and all manner of rich minerals waiting to be discovered in nature's laboratories. There're more railroads being built, one that will connect the United States to its Manifest Destiny, coast to coast. There's never been a time and place like the American West. But much of that West still has to be fought for and won. And we're a part of all that."

"General, you mentioned Manifest Destiny. What about the Indians' destiny? A lot of that real estate belongs to them. You, also, mentioned the transcontinental railroad. The Indians won't like that. And there're rumors of gold in their sacred Black Hills where you're going, and some white miners are already sharpening their pickaxes."

"Reverend, the Indians need too damn much land.

They're movers and hunters, not settlers. There are
going to have to be some adjustments made . . ."

"Mostly by the Indians."

"There were adjustments made between the North
and South. We fought for the Union against slavery.
Some of the Indian ways are worse, much worse, than
the South. They've got slaves, too. They buy, sell,
trade, and steal women and children like horses.
They've got to understand that all that has to change.
Oh, they talk peace, but as Patrick Henry said, 'there
is no peace.' Look, Reverend, from what I've heard
about their chiefs, men like Sitting Bull and Crazy
Horse, they're good soldiers and good men. So were
some of my best friends at the Point, but they were
fighting for a lost cause, like those chiefs. One of
the last things that Lincoln said was 'the West must be
made secure.' It can't be so long as settlements and
wagon trains are being indiscriminately attacked."

"I guess that's why they sent for you, General."

"I'll do what I can."

"But it almost sounds like you'll enjoy doing it . . .
and after all you've seen and done . . ."

"It's *because* of what I've seen and done. I know that
sometimes it takes war to make peace. But, Reverend,
there are different paths that lead to the same place.
In some ways, as of now, war is the engine of my
existence—that and Libbie, of course—the paths of
Hannibal, Caesar, Napoleon, and as for your path,
Reverend—well, a few names come to mind, Jesus,
Buddha, Mohammed . . ."

"Just a minute there, Wolverine, you mention yourself and my husband in the same breath as Caesar,
Napoleon, Jesus, and Buddha?"

"I did."

"Well, then, what does that make Libbie and me?"

"Let me see, now . . . oh, Apostles, I guess."

"Why you shameless . . ."

Libbie threw a tomato at her husband but missed.

"Libbie, I hope those Indians aren't any better marksmen than you."

"Husband, I *meant* to miss."

"I know that."

"But General, the Indians won't . . . *want* to miss, I mean."

"Neither will I, Jon. Captain. Reverend . . ."

"Yes, sir."

"I asked you to wear that Wolverine red scarf today not as a reminder of the past, but for another reason."

"What's that, General?"

"The future. You said you turned to the ministry because of what Reverend Mason did for you and the rest of the soldiers."

"That's a big part of it."

"Well, Sport, I've got a feeling that up there in the Dakotas, with what the Seventh Cavalry is going to have to deal with . . . those hostiles, we're going to have need of a man like Reverend Mason . . . . or you."

"I thought that might be coming, General."

"Well, it came . . . so, Jon, what's the answer?"

"Lorna and I talked about this . . . and because of our friendship with you and Libbie, it's a hard choice, but . . ."

"But, what?"

"Saguaro, it is. We made a promise. Reverend Mason has nobody else. You'll have your choice of a dozen good men up there."

"It won't be the same."

"For us either, but Jon and I think that's the thing to do."

"George and I will miss you so much, Lorna."

"That's true, but in every war there's a last battle . . . and after the one in the Dakotas, maybe I *can* quit soldiering."

"And do what, Autie?"

"Oh, I don't know. But I do know my mission in the military is not over yet. I've been called a glory seeker, and right now the West is where the glory is. Over a hundred years ago a poet wrote, 'One crowded hour of glory is worth an age without a name.'"

"General, you've already had your hour of glory."

"I guess that's true, but sometimes *one* hour is not enough . . . and as I said, maybe after that last battle in the Dakotas I *can* quit soldiering."

"I repeat, and do what?"

"*I* repeat . . . I don't know."

"There's a phrase that's already being rumored around."

"What's that?"

"'Custer for President.'"

"That's a long shot."

"Long shots sometimes hit the mark. And it's happened to generals before: Washington, Jackson, Harrison, and it looks like Grant'll be next. And if it does happen, I'll vote for you, General."

"So would Lorna and I . . . if we could vote."

"Well, Sports, I'll say this for myself, George Custer hasn't talked so much since Sunday school recitation, but it's true, trails do cross, and as long as you have that red scarf . . . I'll be looking for you. We'll have a lot to tell our grandchildren."

* * *

"I know you still have that red scarf, Jonathon."

"Right there on the dresser . . . a little the worse for the wear, but then so am I."

"How do you think the General and Libbie are doing up there?"

"Well, from what I've read in the newspapers along the way, he's already whipped the Seventh into shape and even whipped the Sioux in a couple encounters, to the tune of 'Garry Owen.'"

"What about it, Jonathon?"

"What about what?"

"Do you think we made the right choice?"

"Well, the first choice was my being a minister; that was my choice, and it was the right one for me."

"I know it was."

"But the second choice was Saguaro and neither of us knows what that will be like. At Lincoln there will be other officers' wives, parties, dances, parades . . ."

". . . and the killing of Indians. Do you think you could be a part of all that?"

"I don't think, Lorna, I don't think I could bear watching Indians being killed over land that belongs to them."

"And in a way, it takes more mettle to stand alone and do what you're doing than . . ."

". . . Fight a war?"

"There are different kinds of wars."

"Sure there are Lorna, George Armstrong Custer would point to Caesar and Napoleon . . . and then to Jesus and Buddha . . . I . . . I . . ."

Keyes stopped as he saw the abrupt change that came over his wife.

Lorna gasped, struggled for breath. All color was drained from her face. Her eyelids squeezed nearly shut in pain. Her pale lips trembled. Her shoulders shuddered. Her head fell back against the pillow.

It was uncertain if she were still conscious.

Keyes hurried to the bedside and hovered close to her.

"Lorna, honey . . . can you hear me?"

As suddenly as it had come, at least some of the pain and its effects seemed to subside, but only some. Her breathing became less labored, her face, less pallid, her eyes, more focused.

"Oh, Jonathon . . . I . . . I . . ."

"Lorna, don't talk. Just lie back and rest."

"I will, but oh, Jonathon, I can't help feeling . . . we're in one of those wars . . . right here and now."

Against the azure sky the drifting cloud that had obscured the moon curled slowly into a patternless mist, then vanished into the night so that the outline of the shed was more clearly defined against the darkness of the yard.

Inside, Bethia stood with a clement smile on her face, watching.

The cat on the candlelit table purred as Deliverance's fingers withdrew from the wax figure.

It was the image of Lorna . . . but less recognizable.

CHAPTER 48

Instead of the night's rest and sleep helping, it seemed to have cast Lorna adrift in a sea of listlessness and apathy . . . indifferent to everything and everyone.

Keyes stayed at her bedside and did his best to induce a reaction, touching her shoulder, her face, asking a question or speaking of anything he thought might spark a response.

But her response more often than not was to turn her face away and murmur something unintelligible.

"Lorna, let me get you something to eat, something to drink."

"Don't . . . bother," she finally groaned.

"Lorna . . ."

"Go away!"

"All right."

"No, it's not all right, but go away."

"How's the missus this morning, Reverend?"

"Not as well as expected, I'm afraid, Bethia."

"Oh, so sorry to hear that. I'll go upstairs presently and see if there's anything I can do to be of help."

"That's very kind of you, but Bethia . . ."

"Yes, sir?"

"If she seems, well, a little . . . abrupt, please be patient. Last night she had a . . . well, a sort of spell, and this morning she's just not herself."

"I understand, sir, I understand completely, and would you like me to fix you some breakfast? Eggs and . . ."

"No thanks, Bethia, I'll just have some coffee at the church site. That's where they all are, isn't it?"

"It is indeed, sir."

It was as if they had all been working through the night. That's how much further along the construction had advanced.

After the usual salutations as Keyes passed by the congregation, he reached Caleb Hobbs sitting in his usual shady spot. Just as he arrived so did Deliverance carrying a tray with a mug of coffee and a plate of biscuits.

"Morning, m'boy."

"Morning, Caleb, Deliverance."

"Hot biscuits and hotter coffee, Jonathon."

"Just coffee for now."

"Very good. Let me know if you want anything else later." She turned and glided away toward the serving table.

"Any improvement in Lorna's condition, Reverend?"

"Not much, if any at all, I'm sorry to say," Keyes looked toward the construction. "But there's quite a bit of improvement around here."

"Dedication, m'boy. Dedication, and stalwart shepherding of the flock."

"Yes, well, I'll just finish this coffee and . . . join the flock."

The desert sun, though not yet nearing its daily high point in the sky, still generated heat enough so that about half of the men working had already removed their shirts and were toiling in their undershirts or no shirts at all.

This included Keyes, who wanted to keep his nice fresh shirt nice and fresh. He threw the shirt over a chair and moved toward the building activity.

As he walked past the serving table, Deliverance paused at what she was doing, and took an obviously admiring look at the passerby. Keyes couldn't help but notice; however, he did his best to just look straight ahead and keep on walking.

"Morning, Reverend."

"Good morning, Joseph."

"'Thou shalt exalt in the labor of thy hands.'"

"I am ready to start exalting," Keyes smiled.

Joseph held out a pair of tools.

"Would you prefer exalting with a saw or hammer?"

"A saw will do nicely, Brother Joseph."

"Saw it shall be."

And so it was as Keyes proceeded to take part in the construction of a church in which he would serve only once, then leave behind.

But his mind, his thoughts were not on his work as he sawed, hammered, carried, and fitted beams and wedges into place.

In the mirror of his mind he was sawing through the forlorn image of his peaked wife—and as the saw ripped through the board it was tearing into Lorna's tortured brain—and as he looked up he couldn't help but gaze at the smiling, beguiling, inviting face and figure of Deliverance, who, in spite of the blistering midday heat of the sun, seemed fluent and sangfroid.

Standing, walking, and serving in the sultry desert day among the sweating workers, she seemed fresh as an autumn night wind.

Keyes recalled the conversation with Lorna and Lorna's words about Deliverance.

"Even in the desert she always seems so . . . cool, calm, and composed, so . . . decorous."

Lorna's descriptive words were themselves gracious and flattering, but the tone in her voice, mordant and spiteful, a tone so unlike Lorna.

And yet whenever she spoke of these people of San Melas there seemed to be an underlying tone of uncertainty, even suspicion, in her aspect . . . particularly when it came to Deliverance.

Once again Keyes paused to reach into his pocket, retract a handkerchief, and wipe the perspiration from his face, but in fact the pause was to allow him a better look at the graceful flow of body and beautiful features of Deliverance as she moved toward him.

"Jon, is there anything you'd like now? Lemonade? Tea? Water?"

"No, thanks, Deliverance. I'm fine for now."

"All right, Jon. Well, I'll try again . . . later."

She smiled, turned smoothly, and walked away.

Keyes took a moment to glance around at the other citizens who were working with such enthusiasm and dedication. His glance paused just a little longer at those he had gotten to know better than the rest.

First Caleb Hobbs, their leader and his predominant benefactor, who besides saving his life, had extended hospitality and who obviously wanted them to stay, yet had done everything he could to make it possible for them to continue their journey.

And Joseph, who quoted and practiced the Bible as well as any person Keyes had ever met. A man his age who worked as hard as any man half his years.

The Bryants, William, Pricilla, and of course Ethan, as carefree and brave a lad as Keyes had ever met. Keyes himself would be pleased to have a son like him.

Sam Hawkins, who worked ceaselessly to repair the Conestoga without which they would be marooned in San Melas.

And all the rest.

Hardworking, clean-living, decent, ordinary, God-fearing folk.

And still, there was Lorna, who Keyes in all those years he'd known her, had never heard her express a negative opinion about any man or woman. If she had nothing good to say, she said nothing.

And yet, even in the short time they had been in San Melas, a certain undercurrent of incertitude, doubt, yes, even more than suspicion, surfaced in her spoken, and even unspoken, reaction to this place and people.

Was it the desert sun?

The isolation?

The open idolatry they heaped on him?

Their costumes and customs?

Or was it only one other reason that accounted for Lorna's attitude?

Was that reason Deliverance?

And was she in any way justified?

Keyes hoped not.

He had done nothing and wanted to do nothing that would justify any doubt in Lorna's mind.

Keyes had never loved, or even as much as thought about, any other woman since he first espied the teenage Lorna Benton.

It was a toss-up as to who was the more beautiful young lady in Monroe, Lorna Benton or Libbie Bacon.

Lorna was the more reserved, Libbie the saucier.

Even when she was a pert, dimpled, and beautiful eight-year-old girl swinging on the front gate, as the blond curly haired lad dashed along, it was Libbie who made the first signal—"Hey you, Custer Boy," she blurted and ran into the house leaving him dead in his tracks, but intrigued.

Lorna, at that, or any age, would never be so saucy—or bold.

There was always a certain reserve and dignity about her, although a flash of humor did sparkle through, especially when she and Keyes were together by themselves.

Those occasions were less, much less frequent since San Melas . . . since Deliverance.

Keyes took one more stolen look at Deliverance, then went back to work.

Deliverance made no effort to conceal the fact that she was looking at him.

CHAPTER 49

This time Lorna was not at the window as Keyes and Deliverance walked across the yard toward the shed.

She did not see their elbows touch, nor the smile on their faces, nor hear what was being said.

Lorna was in bed, more comatose than conscious.

She did not see the two of them once again pause at the open door, this time linger a little longer, as Keyes's hand started to move up toward Deliverance's face but stopped in midair as he turned and walked away.

When he entered the room Keyes went directly to the bedside, looked at the untouched tray of food on the bed stand, then at Lorna, whose eyes were closed.

"Lorna . . . Lorna . . . it's . . ."

"I know who it is," she muttered without opening her eyes.

"You haven't eaten . . ."

"I'll eat . . . later."

"I'll bring something up and we'll have supper together."

"NO! You go eat with your friends."

He did.

Of course Caleb asked about Lorna's condition, and Keyes did not want to appear too negative but it was difficult for him to appear in the least bit positive, so he was as equivocal as possible.

"She's resting now."

"Has she eaten any of what I brought up to her?"

"Not yet, Bethia, but she's promised to later."

Bethia nodded and went on serving at the table.

"There's nothing that stimulates a person's appetite," Caleb said, "quite like a hard day's work."

The others at the table did their best not to react to the irony of Caleb's comment since he had seldom, if ever, moved from his shaded seat during the entire day.

Joseph started to say something but thought it better not to.

"Would you please pass the butter, Jon?" Deliverance reached out as Keyes complied and their fingers just happened to converge and stay suspended for a beat more than necessary to make the exchange.

This did not go unnoticed by Bethia, who smiled faintly as she repaired toward the kitchen.

Not much later Keyes rose from the table.

"Well, I'd better go upstairs and see about Lorna."

"And I'd better go out and see about my candles."

"Well, get a good night's sleep both of you," Caleb lit his pipe, "we've got another hard day's work ahead of us tomorrow."

The tray was still on the bedside table and still untouched as Keyes knew it would be. And when he tried to talk to her, she was just as unresponsive as before, with a voice that hardly seemed to be her own.

"Lorna . . ."

"Yes, my husband . . . did you enjoy supper with your . . . friends?"

"I'd enjoy it a lot more with you."

"Is that so?"

"Yes, Lorna, that's so. I wish you'd believe that."

"I wish I . . . could."

Keyes realized that it was hopeless to try and reason with Lorna in her state of mind. He would have to wait . . . but for how long?

Hours? Days? Weeks?

Or . . .

Was it not a matter of time?

Was it this place?

San Melas?

Or was it forever?

Had the Lorna he knew and married been lost in some other realm?

What force was tugging at her, wracking her mind and body?

Deliverance was in the shed, but not working on her candles. On the table directly in front of her were two wax figures, one plainly enough, that of Jonathon Keyes, the other, hardly recognizable except for the hair, Lorna.

As Deliverance kneaded that figure it became even less identifiable.

The nocturnal silence within the shed was rifted only by the pervasive purr of the cat.

* * *

Keyes sat on the straight-back chair near the bed with the Bible in his hand, his head lowered, eyes closed, and lips in near silent supplication for the recovery of his wife.

"'And the prayer of faith shall save the sick, and the Lord shall raise him up.'"

He rose, the Bible still in hand, walked across the room, placed the Bible on the dresser, and removed his shirt. He sponged, then dried himself before almost automatically looking in the mirror.

He instantly wished he hadn't, but it was too late.

He stood benumbed by the reflection within:

The bruised and bloodied man, with anguished face, deep, hollow eyes, twisted mouth, and tortured outstretched arms, straining, running, running, running—but not fast enough to catch Keyes racing just ahead, as the man reached out, desperately trying to grab him . . . words from the tormented mouth cried out soundlessly, racing as before, but this time even more intent.

Once, twice, the man's hand nearly touched Keyes, but instead, he stumbled, lost ground, then regained balance and resumed the chase.

And as Keyes looked ahead, Deliverance was standing within the same doorway . . . beckoning, as a subtle wind pressed the sheer garment she wore against every curve and dip of her flawless form, her flaxen hair drifted gently against the smooth spread of her shoulders . . . a living monument to the mythical sea nymphs who lured sailors from their homeward odyssey.

And Keyes was almost there.

But suddenly . . .

A figure stood between Keyes and Deliverance.

A figure clothed in black.

MOON . . .

Stood laughing.

A mirthless, noiseless laugh . . .

Taunting Keyes.

Keyes stood stone still . . .

And the tormented man who had been chasing Keyes was suddenly frozen, unable to move. But Keyes continued toward Moon, who stopped his advance with a whirlwind backhand to the face that spun him to the ground.

Moon turned and began to move toward Deliverance with Tarquin's ravishing stride.

In that instant there appeared a gun in Keyes's hand. A gun with a gold handle. One of Moon's guns was now missing from its black holster.

Keyes fired the gun in the air. There was no sound, but smoke curled from the barrel.

Moon turned and at the same time in a snakelike motion drew the gun from his right holster and aimed . . . but before he could squeeze, Keyes fired again, this time not in the air but at the black clad target.

Moon fell with the grace of a ballet dancer . . . slowly, symphonically.

Keyes, still holding the gun, ran past the fallen Moon . . . the tortured man now in pursuit.

Keyes managed to make it through the door as Deliverance again shut out the man.

But this time the narrative in the mirror continued to unfold.

As Deliverance held out both arms with an invitational smile, and Keyes stepped closer . . . Moon . . . Moon was somehow alive again, standing inside the room, legs spread apart, gun in hand, ready to fire.

Keyes, holding Deliverance in a protective embrace, fired first.

Then . . .

Fired again . . .

And again . . .

As the mirror cracked.

Keyes stood in front of the mirror, sweating, trembling.

Did the mirror crack, or, was that, too, a reflection of his imagination? He reached out, touched, then passed his fingers across the slivered surface.

The mirror had cracked.

Keyes turned away even though now the mirror reflected only his own image.

He found it hard to breath. He drew each breath with effort. He walked unsteadily to the bed. In truth he didn't know why.

Did he want to tell her what he had seen in the mirror?

The answer was no.

If he did, what could he expect from her? Particularly in her current condition. She had illusions or delusions of her own.

Still, he whispered, then called out her name.

"Lorna . . . Lorna . . ."

As he expected . . . no response.

He might as well have been in the room alone . . . except for the images in the mirror.

He walked to the window and looked out.

Darkness, except for the moonlight that filtered through branches of the trees and spread their shaky shadows on the ground.

He looked toward the outline of the shed.

It was only an outline. No candlelight from within.

But there was a gust of refreshing night air through the bedroom's open window.

If nothing more, he needed the vivifying outdoor air. He needed to get out of this room.

He did.

Keyes, still shirtless, sat on the stump of the tree, his head bent into the palms of both hands in a vain effort to separate reality from illusion.

Who was the man in the mirror? Why was the man trying to catch him? What was he trying to say, or do? Was he a ghost . . . like Moon, come back from the grave to haunt him? But why?

And Deliverance.

Beautiful, beguiling, bewitching Deliverance.

A composition of empyrean elegance and earthy enticement.

A vision out of every man's dream.

"Jon."

Keyes looked up.

Deliverance stood before him, looking much as she did in the mirror. Adorned in a diaphanous white gown. Hair cascading onto her shoulders and breast. But this was no mirror image.

She was real.

"Jon, what are you doing out here?"

"I'll ask you the same question. There is no light in your workroom."

"No, there isn't."

Keyes didn't wait for a further answer.

"Deliverance . . . I have to tell you something. I have to tell someone . . ."

But suddenly the sky crackled and was lit up by a crooked bolt of lightning, then darkness again, and a spatter of rain . . . more lightning, then thunder and a heavier shower burst.

"Summer storm," she said. "Let's get inside."

Deliverance lit two large candles that were on the workbench and glanced at the two wax images now covered with damp cloths, then she turned to Keyes who stood shirtless, his body glistening from the rain.

"Jon, you're drenched."

"So are you," he smiled.

"Yes, but you're half-naked. There's a towel right over here."

She reached on the table, picked up a towel.

He started to take it from her but instead, Deliverance began pressing it gently on his arms, chest, neck, and face.

He stood stiff at the touch of the towel and the occasional touch of her fingers against his body.

"That's fine, Deliverance. Thank you."

"Jon, sitting out there you seemed . . . pensive . . . actually, melancholy . . . and there was something you were going to tell me."

"Now I don't know whether I should."

"Please do, Jon. Maybe, just maybe I can even help you a little, though not like you helped me. I want to try."

"The mirror in the bedroom."

"What about it?"

"Sometimes . . . when I look into it I see . . ."

"Yourself."

"No. A man, burned, blistered, bleeding . . . and he's chasing me . . . why, I don't know . . . whether it's to harm or to warn me. I don't know . . . but I don't want him to catch me . . . and then there's Moon . . . standing between me and . . . you, Deliverance . . . he's alive and I shoot at him again and again while I hold you in my arms . . ."

"But that's just a dream, Jon, a bad dream," she paused and smiled, "except for the part where you hold me in your arms . . . but a dream, nevertheless."

"Deliverance, you dream while asleep in bed . . . not looking in the mirror."

"There are different kinds of dreams. Good and bad. Asleep and even awake . . . day dreams . . . shadows of the soul, they've been called . . . tricks of the mind . . . puzzles within puzzles. . . . There is no earthly answer, any more than there is an answer to the riddle of the Sphinx. No earthly answer, Jon. Your sermons, which have helped so many are all based on a book called the Bible. If there is an answer, perhaps it lies hidden somewhere in there. I want to show you something."

She walked to a corner of the room and pulled back a curtain revealing a cot against the wall.

Keyes did not quite contain his surprise.

Deliverance smiled.

"I use it to sleep on when I sometimes spend the night here. That's why it was dark inside tonight."

She reached down and picked up an object near the pillow.

"Come over here, Jon. Sit down next to me."

He hesitated but not really.

As he sat, she moved even closer to him and held up the Bible.

"This Bible belonged to our last minister, Reverend Courtney Joyner. It was inside the church when it burned down. And it was a miracle, because, miraculously it was the only thing in the church that didn't burn. Ashes all around it, but it lay there untouched by flames. I had read it many times since then, but until you came, until that day when you ridded us all of Moon, could I speak any of the words I had read. And even if I could, I had no one to speak them to. Would you like to hear me speak some of those words to you?"

Keyes looked at her and nodded.

She opened the Bible without even looking at the page and began to quote in a soft, intimate voice as the rain accompanied her with a rhythmic pulsation against the roof above.

How long he sat and listened he could not tell. From the time she began, it was as if he were spellbound by the cadence of her voice, the effect of her fragrance, her nearness . . . the structure of her face and form.

> *The voice of my beloved!*
> *behold, he cometh leaping*
> *upon the mountains, and skipping*
> *upon the hills.*

Keyes, who had been looking straight ahead, slowly turned his eyes toward her.

> *Arise my love, my fair*
> *one and come away . . .*
> *for sweet is thy voice*
> *and thy countenance is*
> *comely.*

Her countenance was more than comely, refined, yet intimate.

Take us the foxes, the
little foxes, that spoil
the vines . . . for our vines
have tender grapes.

There was a tenderness about her, but still a feline stealth.

Awake, O north wind
and blow upon my garden . . .
Let my beloved come
into his garden, and
eat his pleasant fruits.

There are gardens and gardens, depending upon the dwellers, there is the Garden of Eden, the Garden of Evil.

I am my beloved's and
his desire is toward me.
Come, my beloved, let us
go forth into the fields . . .
Let us lodge in the villages.

In which village would he lodge? San Melas or Saguaro. Which was the lily of the desert?

Let us get up early to the
vineyards; let us see if the
vines flourish, whether the
tender grapes appear . . .
there will I give thee my love.

The steady splatter of the rain was followed by the rumble of approaching thunder, then the crack of white lightning framed through the curtained window. Her face turned, almost touching his.

> *Kiss me with the*
> *kisses of thy mouth; for*
> *thy love is better than wine.*

She held out her slender white arms to him.

"It's from . . ."

"Yes, I know."

It was as if he was not quite certain whether this, too, was a vision within a different mirror, or if she was there in the flesh . . . until she reached out and took him in her arms in an embrace . . . then, it became more than an embrace . . . as they kissed and dropped together back onto the cot.

The Bible fell to the floor. Its pages now opened to the Book of Proverbs:

> My son, if sinners entice thee,
> consent thou not.

CHAPTER 50

The night was stunningly clean and clear, having been bathed by the sudden summer shower, which had quit as abruptly as it had commenced, leaving behind a washed-off night with wet leaves, branches, tree trunks, and soaked desert carpet.

And there was only the occasional droplets that fell from the rim of the shed as Jonathon Keyes opened the door, stood looking back inside with a tarnished expression on his face, as the cat scrambled through the door, returning from a nocturnal rendezvous of its own. Keyes closed the door and moved across the yard toward the Hobbses' house.

Somehow, Lorna had managed to make it to the window after observing the unslept part of their bed. Even through the darkness of the night she could make out the familiar figure of her husband as he left the shed and approached.

But just then she was seized by a terrible pain that struck within her head. Both her hands grasped at her temples as she staggered and was barely able to make it to the bed and fall there unconscious.

Deliverance was now at the workbench, her naked shoulders gleaming by candlelight as her supple fingers applied pressure, then withdrew from the wracked temples of Lorna's wax image.

Keyes managed his way through the darkened Hobbs house, up the stairs to the shadowy hallway and into the bedroom.

As stealthily as possible he approached his side of the bed and lay next to, but not too close, to Lorna's inert form.

But he couldn't help thinking of another, more perfect form—of what had happened and how the elements all conspired to make it happen—the visions and events in the mirror with the tortured man, Moon, and Deliverance, the need for fresh air, the appearance of Deliverance in the yard, the sudden summer rain, the Bible salvaged from the ashes of the church, Deliverance quoting in that sonorous voice from the Song of Solomon and then, he, himself unable to resist the song of the Lorelei.

As he lay in the bed next to his wife, Reverend Jonathon Keyes vowed to himself that what happened with Deliverance would never happen again, but still, deep within, there was not complete demurral that it did happen.

Whether he wanted to admit it or not, there was an inward struggle between conscience and enticement.

Reverend Jonathon Keyes resolved to win that struggle . . . if it wasn't already too late.

CHAPTER 51

Last night's rain did not in the least discourage the good citizens of San Melas from going about their voluntary task of reconstructing their church.

But evidently Caleb, Joseph, and Deliverance believed the work could, for the time being, go on without them as they sat in the kitchen partaking of a quiet breakfast being served by Bethia.

Upstairs in the bedroom things were not as quiet.

Lorna looked worse than ever. Her movements and speech were strained and jerky. Her voice shrill.

She stood by the window leaning against the sill, facing her husband across the room.

"Your time is up tomorrow," she spat.

"My time?"

"Tomorrow! We're leaving your playground . . . this devil's sandbox."

"Lorna, what are you talking about?"

"You know what I'm talking about. Don't you think I know what's going on?"

Keyes half sat on the dresser, took a deep breath, and was prepared to confess and beg for forgiveness, to promise . . . anything. But before he could bring himself to speak she tore at him verbally.

"Sneaking back near naked in the dark of the night from her shed, smelling of her perfume, creeping into bed next to me after . . ."

"Lorna, I am sorry . . ."

"*Reverend* Sorry . . . well, never mind! We're leaving! We're getting out of here! Do you hear me?"

Their words tumbled out from both of them against each other.

"Everyone can hear you. Listen to yourself. You're . . ."

"You don't like the way I sound, do you? Or the way I look—is that it? You'd rather look at . . . someone else. What else would you rather do with someone else . . . ?"

"Lorna, please . . ."

"I said we're leaving tomorrow!"

"I heard you, but, please, Lorna just wait until Sunday. Those people . . ."

"Those people . . ." she mimicked, ". . . those people . . . damn those people!"

". . . have worked awfully hard. The church, it's nearly finished, and I promised them . . ."

". . . Them! . . . Them! . . . Them! That's all you care about. I've had enough of them and this place!"

"You're not well enough to travel."

"I'll never get well here! Never! Can't you see that?!"

"Lorna . . ."

"If you're such a miracle worker like they think you are . . . like *you* think you are . . . then heal me!! Go ahead miracle man, *heal me*!!!"

"I want to help you. I do."

"Do you? Or do you want me to die? Isn't that it?!"

"Lorna . . ."

"Then you could stay. Yes, you could stay then. Couldn't you, Miracle Man!? Stay and go back to your Candle Lady!"

"Lorna, I love you . . . please listen . . . I love . . ."

"With, or without you, I'm leaving. I'll walk across that desert alone if I have to . . . either that or we're leaving together . . . TOMORROW!"

"Tomorrow. I'm sorry Caleb, but that's the way it has to be."

"But the sermon, only a few days, can't you wait?"

"I can, but not Lorna, she's intransigent."

"I don't believe she can make it through the desert all those days and nights."

"She doesn't believe she can make it here after the next day or night. She's adamant. She says she'll walk across the desert alone, and I believe she'd try."

Caleb looked at Deliverance, then at Joseph.

"Well, in that case, we have no choice but to do everything we can to make it easier for the both of you."

He rose and tapped the ashes out of his pipe into the ashtray.

"Joseph and I will go to the church and let them know so some of them can help make preparations for your departure. Come along Joseph."

"I'm walking behind you, Caleb."

Deliverance looked at Bethia, who interpreted it as a signal to leave the room and she did.

The room remained silent, but only for a moment as Deliverance gazed at Keyes, and her eyes brimmed with remembrance of last night.

"'I am my beloved's, and my beloved is mine: he feedeth among the lilies.'"

"Deliverance, what happened last night, it shouldn't have."

"But it did. Are you sorry it did?"

"Lorna knows."

"Is that why you're leaving?"

"That's one reason why I'm not staying. It must not happen again."

"Tell me, is that why you're leaving, because Lorna knows . . . or so it won't happen again? Are you afraid that it will if you stay? Do you want . . . ?"

"It was wrong! I'm married!"

"And so was David. He even sent Uriah to be killed in battle so Bathsheba would be free."

"Deliverance, you've got to understand this once and for all . . . Lorna's alive, and I'm married to her, and it's going to stay that way . . . from here to Saguaro and as long as we live."

"I do understand, Jon," she smiled cryptically, "I understand perfectly."

Keyes started toward the door.

"I think I'll go by the church for just a few minutes."

As Keyes walked out the door, Bethia came back into the room having listened to what Keyes and Deliverance had said.

"He seems determined, Miss Deliverance."

"So am I."

"Oh . . . I know."

"He thinks Saguaro is his destination," Deliverance said matter-of-factly, "I think San Melas is his destiny."

Keyes stood unseen behind a tree but close enough to hear what Caleb was saying to the citizens who had ceased working and stood listening, eyes lowered in disappointment.

". . . and so, my friends, I must conclude by informing you that our great friend and benefactor, the Reverend Jonathon Keyes and his beloved wife, Lorna, must leave our community tomorrow . . . I repeat, tomorrow . . . not after the planned service . . . but tomorrow. I know how hard you've all worked and how disappointed and sad you must feel, for I share your disappointment and sadness at his unexpectedly early departure. But so it must be. The work of reconstructing the church will go on but not until after his departure tomorrow. But we'll need some of you to volunteer your help in preparation for his journey. Sam, double check the Conestoga; Mr. Bryant, make sure they have the necessary supplies; Joseph, Jacob, and some of the rest of you help with the luggage and other possessions. If there is anything that any of you . . ."

Caleb Hobbs went on, but Keyes could bear to hear no more; he turned and started to walk away. However, he had been seen by one of the spectators, who ran up to him and called out.

"Reverend Keyes, just a minute, please, sir." The boy was breathless.

"Hello, Ethan."

"Is it true, sir? That you're going away . . . tomorrow?"

Keyes nodded.

"I wish you wasn't."

The reverend smiled . . . tousled the boy's hair.

"My legs are as strong now as they ever were. Did you see how I ran all the way over here?"

"Yes, Ethan, you're doing fine, just fine."

"I just wanted to . . . thank you, and . . . I'll always remember you."

Keyes nodded, turned slowly, and walked back toward the Hobbses' house.

Keyes spent most of the rest of the day with Lorna in their room. She said very little and rarely got out of bed. He did his best to reassure her that everything was in order: the wagon, luggage, supplies, and that Caleb had notified the citizens to stop work on the church until the two of them had left for Saguaro.

She stared straight ahead.

"You understand what I've said, don't you, Lorna? It's just as you wanted."

"I understand . . . Jon, would you hand me our wedding portrait?"

"Of course, dear."

He went to the dresser, picked up the framed portrait and couldn't help looking at it, his eyes unable to conceal the shame of what happened last night.

He handed her the picture.

"Best looking couple in Monroe," he smiled, "and that includes the Custer Boy and his bride."

She gave no sign of agreement or disagreement, just kept looking at the picture.

It was after the sun set that her eyes closed and the picture dropped from her grasp. Still she was conscious but barely.

"Jon . . . take my hand . . . the way you used to."

"Yes, Lorna."

He sat on the edge of the bed holding her hand for what seemed most of the night but actually was less than an hour as she slept, stirred, but didn't waken. Once or twice she murmured unintelligibly, then fell back into a deeper, more troublous sleep.

In a way Keyes, though awake, was just as troubled. He couldn't help remembering last night . . . the words from the Song of Solomon . . . "The voice of my beloved" . . . "Arise, my love" . . . "our vines have tender grapes" . . . "let us lodge in the villages" . . . "thy love is better than wine" . . . and what happened afterwards . . . then this morning . . . "Deliverance, it shouldn't have happened" . . . "but it did" . . . "Lorna knows" . . . "Is that why you're leaving?" . . . "I'm married" . . . "So was David" . . . "Deliverance, you've got to understand" . . . "I understand perfectly" . . .

But did she?

And did he?

Keyes managed to loosen his hand from Lorna's hold. He rose, went to the lighted candle on the bed stand, and blew it out. He looked through the window down into the yard; darkness, except for the light gleaming from the window of Deliverance's shed.

Keyes looked back to the sleeping figure of Lorna, then moved toward the door.

CHAPTER 52

Deliverance was not alone in the shed. As usual her cat was with her. But unlike last night her companion was not Jonathon Keyes . . . at least, not yet.

Bethia stood beside her at the workbench. Deliverance smiled as she performed her nightly ritual on the misshapen wax image of Lorna. But Bethia was not smiling, as the burning candles cast eerie shadows on the walls.

"I'm afraid it's going to happen, Miss Deliverance."

"What's going to happen?"

"That they're going to leave tomorrow."

"Are they?"

"They're all ready."

"Are they?"

"I helped them pack just like you told me."

"Did you?"

"Yes, ma'am. And the Reverend seems agreeable to leaving."

"Does he?"

The smile seemed to be painted on Deliverance's

face as her eyes and hands never left the wax figure of Lorna.

"Bethia."

"Yes, ma'am?"

"Last night the Reverend seemed agreeable to something else . . . didn't he?"

"Why, yes, ma'am." For the first time a smile appeared on the face of Bethia Thorton.

But Deliverance's smile turned to cruel edges as her fingers and thumbs were still at work on the wax image of Lorna.

"'Tomorrow . . . and tomorrow . . . and tomorrow . . . creeps in this petty pace from day to day.'"

"What's that mean, ma'am?"

"It means . . . 'By the pricking of my thumbs, something wicked this way comes.'"

Caleb was at his desk looking at a map and puffing on his ever-present pipe, and Joseph was half asleep on his faithful rocker. As Keyes entered the room Caleb looked up, released a pattern of blue smoke, and smiled.

"Oh, I'm glad you came down, Jon. I was hoping we could have a little farewell talk tonight."

"Caleb," Keyes nodded and sighed, "I'd like a farewell drink of that brandy, if you don't mind."

"Don't mind at all, m'boy, a capital idea. We'll all have one . . . or two."

"'Use a little wine,'" Joseph rocked and smiled, "'for thy stomach's sake and thine infirmities.'"

Caleb rose and moved to the sideboard.

"I'm only sorry that this has to be a farewell drink."

"So am I."

"You know, m'boy, there's an old saying, 'the shortest farewells are the best,' well, I don't believe that. I believe in long, long farewells," Caleb smiled as he poured the drinks and offered them to Keyes and Joseph. "Why can't we linger over this farewell for, say, ten or twenty years at least?"

"Caleb, I know that you're saying that in jest, but . . ."

"Well, I am . . . and I'm not . . ."

"Caleb, please, we've gone over this before, and now my wife's even worse . . . she's near hysteria. There's just no reasoning with her. If we don't leave tomorrow I'm afraid she's liable to break down completely . . . and I've got to get her to a doctor as soon as possible."

"I understand, m'boy." He raised his glass. "Confusion to the enemy."

"Good health and good fortune, gentlemen."

"'Take of the spirit which is upon thee.'" Joseph sipped, then rocked.

Caleb made one last effort, even though he knew it was in vain.

"The pity of it, m'boy, it's just that there's so much you could do here."

"Somebody else'll have to do it."

"Well, in that case, as I mentioned before, we'll do everything we can to help you. The wagon's repaired and loaded with most of your things. You'll have fresh horses, the best in the stable"—he walked back to the desk and picked up a map—"and a map to guide you out of the desert and all the way to Saguaro."

Caleb handed the map to Keyes.

"Thank you, Caleb . . . for everything."

"M'boy, we're in your debt. There's no way of telling you how much."

Keyes folded the map and put it in his pocket.

"Good night."

"By the bye, would you like Joseph and some of the others to ride with you part of the way through the desert, and . . ."

"Thanks. I think it's best we leave alone . . . Oh, good evening, Bethia."

"Good evening, Reverend. I just took a tray out to Miss Deliverance."

"Then she's going to work late tonight?"

"I believe she's going to spend the night there . . . you know she spends the night there sometimes . . ."

"Yes, I know."

"Can I fix you something, sir?"

"No, thanks. Well, everyone, it's getting late; I'd better get upstairs and . . ."

"Aren't you going to say good night to Miss Deliverance, sir?" There was an ever so slight change in Bethia's tone as she smiled just as slightly.

"I'll . . . I'll see you all in the morning. Good night."

Lorna lay sleeping, a fractious, but deep sleep, deep enough so that she would likely be unaware of his coming and going.

He walked to the window and saw that light, the light of transgression . . . of temptation. He stood and watched as does a moth to the flame.

He could not deny the temptation as does "the bawdy wind that kisses all it meets."

Deep within there reined that goodness that had "pleased heaven to try him with affliction" . . . "had rained all kinds of sores and shame on his bare head," as was Othello's plight. But this time Keyes would blow out the candle of the wicked and turn away.

And that's what he did . . . turn away.

But he faced another challenge.

The mirror.

The mirror across the room.

For the first time in a long while he was brimming with courage . . . at least enough mettle to face the mirror.

He walked across the room and tilted the mirror making sure he was looking directly into it . . . face to face.

But not for long.

His image became that of the bruised and bloodied man reaching out in desperation, and to one side stood Moon with a serpentine smile and gunman's stance, ready to draw. On the other side, Deliverance, cool and confident, beckoning without moving . . . a silent, standing summons.

Keyes's gaze went from the bruised man to Moon to Deliverance . . . to the Bible on the dresser, then . . . to the rifle leaning against the wall near the dresser.

He reached out, grabbed the Henry by the barrel with one hand and the other hand grasped the rifle's brass breech. He lifted the Henry shoulder high and slammed it stock first into the mirror with an ear-piercing crash as shards scattered onto the dresser, and the broken mirror fell to the floor with a clatter loud enough to rouse Lorna to her elbows.

"Jonathon . . . are you all right?"

He leaned the Henry against the wall, turned to her, and took a breath.

"Yes, Lorna. I'm . . . all right."

"But this time the mirror is broken. How?"

"I broke it." He almost smiled. "And now maybe we'll have seven more years of good luck."

CHAPTER 53

The bedroom held only a few of the items that the Keyes had brought with them.

Keyes stood in the center of the room with the Bible in his hand, looking around with a sweeping glance; the Henry rifle leaning against the wall with the red scarf now tied around its barrel, the wedding portrait of Jon and Lorna on the bed stand.

Lorna, dressed in traveling clothes, sat on the straight-back chair near the bed. She appeared to be in great discomfort, doing her best not to show it, but failing in the attempt.

Keyes walked past her to the bed stand, reached down, picked up the wedding portrait, looked at it, and smiled at Lorna, who either didn't have the strength or the inclination to smile back.

Keyes placed the picture in a valise on the floor near the open bedroom door.

From the front of the Hobbses' house there came a chorus of singing voices. It sounded as if the entire citizenry had gathered to serenade the departing couple.

They began with a familiar refrain:

> *Should auld acquaintance be forgot,*
> *and never brought to mind?*
> *Should auld acquaintance be forgot,*
> *and auld lang syne?*
>
> > *For auld lang syne, my dear,*
> > *For auld lang syne,*
> > *we'll take a cup of kindness yet,*
> > *for auld lang syne*

Over the last line of the song there was a knock on the open door.

Keyes turned to see Caleb and Joseph.

"May we come in, m'boy?"

"Of course."

But the serenaders were not through. They continued with another familiar refrain:

> *Bringing in the sheaves, bringing in the sheaves,*
> *We shall come rejoicing, bringing in the sheaves,*
> *Bringing in the sheaves, bringing in the sheaves,*
> *We shall come rejoicing, bringing in the sheaves.*

"Well, Jon, the wagon's out front and so is what was to be your congregation. Is there anything . . ."

The answer came from Lorna . . . a painful moan as she clutched at her head with both hands, then fainted and fell to the floor.

Keyes moved quickly, lifted her, and placed her in the bed. She was unconscious and likely worse.

Bethia was at the door and entered the room as Caleb took a step closer to Keyes.

"Well, Jon," there was compassion in his voice, "I'm afraid you will be staying . . . a little longer."

Bethia walked to the head of the bed, looked down at Lorna, then toward the window and the shed below.

CHAPTER 54

Reconstruction of the church had started almost as soon as the citizens of San Melas had stopped singing.

Just after Caleb announced that the Reverend's wife had a relapse and that the two of them would be staying for the time being, the crowd dispersed, and the sounds of sawing and hammering were once again echoing on the construction site.

Caleb Hobbs had assumed his usual shady station and was smoking his usual pipe while overseeing the toilers.

"M'boy, I'm glad to see you out in the open. It does neither you nor Lorna any good for you to stay cooped up in that room when she doesn't even know you're there."

"She seems to, from time to time, Caleb, but Bethia is there for the time being. By the way I'm sorry about that broken mirror."

"Think nothing of it, Reverend. But what happened?"

"It fell," Keyes answered rather awkwardly.

"I see," Caleb nodded just as awkwardly.

"Caleb, there's something I wanted to ask you."

"Please do."

"According to that map . . ."

"What map?"

"The one you gave me to get us through the desert and to Saguaro . . . I've got it right here . . . somewhere," he went through one pocket, then another, ". . . yes, here it is . . ."

"What about it?"

"Well, it looks to me like there's a place less than seventy miles or so, to the southwest, although that part of the map seems rubbed out . . . or something spilled on it. Look here . . ."

"Where?"

Keyes's finger pinpointed the spot on the map.

"Can you make out the name, Caleb?"

"No, Jon, I can't. These orbs aren't what they used to be."

"Looks like Tree . . . Tree Cross . . . sound familiar?"

"No," Caleb shook his head and puffed on his pipe.

"Wait, let me hold it up against the sunlight. Yes . . . Tre-s, Tres Cr-u-s—yes, s-e-s. That's it, Tres Cruses. You must've heard of it, haven't you?"

"Tres Cruses, yes, now that you mention it . . . sounds vaguely familiar. We don't leave this vicinity very often, you know."

"Well, it's on the map and San Melas isn't. It must be more than some small village."

"Jon, what are you getting at?"

"A doctor. That's what I'm getting at. There must be a doctor in Tres Cruses."

"What if there is?"

"If there is, and I can get Lorna there . . ."

"How?"

"In the wagon, how else?"

"The Conestoga?"

Keyes nodded.

"Jon, make sense."

"What do you mean?"

"I mean, less than halfway there in the desert, in her condition, you'd be hauling . . . I hate to say this, m'boy, but you'd be hauling a dead body . . . a corpse."

There was a shrug of acknowledged disappointment in Keyes's shoulders.

"You're probably right."

"Of course I am. But . . ."

Caleb took a contemplative puff on his pipe.

"But what, Caleb?"

"There might be another way."

"How's that?"

"If we send a rider to Tres Cruses, our best rider . . ."

"Who would that be?"

"Sam Hawkins . . . he'd bring back a doctor, if there is one in Tres Cruses . . . maybe even in time for your sermon. But either way it's a better chance than trying to transport Lorna all those miles through the burning desert. Meanwhile, the best thing for her is rest."

"You're right, Caleb, absolutely right." Keyes smiled. "When can Sam get started?"

"Right now, m'boy. Sam!" Hobbs held up his pipe and motioned. "Sam Hawkins, come over here and come a'running."

It didn't take long for Caleb to explain the mission to Sam Hawkins as Keyes handed him the map.

Less than an hour later Hawkins mounted his best horse in front of the stable as Keyes and Caleb watched.

"Mr. Hawkins, I can't tell you how obliged Lorna and I are for what you're doing. God bless you."

"Reverend, after all you've done for us, I'd ride through hell's thorns for you. If there's a doctor there I'll bring him here one way or t'uther, even if I have to hog-tie and carry him on my back."

Sam Hawkins rode off to beat the devil.

Joseph and a couple of other men had brought up the trunk and some of the other items that had been loaded on the Conestoga.

Bethia had cleaned up the mess from the broken mirror.

Keyes sat on the straight-back chair near the bed holding the wedding portrait while Lorna still lay on the bed, her face twisting in pain from time to time but unaware of anything or anyone in the room.

"Is there anything else I can do to help, sir?"

"No, thanks, Bethia."

She nodded and left the room.

"I'll ask the same question, Reverend," Joseph said, "we've brought up everything we think you'll need while you're here . . . unless you can think of anything else."

"No thank you, Joseph. I'll just sit here in case she regains consciousness."

"Yes, Reverend, 'until the spirit be poured on her from on high.'"

Keyes looked at the wedding portrait in his hand then at Lorna. He spoke to her knowing she was mostly unaware of what he said but hoping that just the sound of his voice might be of some comfort.

"Our wedding day, Lorna. Custer, Best Man, Libbie, Matron of Honor. I was as nervous as a crab in a heated pot . . . Custer's words of advice . . . and I guess you could call it encouragement: 'Sport,' he grinned, 'remember what I always said going into battle? I said 'charge to the sound of the guns,' well, at my wedding and now at yours, all I can say is 'charge to the sound of the church organ.'

"And that's what I did, Lorna . . . what we did . . . and our path through life together has been a very gracious thing. And it's going to be even better. Lorna, I hope you can hear this . . . we've sent for a doctor . . . a doctor on his way with medicine to help you recover so we can be on our way to Saguaro. It won't be long now—so hang on, Lorna . . . hang on."

The daylight hours crept by into the tenderloin of night when Bethia came back into the room.

"Sir, you've been here all hours of the day. Can I fix you something to eat? The others already have . . ."

"No, Bethia, thank you, but I have no appetite."

"Then I suggest you get a little night air, Reverend. And a good exercise of the legs will be beneficial. You've been sitting in that chair till you're all cramped up. Go on now, I'll sit here with the missus."

"Maybe you're right, Bethia." He rose and put the wedding portrait on the bed stand. "I'll be back soon."

When Keyes left the room, Bethia went to the window and looked down at the backyard.

Downstairs he started for the front door where he might have sat on one of the porch chairs, or even

Joseph's rocker, or on one of the steps . . . but he stopped. Out front he knew he would avoid Deliverance, however, since they would have to stay in San Melas for days, maybe weeks more, it would be impossible to avoid her all that time. If, on the other hand, he went out back, there was the possibility of seeing her.

He decided to go out back.

Not because he was tempted, but because, if he did see her, he wanted to test his will. To be able to look at her, talk to her, and turn the other way.

That's the reason he gave himself for deciding to move toward the back door.

The setting was out of an Arabian Nights tale. Quiescent. Timeless. With an armada of stars floating in a sea of marine blue serenity.

Keyes sat on the tree stump, his head immersed in the palms of both hands, with drifting thoughts of things to come.

"Jon."

Her voice.

He looked up.

She stood as before, as if challenging him to look away.

He didn't.

"I thought you might have . . ." she smiled, ". . . forgotten me."

"I've been with Lorna as much as I could . . ."

"Does she know it, even if her eyes are open, but her senses shut? Is she aware of anything?"

"I'm not sure. I've been doing what I think is best."

"Best for whom?"

"For all of us."

"Sometimes, Jon, you just ooze of goodness. Sometimes . . ."

"Deliverance, please . . ."

"The poet wrote it, 'the world's a stage' . . . peopled by mummers who can make it a tragedy, or a fairy tale where the leading players can live happily ever after."

"Yes, but . . ."

"But, what, Jon?"

"In this fairy tale . . . who are the 'leading players'?"

"That . . . is the question."

It wasn't a question; it was an invitation.

Keyes rose.

He looked into her eyes.

Paused.

Then walked past her toward the Hobbses' house.

Deliverance remained sangfroid, confident that there was more to come.

CHAPTER 55

In the days that followed, Keyes did his best to avoid the company of Deliverance. He succeeded to the extent that if they were together there was someone there with them. He avoided the shed area altogether, day or night. He spent as much time as possible with Lorna, except for an evening drink with Caleb and Joseph, while Bethia stood watch over Lorna upstairs. Usually it was not more than a half hour or so in an aromatic room redolent of pipe tobacco and traces of patternless blue smoke, while Joseph was rocking, half asleep between sips of brandy.

"Caleb, may I ask you something that's a bit contradictory here in San Melas?"

"I hope I can provide a satisfactory answer, m'boy. Go ahead."

"It didn't take long to notice that there was not one . . . 'saloon,' here in town, yet you have no qualms about keeping a stock of brandy—by the way—very excellent brandy, in your home . . . actually there are two questions. Are you the exception, since you're the mayor, or do the rest of the citizens, also, lay up a supply in their households?"

"You're right, of course, Jon, there is no saloon here. But the Good Book contains no prohibition against an occasional libation, does it, Joseph?"

"'. . . eat thy bread with joy, and drink thy wine with a merry heart.'"

"Ah, but a 'saloon' as you call it, without a family setting can soon lead to, well . . . you don't need much imagination to imagine to what. So we thought it best not to strew our citizens' pathway with any such temptation. Would you care for a refill?"

"Well . . ."

"A 'cup of kindness' to quote the Scottish poet. Just one more cup?"

"All right, just a touch."

Caleb smiled as he poured.

"I mentioned 'family setting.' We strongly believe in family. There is no such thing as divorce in our faith. It's strictly till death do us part.' Unfortunately, that's what happened to my beloved Amantha, when she was much too young."

"I'm sorry, Caleb. Amantha, I'll remember her in my prayers."

"Very good of you. You know, Jon, these farewell drinks are getting to be a splendid ritual."

"Speaking of rituals, I've got to work on the sermon for Sunday. Only two more days, and the church is in good enough shape to . . ."

"Not quite . . . and I'm going to ask one more favor after all you're done."

"Of course. What can I do, Caleb?"

"What do you know about Summer Solstice?"

"Summer Solstice? Not much. Actually, very little. I'm not much on astronomical manifestations. Isn't it the longest day of the year?"

"That, and much more to us, to our religion . . . the most hallowed of all days, except for the birth. Let me explain briefly as possible, if you don't mind."

"Please do."

"Summer Solstice: Latin, *'sol'* for sun. *'Sistere,'* or stand still, but dating back before Neolithic times—from dwellers in caves, to the clusters of civilizations, across the sands of mystic Egypt, the gardens of Babylon, the span of the Ottoman Empire, to the glory of Alexander, and the grandeur of Rome with the coming of Christendom, when it was—and still is—celebrated as Saint John's Day, also known as the Feast of Saint John. Quite a coincidence, isn't that, Reverend?—maybe even more than just a coincidence." Caleb relit the tobacco in the bowl of his pipe. "Jon, we celebrate the outer and inner fire of each of us, at the altar of light and gratitude. It is the hallmark of brighter and better things to come. I cannot tell you how much each Summer Solstice means to us . . . and on this occasion you have been sent to us. You see, this year the Summer Solstice falls on—not this coming Sunday, but on the next, June twenty-sixth. We've done without a Sunday service in the church since it burned down. Please let's wait for that service in the new church until the twenty-sixth. It will be completely finished by then and maybe

Sam will be back with the doctor, and likely even Lorna will be well enough to attend. You've done so much. Will you do this as a final goodwill gesture for all of us?"

"Caleb. How could I refuse?"

CHAPTER 56

To Keyes that next week seemed to have more, many more, than seven days.

There in San Melas, he recalled and relived, most of his life, before, and since meeting, then marrying Lorna—from farm boy—to law school student—encountering Custer—to soldier, war—wounded at Yellow Tavern—and Reverend James Mason—to becoming a man of the ministry—and husband—the journey toward Saguaro as far as the punishing desert would allow—the rescue by Caleb, Joseph, and Deliverance, taken to San Melas—Lorna's sickness—the menace of Moon—the "miracles" of the crippled Ethan—and the mine—the vision of the burned and battered man in the mirror—Moon's death and the first time he heard the sound of Deliverance's voice—her allurement and the torment of his own guilt—Lorna's relapse—sending for a doctor in Tres Cruses—and waiting for the Summer Solstice service in the resurrected church—just more than a week—in the kind of time not made in calendars.

By now, that, too, had passed.

CHAPTER 57

June twenty-sixth. The day of the Summer Solstice.
The longest day of the year in the Northern Hemisphere.

In San Melas the spotlight of the sun streaked over
the rugged peaks of the distant mountains with a
glowing brilliance onto the hardpan of desert.

Caleb Hobbs had not exaggerated the effect that
the Summer Solstice service would have on the citizens of San Melas. Mayor Hobbs had made the
announcement at the town hall meeting, and the
news met with a most enthusiastic response, gratitude, and appreciation. The word spread like a welcome breeze. There was even a bulletin posted on a
pillar outside of the Bryants' store, where notices
were placed to inform passersby of special events.
The news was on everyone's smiling lips.

In those last few days Caleb Hobbs was even more
at ease than usual, as if he actually took on the role as
captain of a ship, enjoying his pipe, while in peaceful
waters, entering a safe harbor.

The sinewy Joseph continued his rocking with a dreamy, contented smile on his elfin face.

Bethia was her usual efficient self, always there, quietly in the background, ready, willing, and capable of performing her duties.

In the meantime, Keyes had worked and reworked his sermon. Writing and rewriting—even taking long walks while rehearsing and rephrasing the message.

And he had spent hour after hour at the bedside of Lorna, hoping, and yes, praying for any sign of improvement—but if anything, the sign pointed in the wrong direction. If the doctor did not arrive soon, it was apparent that her condition would continue to deteriorate until the inevitable end.

But during those last few days it was almost as if Deliverance were deliberately avoiding Keyes. It was she who departed when he entered—and entered when he left—as if her absence might become more enticing later.

That morning of the Sunday Solstice service, he caught a glimpse of her as she was prepared to leave, and it seemed to him she was not dressed for a church service, but more as she had appeared to him in that first dream—more like a pristine vision in white.

Beneath the towering, sun-splayed cross, from inside the church with the fresh smell of paint and gleaming newly polished pews, came the spiritual chorus of uplifted voices.

> *Amazing grace! How sweet the sound*
> *That saved a wretch like me.*
> *I once was lost, but now am found,*
> *Was blind but now I see.*

Shout, shout for glory,
Shout, shout aloud for glory;
Brother, sister, mourner,
All shout glory hallelujah.

Caleb stood behind the pulpit singing, his voice, even louder and more distinguishable than the others in the congregation, which consisted of every man, woman, and child of San Melas.

Keyes was seated to the side of the pulpit holding his Bible and the papers on which he had labored over his sermon. His face was flushed with despair, his eyes desolate but occasionally glancing up to the parishioners who filled all the benches. Joseph in his shiny Sunday suit, William, Pricilla, and young Ethan Bryant—still absent was Sam Hawkins, who had yet to return from his mission of mercy—and Bethia, who tended to Lorna, too weak to rise from the confinement of her bed—but all the rest were there with devout faces gazing eagerly toward the pulpit. All except Deliverance, whose eyes never left Keyes . . . her slim, serene figure, dressed in Circean garb, was distinct from all the others.

Caleb clutched each side of the pulpit, this time without his faithful pipe, and began to speak with supernatural earnestness.

"Fellow citizens of San Melas, my friends, and fellow wayfarers—we have come here today to dedicate this new edifice on this day of our deep piety, the Summer Solstice—and at the same time to express our appreciation to a man who came to us only recently—a man for whom we have waited a long time—but more than a man, a presence who has wrought what many of us believe to be a wealth of good fortune. Yes, a man who has made this day possible.

"Although his beloved wife is ill and cannot be with us, except in spirit, he has come to give us the first sermon within these walls . . . and regretfully the last sermon that we will hear from him."

Caleb looked admiringly at Keyes then back to the congregation.

"I give you the finest, bravest, most decent man who has ever come to us here in San Melas. Reverend Jonathon Keyes."

Caleb Hobbs nodded to Keyes, left the pulpit, and took his seat next to Deliverance.

Keyes breathed deeply, rose, stood for a moment with the Bible and his sermon in hand, and moved toward the pulpit.

He looked out at the congregation, his face sweating, his fingers trembling, then braced himself against the pulpit. Finally he started to speak, his voice hoarse and hesitant . . . but slowly gathering urgency.

"I am a stranger in your midst and a sojourner among you. And who among us can look into another's heart . . . and know what is there? As I look into your faces . . . faces of trust, of friendship, of belief . . . I must reveal what is in my heart . . . to you and to myself . . . for the heart can be deceitful."

This was, and yet, was not what they had expected to hear. He had not referred to his written sermon, nor opened his Bible, but they sat, enthralled, with eager anticipation. Caleb, Joseph, the Bryants with Ethan, the young towheaded boys, Deliverance, and all the rest, waited.

"On this revered day of the Summer Solstice, the subject of my sermon to you . . . was to be . . . the Ten Commandments. The laws that were handed down for each of us to live by. But now I am setting aside that prepared sermon and speaking from my own heart.

"Because as I stand here and think back . . . on what has happened . . . on what I've done . . ."

He paused.

". . . I cannot find it in my heart to speak of those Commandments. For I myself have broken too many of the Lord's laws."

As he spoke those confessional words and looked out, Keyes seemed to discern, not the reaction he expected, but traces of slight smiles on the faces of Caleb, Joseph, the Bryants, including Ethan, and even the towheaded children. Deliverance, and the rest, were all leaning forward, eager to hear more.

He continued, painfully and slowly.

"I have allowed myself to become the subject of your idolatry . . . I have deceived . . . I have lied . . . I have coveted . . ."

He shuddered as his eyes went to Deliverance looking even more beguiling than she did in that first dream.

". . . I have coveted . . . that which is not mine. I have . . ."

By this time all in the congregation were not trying to conceal their smiles, which had become broader and on the brink of laughter.

". . . I have killed . . . and I have . . ."

Suddenly, it was as if he were not in a newly constructed church that had been so carefully built with precisely measured and fitted timbers. It was more like an asylum, a bedlam, peopled with inmates who were all deranged except for him. Or was it the other way around? Was it he who was deranged and all of them completely sane?

Then why did they all have that look on their faces—partially amused but mostly wicked?

Was it all in his mind or did the walls actually waver and bend?

Instead of the purifying incense, he breathed in the odor of acrid sulfur.

Even the flames from the candles leaped higher, and instead of yellow and white, the flames blazed a bright red and baneful black.

Had these common, decent, hardworking worshippers turned into wide-eyed smirking mockers in a garden of grace—gargoyles as in a Philistine temple?

He struggled to continue his confessional.

"I have been corrupted!"

The congregation broke out in ruckus laughter. And instead of their mocking faces, there loomed the visage of his wife in front of him obscuring everything else—a face twisted in pain, with eyes burning in agony, a lipless mouth pleading for help but unable to make a sound.

He didn't know what had happened or what was happening, but he knew that he had to get out of there.

He had to be with Lorna before it was too late—or was it already too late?

There came from him an unearthly repentant cry. "L-O-R-N-A!!!"

And then he saw the figure of Sam Hawkins with a

crooked smile on his contumacious face standing in the aisle near the doorway.

With anguished effort he left the pulpit and stumbled down the aisle toward the unblinking blacksmith.

"Sam! Sam, you've come back. Did you bring the doctor?! Is he with Lorna?!"

Hawkins's expression remained the same, as he spoke.

"Reverend, why don't you go and see for yourself?"

At first when Keyes tried to move it was as if his ankles were buried in cement.

He summoned all the strength, all the will in his body and brain, then sprang free.

He raced toward the door without looking back, but could hear the callous laughter careening through his head.

CHAPTER 58

As he raced from the church toward the Hobbses' house, his major concern, of course, was the condition of his wife.

But invading that concern was the riddle of why all of this was happening.

What was truth, and what was madness?

Much of what had happened since these people rescued them from certain death and brought them to this forsaken desert island of sand and stone didn't make sense.

After all the praise and gratitude that they had heaped on him for the so-called "miracles" that they had attributed to him: young Ethan's recovery and rescue at the mine, his first confrontation with the evil Moon, the rediscovery of the vein of gold, his part in the death of Moon, the rebuilding of the church.

And in the midst of all this . . . the bruised and agonized vision of the man in the mirror. Was he one of them?

Why? Why? Why?

Was it his sermon?

He had meant that his confession from the pulpit should have a cleansing effect, not only on himself, but, also, on them.

Why? Why? Why?

But more important than the answers to all those questions was the question of Lorna's condition.

He made a last, desperate effort to reach her side.

CHAPTER 59

He ran into the room, past Bethia, who stood passively near the doorway as if she were anticipating his arrival.

He knelt at Lorna's bedside holding her in his arms, tears in his eyes, his voice sobbing, trying to get through to her.

"Lorna . . . oh, Lorna, I'm sorry. Please Lorna . . . come back to me."

But she could not hear him.

He realized she was never coming back.

But he, also, realized something else. Still holding her he felt the presence of others in the room.

And that the room was growing darker by the minute.

Standing near the entrance were Caleb, Joseph, the Bryants with Ethan, Hawkins, and Deliverance holding the twisted wax image of Lorna. The cat beside her leaped on the dresser for a better view.

There were more from the congregation at the door and hallway. Not a trace of sorrow, of sympathy on any of their faces, and there was a row of children holding animal masks in front of their faces and softly chanting just as Lorna had described in the yard. The men and women were smiling diabolically as the room grew still darker.

Was the gathering darkness all in the encampment of Keyes's mind? Had the corridors of his brain become a labyrinth of madness?

He looked from them to the dimming window and then back to the citizens of San Melas.

"What . . . is it?" Keyes stammered, "What's happening?"

"It's an eclipse, Reverend," Joseph grinned, "That's what we've been waiting for, isn't it, Caleb?"

Caleb Hobbs smiled what appeared to be a benevolent smile.

"That's why I wanted to delay the sermon. You see, m'boy, this year the eclipse falls on the day of the Summer Solstice."

"But why . . . why are you doing all this?"

"Why? I will tell you *why* soon enough. We didn't just find you. We changed several signs along the way . . . as we've done before."

The room swayed and so did the people in it. Their faces billowing in festive contentment or so it seemed to Jonathon Keyes.

"And," Caleb nodded toward Hawkins, "you must be wondering about the doctor in Tres Cruses, if there is one. We still don't know. Sam took a short ride into the desert, then doubled back, out of sight until today. And now it is nearly time for *our* ceremony."

Caleb Hobbs took a step forward, then turned slightly toward the doorway.

"But first we want to reintroduce you to one more

member of our congregation. Come in friend. We've been expecting you."

From out of the crowd by the darkened doorway, another figure emerged.

MOON.

The others laughed even harder.

Keyes was frozen.

"No! You're dead! I killed you! You're dead! I saw your grave! I . . ."

"The grave is empty," Caleb said. "It was all a game . . ."

"A game?!"

". . . A sham to keep you here."

Moon had the same malevolent smile on his face as he withdrew both guns and held them waist high.

"They're beautiful aren't they . . . and deadly . . . but sometimes quite harmless, as when filled with blanks, like the one I threw toward you."

"But *WHY*?!"

"We have made a covenant with death," Joseph's eyes took on the look of evil incarnate, "and with hell are we in agreement."

"Some call it a Sabbat," Caleb's voice was mellow as always. "And for our ceremony we need a man like yourself . . . who in the eyes of your world is pure and uncorrupted. Ah, but were you, Reverend Keyes?"

Caleb paused and let the question sink in before answering his own query.

"No. Reverend, within you was the seed of corruption. We merely tended that seed and nourished it . . . all of us . . . Joseph, Bethia, Moon, the Bryants, even

Ethan, Sam Hawkins, and of course, Deliverance . . .
until you fell from grace."

Joseph picked up the wedding picture from the
desk, then took another picture from his pocket and
held it up.

"Last time it was *him*."

It was a picture of the man in the mirror. But
young, handsome, clear-eyed and smiling.

Keyes looked at the picture, then at the place where
the mirror had hung.

His hand went to his head, covering his eyes for
just a moment in sudden realization.

"He . . . was trying to . . . warn me!"

"So it seems. But you see, m'boy, we are not from
Connecticut. We are from a village in Massachusetts . . .
a long time ago."

Keyes looked at the placid, smiling face and uttered
her name.

"Deliverance . . ."

"My name is Lilith . . . 'the witch that Adam loved
before the gift of Eve.'"

She opened her hand and let what was left of the
image of Lorna drop from her hand.

Keyes screamed.

"No!!!"

The scream echoed through the veil of darkness.

NOON.

But a Black Noon.

The sun completely eclipsed by the moon in a
sable sky.

Reverend Jonathon Keyes, stripped to the waist,

was hung upside down near the pulpit inside the church.

Leaping flames had already seared his body—but not his open Bible on the pulpit.

And he could hear the chanting voices of the congregation.

> *Go blat . . . som blat . . . carradon . . .*
> *go loos. Com blat . . . go blat . . .*
> *go loos . . . carradon . . .*

In a final, fading effort he managed to whisper.

"Father . . . I am prepared to enter . . . heaven or hell . . ."

CHAPTER 60

Reverend Jonathon Keyes awoke from the dream with a start.

Neither in heaven, nor in hell.

He was lying in the Conestoga under the canvas cover of the wagon with his wife, Lorna, now awake at his side.

This was not the first time since he had come home from the war with a head wound that his sleep had been breached by a bad dream.

"Jon . . . are you all right?"

"Yes, I'm . . ."

"You're trembling, wringing wet."

She reached out and gently touched the back of his head as she had done before.

"Jon, was it that dream again? The war? The battle of Yellow Tavern? The wound . . ."

"No, Lorna. It was a dream but not the war . . . something else this time." He tried to smile.

"Tell me what it was, Jon. Maybe you'll feel better."

"No. I'm really all right, but if you want, I'll tell you tomorrow."

"I want . . . promise?"

"I promise."

From the desert darkness there came the cry of an animal.

"Did you hear that?"

This time he did smile.

"Probably some lonesome coyote."

"Not as lonesome as I was when you were away."

"That makes two of us." He moved closer and kissed her forehead. "Now go back to sleep. We've got a ways to go before we get to Saguaro."

"All right, but I still want to hear about that dream."

"I'm not so sure you do . . . but I'll tell you on the way to Saguaro."

It was not possible to differentiate the next day from the scores of other desert days they had traveled across the burning sands under a scorching sun in the bald sky. Miles and miles of endless espadrille rimmed by distant purple peaks, a lost, silent land with the rising sun pulling the heat up with it.

The Conestoga's canvas top, ribbed with curved metal frames, swayed gently like billowing sails as the creaking wagon rolled southwest toward the barren horizon.

Jonathon Keyes had been unusually silent, still partially under the spell of last night's torturous vision.

By midmorning Lorna had twice brought up the subject of his dream. Each of those times Keyes had managed to avoid answering, changing the subject by pointing out some scurrying rabbit, or peculiar rock formation.

"Look there, Jon."

"Where?"

"That sign, 'San Melas 5 miles.' It's pointing south."

"San Melas," he whispered almost to himself. He had never even heard of a place called San Melas until the dream. It actually existed. Did those same people he dreamed about exist?

As he stared at the sign a troubled look overcame his face, more than troubled—he shuddered with fear and dread, doing all he could to regain control over the frightful image still burning in his brain. *San Melas. San Melas. San Melas.* Was it all just a dream—or a foreboding—a precursor of things to come? Things that ended in a fiery death? Whatever San Melas was, it was something he had to avoid.

"Jon, do you think we ought to spend the night there, refresh the horses and check our supplies?"

He snapped the reins hard.

"The horses are all right, and we've got enough supplies. I thought you were anxious to get to Saguaro."

"I am. But I just thought you . . ."

He snapped the reins again, harder.

"I think we ought to keep going," he said in a manner she had never heard from him before.

Then he quickly softened and even managed to smile.

"Lorna, let's not tarry. It's already taken us longer than we expected, and . . ."

"It's perfectly all right, Jon, and you're right, we should get there as soon as possible, but you've been at those reins a long time. I thought you might feel . . ."

"I feel fine . . . and I'm sorry I was . . . abrupt."

"If you were, I didn't notice. You're the captain of this ship, my husband. Sail on!"

Captain of the ship, Keyes thought to himself, that's what Caleb Hobbs had called himself at the construction site.

"Captain of the ship," Keyes said out loud, "out here in a sea of desert?"

"Why not?" Lorna bantered. "They call these Conestogas 'Prairie Schooners,' don't they?"

"They do," Keyes did his best to paint on a happy face.

He looked at her and began to sing.

> *A capitol ship for an ocean trip*
> *With a walloping wind o'blind;*
> *No wind that blew dismayed her crew*
> *Or troubled the captain's mind . . .*

"That's better, Jon, 'no troubled mind . . .'"

"Not as long as I've got you, Lorna . . . and my Bible . . . and the Henry."

He pointed to the rifle leaning against the seat and the Bible next to it.

"Yes, Jon," she smiled, "but have you forgotten your promise?"

"What promise?"

"That's exactly what I mean," she teased. "You know exactly what I mean. That dream that was *not* about the war. *Not* about Yellow Tavern and Custer, or Stuart. *Not* about the wound you suffered there. *That* promise."

"Oh, yes," he feigned, "*that* promise. Thanks for reminding me."

He was a sunk duck and he knew it.

But Reverend Keyes had decided that in the telling he would be better advised to either omit, or edit some of the events—even though they weren't actual events—in the abridged version that he would relate. In fact he would almost make light of the whole thing. He saw no reason to mention his ties with Deliverance in the yard, the Secret Garden, and in the shed.

"Well, it seems that we had lost our way . . ."

But suddenly it was no longer a desert day like all the scores and scores of other desert days they had come through.

Luckily, Keyes had seen it coming.

He pulled up the reins and the team reacted, slowing down abruptly. He jerked one of the leathers to the right, and the Conestoga veered in that direction.

"What is it, Jon? What's the matter?"

"The matter is that swirling cloud of dust coming at us. See it?"

"I see it now."

"Dust devil . . . I've seen worse . . . but this one's bad enough."

He whacked the ribbons, and the horses picked up speed.

Keyes nodded toward a semicircled outcrop of rocks, brown boulders ahead. They made it to, and inside, the sheltering formation.

"We won't get much of it in here, but we'd best get inside under cover. I've headed the horses against what's coming. I think they'll be all right."

They both scrambled over the bench and to the area where they had slept, and Lorna snuggled close to him. They could hear and feel the whirling wind and sand, but with a minimum effect within their rocky haven.

"My hero!" Lorna smiled and cuddled closer.

"Well, your *husband*—I don't know about the *hero* part."

"I do," she patted his shoulder, "and always have, Jon," she paused, "this is a good time for it."

"For what?"

"For . . ." she smiled, ". . . for you to go ahead and tell me about that dream. We're so nice and cozy in here, aren't we?"

"I guess you could call it that."

"Then go ahead."

"Well, let's see, where were we?"

"It seemed," she said, "that we had lost our way."

"Oh, yes, lost our way . . . missed one of the signs I guess. We were in bad shape, especially you. Unconscious, and I nearly was, too."

"That *was* bad. Go on."

"Just before it was too late we were rescued by three people; a man named Caleb, the other was Joseph, and there was a young woman with them, Caleb's daughter, Deliverance . . ."

"Was Deliverance . . . attractive?" she chided.

"Well, sort of, I guess you could say that, but she was mute." He omitted the fact that she looked like the woman in his dream.

"They took us to their nearby village. It was a strange sort of place . . ."

"What was strange about it?"

"Well, it didn't look very much like a western town, more like New England, where they had come from, and they had suffered a series of misfortunes."

"Misfortunes?"

"Church burned down, lost their minister and doctor . . . a mine they depended on had played out, and there was a young boy, Ethan, who had an accident and couldn't walk . . ."

"Reminds me of a line from Shakespeare, how does it go? 'When troubles come they come not single spies, but in battalions.'"

"You know your Shakespeare better than I do; at any rate, they did the best they could to help you recover."

"Seem like nice people."

"Seemed nice . . . except for a creature called Moon, who had been extracting tribute from them and still demanded payment even though the mine was no longer productive. They couldn't fight back because their religion was nonviolent. . . . They didn't even have weapons."

"General Custer would have settled Moon's hash."

"Yes, but Autie was not around; however, good fortune did smile on them."

"Was that *your* smile, Jonathon?"

"No, but they did ask me to do a sermon in an open field, and in the midst of it the young boy rose and walked . . ."

"So far, so good."

"Not only that, but later when Ethan and the other children were playing in the mine some timbers collapsed, and Ethan was trapped under a beam . . ."

"Not so good."

"No, but we managed to get him out."

"We?"

"Well, I was there to help."

"I don't doubt that," she nodded.

"Not only that, but a rich new vein was discovered in the mine, and they decided to rebuild the church."

"More good fortune."

"Except for your condition. You didn't get much better, in fact, quite worse . . . and strange things began to happen . . ."

"What sort of strange things?"

Keyes paused. He decided not to tell about her seeing the masked children chanting in the yard and the man he saw in the mirror.

"Oh, I don't really remember all the details, but the church was being rebuilt, and then Moon came back and there was a terrible confrontation and . . . he was killed."

"Who killed him?"

Another pause.

Then he answered.

"I did . . . with one of his own guns . . ."

"You, Jonathon?"

"But it was in self-defense. In the dream I had no other choice."

"I'm sure it was the right choice . . . in the dream. Please go on."

"I was asked to give just one more sermon in the rebuilt church during one of their . . . holy days, and then . . ."

"And then, what?"

"During the sermon there was an even stranger change . . . in the congregation . . . and . . ."

"And?"

Keyes lifted himself to his elbows and listened.

"The storm stopped."

"What storm?"

"The dust devil outside. We'd better get going while the going's good."

"But . . ."

"No 'buts,' Lorna, let's get a move on."

Keyes rubbed down the horses, fed them grain and water from the barrel tied to the side of the wagon.

In the aftermath of the storm, as they rolled away from the shelter of the rocks and were on the road west again, the sky was almost clear, but there were still particles of sand and dust drifting in the air.

"Well, go on, Jon," she said.

"I am going on."

"You know what I mean . . . go on with the story."

"It wasn't a 'story,' it was a dream."

"Jon," she smiled, "let's not quibble over definitions. What happened?"

"Not now, Lorna, there's still quite a bit of dust floating around."

He pulled the red scarf up over the lower part of his face.

"And you cover your nose and mouth with a bandana or you'll be breathing and swallowing a lot of this desert."

An hour or so later the air was clean and clear, the sky its usual cloudless granite gray as they approached a divide in the road. Keyes tugged at the reins and the wagon came to a stop.

"Well, Lorna," he said as he lowered the red scarf from his face, "this is the last chance."

She did the same with her bandana.

"Last chance for what?"

"To change our minds. That's Eagle Pass just

ahead . . . and Saguaro. The other road would take us up north toward Fort Lincoln and Custer and Libbie."

"I thought we already decided," she said with obvious surprise.

"Sure we did. But we can still undecide."

"You wanted so much to be of service to Reverend Mason and his congregation in Saguaro."

"I still do, but . . ."

"But what, Jon?"

"I can, also, be of service to the soldiers of the Seventh Calvary," he touched the scarf around his neck. "The fort is not all savagery; there is society. And you'd have the company of the ladies at the fort, officers' wives. There'd be parties and dances, old friends and new ones."

"I don't need any of that and neither do you. Don't you think Autie and the Seventh can get along without you? Why Custer and the Seventh will be riding to glory to the tune of 'Garry Owen' and you know it."

"You're right about that, and I do know it." He smiled. "I just wanted to make sure about how you felt."

"Was there ever any doubt?"

"Not really, sweetheart. And ol' Custer will teach those Sioux a thing or two about strategy, he'll spank their chiefs and send them back to their teepees or up to their happy hunting grounds."

"I'm not sure who'll teach whom," she said, "but we promised Reverend Mason, and a promise is a promise."

"Well, then, Saguaro is our promised land . . . and the Dakotas are Custer's promised land."

He snapped the reins and the wagon rolled toward Eagle Pass.

"We'll have a lot to tell our grandchildren . . . and so will Custer after he tames all the Indians in the West."

But just ahead at the narrow gap to Eagle Pass, more than a dozen mounted Indians, some with rifles, some with bows and arrows, others with lances, commanded the passageway like silent sentinels. Their flat faces grim with dark eyes glaring in the sun.

As the wagon stopped, their obvious leader, a man of narrow body and indeterminate age on a dappled steed, approached, followed by three younger braves.

Keyes looked down at the rifle leaning close to the Bible on the bench.

He held onto the reins with one hand and raised the other in what he hoped was a universal sign of peace among the tribes.

There was no response, physical or verbal. Only silence. An ominous silence and the same inscrutable mask of the leader.

Keyes pointed to himself, then at Lorna.

"Jon Keyes, my wife Lorna, from the East. Do you understand? Savvy?"

"I talk your language, American," the Indian pointed to himself. "Touch the Clouds," then around to the other Indians. "Navajo."

"Good, Touch the Clouds, we were . . . we are on our way to Saguaro."

"Maybe . . . you come in peace?"

"Yes."

Touch the Clouds pointed at the Henry.

"The rifle? I use it for hunting."

"Hunting Indians?"

"No, no. For food . . . until we get to Saguaro."

"We know Saguaro."

"Very good," and under his breath, "I hope."

"Why Saguaro?"

"To meet a man there named Mason."

For the first time there was a different look in the Indian's eyes, and a different tone in his voice.

"Jimmy Mason?"

"Yes."

"We know Reverend Jimmy Mason."

"You do? He's . . ."

"He brings us medicines and seed to plant crops. Jimmy good man. Navajo grow crops. Fight no more forever." His eyes narrowed. "You soldier?"

"Not anymore . . . Now I'm *Reverend* Johnny Keyes . . . forever." He looked at Lorna, then at Touch the Clouds. "We're on our way to help Reverend Jimmy Mason."

"Good." Touch the Clouds nodded, then pointed toward Eagle Pass. "Go in peace."

"Very good," Keyes slapped the reins over the team, and the Conestoga started to roll. "We'll be seeing you, Touch the Clouds."

When the wagon entered the pass, Keyes and Lorna looked back and each took a deep breath, then she touched the barrel of the rifle.

"Jon, if things were different, would you have used the Henry?"

He hesitated.

"Probably," he shrugged, "but I'm really not sure . . . and I'm glad I didn't have to."

"So am I . . ." She held up the Bible in her hand, ". . . but I did pick up and use this."

"A mighty weapon . . . and it never runs out of ammunition."

"Amen," she said and smiled, "but will you tell me about one more thing?"

"About what?"

"That dream . . . it didn't have a happy ending, did it?"

"Sure it did," he nodded, "I woke up, didn't I?"

EPILOGUE

One hundred years later

The same summer sun on the same mountain desert, rimmed by the same cathedral mountains and rocks.

But now there was a two-lane road paved with seething concrete.

A lone eagle circled high in the pearl gray sky, and a mausoleum silence permeated the limitless terrain.

Heat waves rose from the surrounding sands in the blaze of noon.

A late model station wagon with lifted hood and loaded with luggage and camping gear, obviously in distress, stood half- on—half-off, the road.

A handsome, well-built man, about thirty, labored on the exposed engine as a lovely woman and young child, a boy of four or five years, watched and waited.

The man lifted his head, looked at his wife and

son, and then shrugged his shoulders in a negative manner.

In the distance a dusty pickup truck appeared and slowed down as it approached.

"Look, Daddy," the boy pointed, "somebody's coming. Maybe they'll help us."

The man stepped away from the station wagon onto the road and waved at the pickup truck.

The truck, with three people in the front seat, braked and came to a stop.

The driver had rolled down the window.

He was middle-aged, tall, and clean featured, with a smooth, almost saintly face.

On the other side sat a rope-thin man with an elfin visage, creased by a thin-lipped smile.

Between them, a beautiful young lady, her hair pulled back, revealing a soulful, suasive appearance.

The driver smiled as he called out.

"Can we give you a lift?"

The pickup truck towed the station wagon as they approached and passed a road sign.

SAN MELAS

The three people inside the truck looked at each other with contented anticipation, then at the sign again.

Through the side-view mirror the words on the sign were, of course, spelled backwards.

SALEM

Turn the page for a bonus short story
from the award-winning

Andrew J. Fenady

THE WISE OLD MAN
OF THE WEST
and
The Fountain of Youth

Across the campfires he was known only as the "Wise Old Man." Most of the time he would appear out of the dark and disappear before first light.

He didn't talk like any of the cowboys, more like a college professor; dressed as if he had just stepped out of a San Francisco opera house—at least to the cowboys—complete with malacca crosier and high-toned homburg. Clear-eyed and clean-shaven, except for a meticulously trimmed military mustache.

Countless campfires like this one dappled the inconstant landscape, afterglows of an uneven link of cattle drives out of bankrupt Texas to bankable Kansas.

Raw-boned, saddle-worn men of all lineage, some known to each other only by tags such as Slim, Baldy, Buster, 'Bama, Clay County, Misery, Hondo, and Ofty-Ofty, wore out remudas and themselves over a venturous trail blazed by a half-breed Cherokee called Chisholm.

Indispensable to each drive was a range cook

sometimes dubbed Belly Cheater, Biscuit Shooter, Dough Puncher, but most often, Cookie. This camp's Cookie couldn't have topped out at five and a half feet, from the bottom of his Justin boots to the tip of his Stetson, and didn't weigh in at more than one hundred and thirty pounds including his gun belt and loaded Colt. He had a voice like a constipated canary, but he was the cock o' the walk. Nobody crossed or back-talked him. And when they choked down his chow they'd best grin and sing out "Just the way I like it, Cookie."

The Wise Old Man never asked for anything, but all the different Cookies of each camp, as well as the drovers, were pleased to supply him with coffee, beef and beans, plus tobacco for his curved Meerschaum, just to hear him talk.

Talk came easy to the Wise Old Man.

And in what the wrangos considered a fair swap for the coffee, beef and beans, plus tobacco, the Wise Old Man would spin a yarn or two. Sometimes in answer to a cowboy's question, or, he'd just talk about something he felt like talking about.

But that night the Wise Old Man did look around and make an inquiry.

"Where's Tom Riker? Isn't he the trail boss of this drive?"

"He sure as hell is," Cookie nodded, "but ol' Tom went up ahead with Hondo, lit out at noon, took some grub and extra canteen to where the trail divides, to figure which of the two he's gonna have us follow. Makin' dry camp tonight. We'll meet up tomorrow. Left Red here as the high hickalorum."

Red Flannigan was dependable, had the most schooling in the outfit—all the way through the sixth grade, he claimed. He could read without moving his lips, and do pretty good with his sums.

Flannigan was not reluctant to display his erudition. It didn't take him long to make a show of it in front of the Wise Old Man. He commenced by saying he'd heard about a fella, a Spaniard named Poncho de somethin', who searched for a fountain of youth. Did the Wise Old Man ever hear of such a thing—or place?

"Yes," the wise Old Man recalled, "Ponce de Leon, of course. He sought the magic waters that would prolong life, keep a man young and fit till the end of time."

This grabbed the heed of the cross-legged cowboys, most of whom were somewhat stove-up and looked at least a decade older than their birthdates.

"But," the Wise Old Man went on, "that puts me in mind of another tale concerning another man involved in that same elusive quest."

"How about tellin' us about it," Red suggested, and pointed to the empty tin cup the Wise Old Man held in his firm, ropy fingers, "while we fill 'er up with some of ol' Cookie's hot tar?" Red said it with a grin.

"Fair exchange," the Wise Old Man smiled, while Cookie reached for the pot and poured, as the circle of drovers leaned closer. Most of them had heard, or heard tell, of the Wise Old Man and his tales.

From some not too far but unseen ridge, a lonesome coyote wailed into the night, and waited for an answer. It never came.

The Wise Old Man sipped the bitter brew between his pale lips, cleared his scratchy throat, and went at it.

"A man, very successful, let's call him Claude, at the peak of life, wanted to go on living for a long, long time. Claude had been convinced that somewhere there was a fountain of youth." The Wise Old Man pointed the stem of his Meerschaum toward Flannigan. "Like you, he had heard about de Leon. But where was that liquid treasure?

"He was determined to find the answer.

"His determination became an obsession. He spent days, nights, weeks, and months looking for clues, confirmation of any kind. From the Bible, from sources before the Bible—and since Gutenberg, to the latest periodicals. On walls of caves, scrolls in basilicas of ancient Greece. He left no evidentiary stone unturned—no writings unread—and with the aid of interpreters—even in seven different languages.

"But his quest was not only literary, it became widely geographical—on foot, rail, sailing ship, horse, camel, and caravan."

"Get to the nub!" One of the young drovers called out through a haze of cigar smoke. "What the hell happened to him?"

"Shut up, Curly!" Flannigan ordered. "Let him tell it in his own way."

"A failing of the young fellow's generation," the Wise Old Man puffed on his Meerschaum, "impatience to proceed in an orderly fashion. But there is something to be said for young Curly's point of view—and even Shakespeare advised, 'hasten thy story'—besides, it's getting late, and you good fellows are entitled to a good night's sleep after a hard days labor. How many miles did you cover today? Fourteen? Fifteen?"

"Closer to nineteen." Curly said.

"Very good. From now on I'll do my best to summarize without losing the gist and flavor of the narrative . . ."

"Like I said," Red pushed back the brim of his hat on his forehead, "you tell it in your own way. If pipsqueak Curly needs his sleep so bad, he's always got his saddle for a pillow waitin' nearer than further."

"Nah, I'll finish the rest of this cigar." Curly inhaled. "Go ahead, ol' timer. What happened next?"

"'Next' turned into a long, long, time, even though it was just a blink in the eye of eternity—but years and years, as men count it. And he covered thousands more miles than you fellows did today—searching the world and drinking the world's waters.

"Near freezing waters of the icy north, to gurgling hot waters of the unforgiving desert. From the mystic birthplace of the gods, Olympus, to the Valley of the Kings in Egypt. From Babylon, where once there hung those gardens considered one of the wonders of the ancient world, to India, where Alexander had no more to conquer.

"Through Asia, across the steppe and into the Kerulen Valley, homeland of the Mongols, once led by Genghis Khan."

The Wise Old Man drew deep through the stem of his Meerschaum, then continued.

"This, and more for his travel's history—perhaps best chronicled by the Bard's black Moor, Othello:

'Wherein of antres vast and deserts idle, rough quarries, rocks and hills whose summits touch the heavens . . . And of Cannibals that each other eat, the Anthropophagi, and men whose heads do grow beneath their shoulders.'"

There was a silence of uncertainty among the drovers until Cookie chirped.

"Could you chew that a little finer—what the hell does it mean?"

"It means, my liege, roughly speaking, that in his sojourn he had audience with the most pious—from monks in monasteries to even the Holy Father at the Vatican—and with their opposites: scoffers, apostates, and Satanists. The good, the bad, and the in-between. That's about as fine as I can chew it."

"Good enough," Cookie nodded, "go on."

"And Claude went on, to one disappointment after another. At times it seemed otherwise. He heard of a place in Anatolia where men and women lived a long, long time. He sought it out and they did. But not nearly long enough—one hundred to one hundred and twenty years—not nearly span enough for him, and not because of any special water, but from digesting an abundance of yogurt, which he tested—and detested."

A rapid volley of voices shot out from around the campfire.

"What the hell is yo-gert? Never heard of it . . ."

"Has anybody . . . ?"

"Not in this outfit . . ."

"I sure as perdition did." Cookie's chirpy voice

declared. "It's spoiled milk . . . milk with a disease. Goat's milk."

"*Goats*?!"

"I can't abide goats. Goats is dirty . . ."

"Goats stink. "

"Might as well try to milk a skunk . . ."

"Goats eat cardboard, leather, timber . . . tin cans . . ."

"Tin cans? Then what kind of milk can goats give . . . ?"

"Spoiled milk that makes you live over a hundred years, I guess . . ."

"It ain't worth it . . ."

"Who the hell wants to milk a stinkin' goat?"

"I guess some women do . . ."

"What kind of women milk goats?"

"*My* kind is any kind . . . after a long drive . . ."

"Yeah, even women with whiskers—like goats have . . ."

"Boys, you got it all wrong," Cookie wiped at his nose, "it don't come out of the teat spoiled. They let it ferment like whiskey . . ."

"I'll stick to whiskey that don't come out of a teat, you can shuck your goats and their yo-gert . . ."

As the chatter subsided, the Wise Old Man smiled and continued.

"Nevertheless, yogurt can be traced back thousands of years and in spite of, or even because of, its bacterial content, is still considered salubrious nutrition. But for Claude it was no substitute for what he sought, the fountain of youth—everlasting youth— and so, his search went on.

"And so did one disillusion after another, sometimes with humorous consequences, and at other times with more disagreeable effect.

"From the diary of a ship's captain, Claude ascertained that at a remote village there flourished a tribe where no one, man or woman, appeared older than approximately forty-five years of age. The captain wrote that he had even taken photographs, with a camera obtained after the recent U.S. Civil War, as evidence of what he had written. Unfortunately, such evidence had been lost, but the diary did include the latitude/longitude of the tribe's location. The captain had, also, written that the tribe had a secret, which he had vowed never to disclose.

"It was not easy, but eventually Claude managed to locate and enter the remote settlement. What the captain had described was true. No one appeared to be over forty or so.

"The tribe was not unfriendly. Claude sought out an elder who seemed no more than forty years of age and was obviously their spiritual leader. The elder was called Sonsiri and even managed some semblance of English, which he had acquired from the ship's captain.

"Most promising, there was a waterfall that plunged into a radiant body of water beneath.

"Claude's expectation soared. After gaining the confidence of the elder, he feigned thirst and mentioned that he'd appreciate a drink from the waters below.

"A dark reaction clouded the elder's visage. Not from those waters, he managed to explain. Those waters were holy. Nobody drank from them. There was a well in the village for drinking and other purposes.

"After pledging himself to secrecy, Claude pressed for further explanation.

"Sonsiri took him at his word and confided to Claude that the tribe worshiped Wotam, the God of Youth. There was, in their religion, only one way to achieve eternal youth. Not from *drinking* the water.

"First of all, no one was ever allowed to learn how to swim. And on the day of each individual's forty-first birthday, he, or she, must enter the water just above the precipitous cascade, and in order to make sure of their fate and destiny to live eternally, be weighted down with a belt of iron.

"The elder, himself, was already preparing for the ritual—to make his voyage to the bottom of the waters—and had chosen his successor, a youth of twenty-one years.

"Sonsiri went so far as to show Claude the iron belt that had been fashioned for his own transitional journey—to be transported into the sacred waters below."

After a stunned silence, some of the drovers voiced their reactions that ranged from laughter to incredulity, to contempt, including Red Flannigan's comment:

"What kind of mumbo jumbo religion is that?"

The Wise Old Man only smiled as he answered.

"There are many arcane beliefs concerning the path to eternal life. That was only one of them."

"Not mine!" Curly smirked.

"Nor Claude's." The Wise Old Man intoned. "And so his excursions ensued.

"He even retracked de Leon's Floridian expedition from the dank swamplands of Okefenokee, where grew the rare ghost orchid on trunks of cypress trees, and through the perilous territory of the unsurrendered Seminoles, to the sun burnished white water lilies of the Everglades—more disappointment for both Ponce de Leon—and Claude.

"But Claude proceeded south, deep into Mexico and the ruins of the once great civilization of the Mayans on the arid Yucatan Peninsula where its underground waters fed sink wells called *cenotes*. And though the wells provided plentiful water, it was not the *kind* of water Claude had sought—and continued to seek.

"But his travels, travails, and the years kept taking their toll.

"At last, when he had become a weary, wrinkled, old man, he became convinced—perhaps because he wanted to *be* convinced—that he had discovered the object of his seemingly endless search. One story goes that he came across the answer in an obscure quatrain from a little-known translation of Omar the Tentmaker's *Rubaiyat*. The miracle waters of eternal life awaited discovery at a hidden oasis in the parched sands of fabled Persia.

"But the entire crew of a caravan he had hired ultimately gave up and abandoned him. Still, he went on alone. Through frozen nights and furnace days—until one of those days, with the sun directly above, an oasis shimmered not far in front of him. But was it real—or a desert chimera?

"He approached with fervent trepidation.

"And, no, it was not a mirage. He dipped both trembling palms into the clear water and splashed the refreshing liquid onto his aged face.

"Then Claude eagerly cupped his hands and drank, again and again, of what he believed to be the source of eternal youth—and waited for the result.

"But, as he waited, he grew weaker and weaker—and then, he died."

The listeners were obviously caught short by the abrupt climax of the Wise Old Man's account.

There was a spell of deep silence among the drovers, with only the crackle of the campfire and a vagrant whistle of wind to be heard—until Curly exclaimed.

"He *what*?"

"He died." The Wise Old Man repeated.

"What kind of an end to the story is that?" Red Flannigan asked in a hoarse whisper.

"Well," the Wise Old Man smiled, "that's not exactly the end of the story."

"Then go on." Cookie prodded. "What else could've happened?"

"Shortly afterwards a wayward caravan came upon his body.

"But a strange transformation had taken place.

"His gray hair had turned dark again. Wrinkles on his face, neck, and entire body had disappeared—and he looked exactly as he did at the peak of his life."

The Wise Old Man tapped the residue from the bowl of his pipe onto the palm of his hand.

Once again a quizzical silence pervaded the camp.

This time it was Red Flannigan who first spoke.

"Well, is *that* the end of the story?"

"As Omar Khayyam's *Rubaiyat* closes, '*Tamam*' The End."

"Then," Flannigan pressed, "what's the point of the story?"

"Did you ever hear of the man who drowned chasing the moon in the ocean? *He was chasing an illusion.*"

"But," Flannigan persisted, "if it was an illusion, why did the wrinkles fade and his body come back to its youth?"

There was no immediate response.

It was Cookie who spoke.

"They don't call you the Wise Old Man for nothin'—so give us the answer."

"The answer is . . . I am not *that* wise."

Once again, from a ridge, the lonesome coyote wailed, and waited, and, once again there was no answer.

Somewhere, west of the one hundredth meridian, there was another campfire . . . Or a snow-bound shack . . . A seemingly abandoned ghost town . . . An army fort squatting in a savage desert . . . A sealing schooner about to cast off for the northern coast of Japan . . . A miner's court preparing to hang a deaf-mute . . . A range war flaring between cattle barons and squatting settlers on the grazing fields of

Wyoming . . . George Armstrong Custer in the Black Hills of the Dakotas, at his last camp along the Little Big Horn . . . A near-starved Wagon Train on the Oregon Trail, already subjected to an Indian attack, and anticipating another . . . Tombstone on the twenty-fifth of October in a Fleet Street saloon near the O.K. Corral, with the Earps and Doc Holliday on one side of the room, the Clantons on the other, and the Wise Old Man in between . . . The legend of the Hanged Man, James Devlin, gunfighter not always on the right side of the law, but hanged for a crime he did not commit. Properly pronounced dead, however— Fate? Destiny? Chance? He survives. Why was he spared? What did this Lazarus of the West do with the rest of his life—and his gun? . . . A solitary camp-site as the War Between the States has recently ended, the Wise Old Man sits alone near the warmth of his fire when a stranger, well dressed, but travel worn, approaches on a lathered horse, both in need of respite—the stranger does not introduce himself, but the Wise Old Man has, more than once, seen a theatrical performance by John Wilkes Booth.

The Wise Old Man is no stranger to the hospitality, or the hostility of the West, where bone-weary sons and daughters of the frontier will chance to hear his stories, some brutal, or tender, some historic, or mystical—all tales of the American West—a time and place that can never happen again. Tales told by the Wise Old Man who might appear in the dark and disappear before first light.

not
THE END